DRUID'S CURSE

A DRUIDVERSE URBAN FANTASY NOVEL

M.D. MASSEY

1

Well, here's another fine mess you've gotten me into.

"Druid." Crowley snapped his shadow-shrouded fingers in front of my face. "Druid, snap out of it. Dangers lurk near these gates. We need to move."

"Huh? Oh, right."

I tried to remember why we'd come to this place, this seemingly bottomless hole in the Earth. Something about going to Underhill for help. Yeah, that was it. We needed to find the Dagda.

"I think he's in shock," Crowley said.

"S'understandable. He's not o' an age ta' consider his mortality, yet."

I shook myself to dispel a sinking feeling that I might soon be descending to my doom. Click, the immortal wizard once known as Gwydion, had just popped in to inform me that I was dead. Not here, of course, but back in my original timeline. Meaning, I'd been killed here, at some point in the very near future. To say I was shook was an understatement.

"I'm fine," I said, pushing myself to my feet. "It's just a little weird to learn that I might be dead in another timeline."

"Or soon ta' be in this one," Click added in an inappropriately cheerful tone.

"Perhaps the trickster might consider his words before contributing to the conversation," Crowley said as he arched an eyebrow at Click. "I need the druid to be on his game if he's to help me destroy the vampire faction in this timeline."

"Right ya' are, necromancer."

"At least one of you is right in the head," I muttered.

"Whazzat?" Click asked as he drew a cigarette from the pack he kept rolled up in his t-shirt sleeve.

"Nothing," I replied.

Considering what I'd just been told, I figured I had the right to grouse about it. Especially since I was ninety-nine percent sure it had something to do with Click.

"Oh, don't go lookin' at me like that," the trickster said as he waved his cigarette-laden hand back and forth. "I had nothin' ta' do with this mess. Not one thing, lad."

"Except for teaching the druid time magic and encouraging him to use it, that is," Crowley muttered as he scanned the surrounding terrain for threats. "As I said previously, we should move. This is no place to linger at night, even in the presence of a master druid and an even more proficient necromancer."

Click leaned toward me as he whispered behind his hand. "Wait a minute—he knows 'bout the ime-tay agic-may?"

"Yes," I said in an exasperated tone. "He saw me die —this timeline me, that is. When I showed up, it didn't take much for him to figure it out."

"We should kill him," Click said, still whispering behind his hand.

"I can hear you," Crowley said dismissively. "And you might find that to be a difficult task, magician."

"Pfah! I eat necromancers fer' breakfast, six pence a dozen," the trickster replied.

Crowley made a wicked, hollow sound that might've been a chuckle. "I'm a master necromancer, and we're in the midst of an undead apocalypse. The field favors me greatly, despite your many centuries of experience."

"Oh yeah?" Click discarded his cigarette, then he crouched in a goofy kung fu stance with one leg extended, the other bent, his hands held in front of him in "judo chop" fashion. "Come at me then, Lurch, an' we'll see how ya' fare against a magician wit' real talent!"

Crowley raised an eyebrow at the slight, skinny immortal's display, then darkness began to swirl in the black depths that served as his eyes. The wizard-slash-necromancer cut an imposing figure, even without the shadow magic that shrouded him constantly these days.

He resembled a young, scarred Jeff Goldblum—and he was twice the magic-wielder he appeared to be.

Based on the set of his shoulders and the look in his dark, fathomless eyes, Crowley meant business. Before the confrontation could go any further, I stepped between him and Click. As much as I'd like to see the outcome of that match, we had greater concerns. Namely, getting to Underhill and finding the Dagda so I could either bond with my druid oak in this timeline or plant a new one.

My recent confrontation with the ancient vampire known as Alarngar had proven beyond a doubt that I needed to be at full strength to defeat the vampires. I'd feel a lot better about preventing my own death after I acquired a nearly unlimited magical battery to draw on—namely, my druid oak. The longer we lingered here, the more likely we were to be delayed in that task.

"Knock it off," I said as I extended my arms as if to hold them apart. "You two knuckleheads can have a wizard's duel later. Right now, we need to get to Underhill."

"Another time, then," Crowley said with casual amusement in his voice. "Come, druid—the descent to Maeve's portal is long and treacherous. We should be on our way before—"

A howl rang out in the distance, cutting the shadow wizard off. Another followed, then a third, both closer than those previous.

"Well, that doesn't sound good t'all," Click stated as he lit another cigarette.

"It's okay," I said. "I know all the werewolves in the Austin Pack."

Crowley shook his head. "Many of their number went feral after the bombs fell. They've since made more of their kind, and now they hunt the ruins of the city, devouring any humans they come across. I doubt these weres will listen to reason."

"You don't know that these 'thropes are feral," I protested. "Give me a chance to talk to them before you start setting them on fire or siccing your undead army on them."

Crowley rolled his eyes. "I will prepare for our descent, then, while you avoid being eaten. At any rate, we need a sacrifice. A feral werewolf will do nicely."

"Right," I said with a nod before his words fully registered. "Wait a minute—we need a what?"

Click tugged on my sleeve as he faded out of sight. "Ya' got company, lad. Don't mind me, I'm jest gonna watch at a safe distance."

"Of course you are," I said as I turned to face the trio of werewolves that vaulted over Maeve's garden wall.

It's not like I was friends with the whole Pack. In fact, most of them hated my guts. But I didn't want to kill any of them, either—not if I could help it.

The werewolves that stepped into the clearing were in their half-human, half-wolf form. They walked on their hind legs, and they were somewhat humanoid in form, but that's where the resemblance to humankind ended. The 'thropes had elongated lupine faces, pointed ears, and piercing, forward-facing eyes set on either side of their nasal bridge.

Of course, they were covered in thick, shaggy wolf fur from head to toe—or claw, to be specific. Adding to the overall effect, their legs had an extra joint at the ankle, making their bipedal gait a strange, almost awkward exercise in balance and motion. Yet they landed nimbly before stalking toward me through the undergrowth, spreading out in a half-circle with teeth bared.

"Greetings," I said with a wave and a smile. "One Pack member to another."

I didn't recognize any of them, which did not bode well for my plan to negotiate a truce. Of the three wolves, the one in the center seemed to be the leader. She was tall for a female werewolf, with mottled brown, gray, and blond fur that faded to a dirty-white blaze on her chest. Rather than respond, she growled menacingly as the trio continued to advance.

"Keep goin', yer' doin' great, lad," a disembodied voice said from behind me.

I ignored Click, locking eyes with the she-wolf. "Maybe you don't remember me, but I'm a member of the Austin Pack. I went through the initiation, trials, and everything. Samson trained me himself."

"Samson is a coward and a traitor," the female werewolf growled. "He abandoned us, left us to fend for ourselves. The Pack's still here, but we have new leadership."

"You?" I asked.

She chuckled, and it came out almost as a growl. "No, not me. Someone new."

"Ah." I scratched my stubble. "You're going to try to eat me, aren't you?"

"Just figuring that out?" she asked, somehow managing a wicked grin despite her malformed jaws and mouth.

"Eh, I was holding out hope you weren't feral," I replied. "But I'll give you the benefit of the doubt and offer the opportunity to reconsider. I really am a full-fledged member of the Pack."

She sniffed the air. "I think not. You stink of fae magic. You're not a 'thrope, and not Pack." She licked her lips again. "Food."

"Unless..." the smaller black male wolf on my right said.

"What?" the female demanded.

"Unless he's the druid."

The third werewolf, an average-sized male with white fur, grunted his dissent. "The druid died in the blast," he growled. "I say he's food."

"So, I died, did I?" I asked. "Where's your proof?"

The wolf with the black coat shrugged. "The bombs fell, and no one saw him after that. Other Pack members said he was killed in the blast downtown."

I crossed my arms over my chest. "Apparently, rumors of my death have been greatly exaggerated."

"Good one," Click whispered from somewhere behind me.

"You do kind of look like him," the female werewolf said.

"That's because I am him—er, me. I'm Colin McCool."

"Doesn't matter," she said. "From what I hear, most of the Pack hated you, and they resented Samson's decision to welcome you with open arms."

I sensed a change in their demeanor at that. The two smaller werewolves had nearly flanked me, so I had one to each side and the third, larger wolf in front. The she-wolf shifted her weight, crouching slightly, and I saw the other two tense in my peripheral vision.

Great.

"Don't do it," I advised.

Despite my warning, they pounced. I'd already stealth-shifted long before the wolves showed up. Meaning, I was at least as fast and durable as they were—on the inside, at least. And having anticipated the attack, it wasn't difficult to evade them.

Could I take three werewolves at once? Sure. Did I want to? Not really.

Time to Plan B this shit-show.

Instead of counterattacking, I ducked and rolled out of the way at the last second. The three wolves converged on empty space, colliding with each other and landing in a jumbled mess of fur, limbs, and teeth. I rolled to my feet, facing the trio of werewolves as they disentangled themselves from each other.

"Um, guys? A little help here?" I said as I glanced around to find Click and Crowley.

"I'm right here, lad, cheering ya' on," Click's disembodied voice said. "Keep it up!"

"Of course, what was I thinking, asking you for help?" I hissed.

"Eggs-zactly," Click replied.

Click was, of course, still invisible, and likely as not I was the only one who could hear him at the moment. I doubted he'd step in to assist me, not unless I was really on the ropes. Although I'd yet to witness the full extent of his power, I'd seen enough to know that the quasi-god was incredibly powerful—and very full of himself. Thus, he felt that physical altercations were beneath him.

Moreover, as my erstwhile mentor in all things magical, Click preferred to let me sort my own messes. In the past, the immortal magician had revealed a preference for a "trial by fire" method of teaching. To him, hopeless situations and lopsided battles were the ideal proving ground for his lone pupil, and his lessons were very much sink or swim in nature. If I failed, then I must not

have been worthy of his instruction in the first place—
que será, será.

As for Crowley, he'd hidden himself in shadow near
the entrance to the pit. I took a moment to look for him
in the magical spectrum, and my magesight revealed
that he was working on some sort of ritual. In the short
time since the werewolves had arrived, he'd created a
summoning circle around the pit.

Although its purpose was a mystery to me, the
runes, glyphs, and lines appeared to be etched in
shadow magic, flickering here and there with the sickly
yellow-green of death enchantments. Whatever he was
doing, it seemed to require a lot of power and quite of
bit of his attention. I'd not be getting an assist from him
anytime soon, and that was a fact.

Fine then, I'll deal with this myself.

I backed away from the lead werewolf, as she was the
first to reorient herself after colliding with her pack
mates. "Trust me, you don't want to do this."

"I believe I do," she said as she stalked toward me
with saliva dripping from her slavering jaws. "If you *were*
the druid, you'd have used your magic already, or
shifted into a more powerful form. That you haven't tells
me you're an imposter, which means you're—"

"I know, I know—'food.'" I sighed, cracking my neck.
"Don't say I didn't warn you."

The female werewolf sprinted at me, closing the distance between us much faster than I expected. Either she was an older 'thrope, or she'd been turned by a primary, because the only other 'thropes I'd seen move that fast were Samson and Fallyn. That said, I was just as fast. As she neared me, I sidestepped to my right and cuffed her across the left side of her snout with a downward, open-handed blow.

"Bad dog. Bad!" I said, hoping to enrage her further.

Things could turn against me quickly if I made a mistake, so the more I could stack the odds in my favor, the better. The female werewolf didn't miss a beat, and if that strike had any effect, she didn't show it. Instead of staggering, she rolled with the force of the blow, spinning midair in a Matrix-like move that ended in a downward, left-handed slash that caught me across the face and chest.

Damn, she's good.

The slash shredded my right cheek, and it left a trio of deep gashes in my right pectoral muscles. The facial injury was merely an inconvenience, but the damage to my chest muscles was a problem. Based on the way my right arm dangled awkwardly, I knew she'd partially severed the pectoral tendons where they connected to the humerus. Until it healed, I was going to have a damned hard time using my arm.

Well, shit.

I staggered back as the female werewolf pressed her advantage. Adding insult to injury, her companions were now back in the fight. The black-furred werewolf was hot on his leader's heels, while the one with the white coat was circling to flank me on my right.

Attacking my weak side. Smart.

"Any time now, Crowley!" I shouted as I shoved my left hand in the female werewolf's face.

"Come now, lad—there's no need for an assist yet," Click chided from somewhere to my right. "I say it's high time to show these tossers what ya' kin do."

"You're not helping," I growled.

Since my return to the Hellpocalypse, I kept a couple of spells queued up at all times. One of them was my sunlight spell, which I normally reserved for dealing with vampire mobs. It was excellent for crowd control against leeches, but it could do double-duty as a flash-bang in a pinch.

Since it was the only thing that I could think of under pressure, I squeezed my eyes shut as I let the werewolf have it full in the face. For a split second, the spell lit up the clearing like the midday sun, and the 'thrope roared in surprise. While the light did little to harm the 'thrope, werewolves had exceptionally good night vision, which also meant their eyes were quite sensitive to bright lights at night. She'd be blinded for several seconds, until her werewolf metabolism dealt with the insult to her vision.

Time enough for me to deal with the other two.

The werewolf with the dark coat had been right behind his leader, and though he didn't get the full brunt of the sunlight spell, it still caught him off guard. When the female shied away and covered her eyes, he ran right into her back, effectively tackling her to the ground. Rather than attack them while they were down, I turned to face the more immediate threat: the white-furred werewolf sneaking up on my right.

He was coming in low, most likely to hamstring me with a quick snap of his jaws or a swipe of his claws to the back of my leg. Instead, he ate the second spell I kept spooled up—100,000 volts of druid battle magic.

As usual, conservation of energy was in full effect. First, the 'thrope's eyeballs burst outward as his brain boiled inside his skull. A millisecond later, his head exploded, leaving nothing but a bloody, charred mess of flayed skin, muscle, and bone that sat atop his neck like a gory, red flower.

Yeah, that's gonna leave a mark.

As his lifeless corpse toppled to the ground, I leapt over him, landing and pivoting to face the other two 'thropes behind me. The female still appeared to be blinded, growling and snarling as she attempted to blink the spots from her eyes. As for her companion, he'd recovered nicely and currently stalked around my left to position me between himself and the female were.

My right arm still dangled uselessly at my side, and it'd be several minutes before my Fomorian healing factor repaired the damage. Besides that, I'd just spent the only two insta-cast spells I had in my arsenal. While

I could call on even more powerful magic, it'd take time to prepare another druid battle spell.

Also, the fight had taken quite a bit out of me, and my innate magical reserves were running low. I had maybe one or two offensive spells left in me, and then I'd be forced to fight hand-to-hand with the assistance of minor cantrips. The male 'thrope must've sensed my hesitation to engage, because his upper lip curled in a snarling grin.

"We gotcha' now, magician," he growled. Then he shouted past me to his leader. "Get ready, Eve—I'm going to drive him your way!"

Another fine mess, indeed.

2

In my opinion, among all the supernatural races, werewolves were the species most like humans. I hadn't known for a fact that these 'thropes were feral until they attacked, and frankly I'd hoped they weren't. I didn't really want to kill them, but they'd left me little choice.

Time to finish this.

I reached into my Craneskin Bag for Dyrnwyn, just as Click spoke from somewhere behind me. "The necromancer says he's ready, lad. He wants ya' ta' lead one o' the 'thropes ta' that great hole in the ground. Said he'd handle it from there."

"About time," I said.

"Are you nuts?" the dark-furred werewolf asked. "Who the hell do you keep talking to?"

"To the voices in my head," I said matter-of-factly as I glanced around. "Click, did he give you any further details? Am I supposed to push him in, or just get him in the general vicinity?"

Click didn't respond, so I assumed he'd left the scene. He was like that, always popping in and out without so much as a hello, or goodbye, or even a fuck you. Tricksters were a real pain in the ass when it came down to it.

"Right—horseshoes and hand grenades it is," I muttered.

I was already in a very "fuck it" mood and talking to empty air hadn't improved my attitude—never mind my injuries. While it was my fault for taking it easy on the 'thropes, it irked the hell out of me that neither of my companions had raised a finger to help.

Then again, Crowley did pull me out of that dungeon in Dallas.

Rather than dwell on personal slights, I decided it would be best if I wrapped things up so I could heal and get on with finding the Dagda. The problem was, the female 'thrope looked to be nearly recovered, and the other remaining werewolf was in top shape and closing on me rapidly. On the plus side, the male stood between me and the pit. All I had to do was push him into it.

I might not have had a ready-to-use spell queued up, but he didn't know that. I screwed my face up like I was in serious concentration—or holding in a fart, take your pick—then I wound up with my left arm like I was about to cast the world's biggest *hadouken*. When I thrust my left arm out at the end of the motion, the werewolf shied away, covering his face in anticipation of being on the receiving end of an offensive spell.

While he was distracted, I stepped forward quickly, planting a front thrust kick on his chest that would've made King Leonidas proud. Perfect form and timing combined with my Fomorian strength and speed resulted in an attack that sent the werewolf stumbling backward, straight toward the pit. Since I wasn't certain what Crowley was up to, I switched from mundane vision to magesight so I could see what he'd cooked up.

Now that his spell was complete, I realized that the magic circle Crowley had been creating wasn't a summoning circle after all, but a circle of containment. And it was a doozy. We druids didn't mess with conjuration magic, as it mostly involved summoning powerful and very evil entities of the kind that didn't belong on this plane of existence. But based on what I knew of the practice, the circle that Crowley had laid out was designed to contain an extremely powerful entity.

Holy motherfucking gates to Hades... just what the hell is that creepy wizard planning?

As soon as the male 'thrope stumbled into the circle, a half-dozen ropy tendrils of shadow magic shot out of the ground, wrapping around the werewolf's arms, legs, and torso. The shadow tentacles lifted the 'thrope up, conveying him toward the hole in the ground by handing him tentacle over tentacle to the center of the circle. Within seconds, the werewolf was suspended above the pit, stretched and splayed spread eagle over the hole.

That's when the pit started glowing. Or rather, a soft glow began to emanate from its depths. It started as a deep purple light that was almost black, then it grew in intensity as the tone shifted from plum to grape, then from magenta to a sickly violet color that made my vision swim and my skin crawl. Finally, the light coalesced into the vague outline of something that bore absolutely zero resemblance to any creature from the natural realm.

The closest I could compare it to was the eldritch godspawn I'd killed in the Void some time back, as that creature had no definite shape except for that which suited it at any given time. The entity in the pit was similar in the sense that it too lacked a definitive form, instead seeming to shift and flow from one form to the next. Each new iteration defied logic and the laws of physics—a marriage of a Fuseli and a Goya, come to life.

I was at once horrified and yet unable to turn my eyes away, enraptured as I'd become by the other-worldly presence of the thing Crowley had summoned. As the light intensified, the male werewolf strained to look over his shoulder into the depths of the pit. On seeing what lurked beneath him, he unleashed a scream that was entirely human and altogether bone-chilling in the despair and fear it conveyed.

As if spurred by some primitive prey drive triggered by the 'thrope's shriek of terror, multiple tentacles and pseudopods shot out of the pit to ensnare the sacrifice Crowley and I had prepared. At that, the werewolf's cries increased in volume and intensity, his eyes darting this way and that as the wolf-man searched in desperation for some reprieve or escape.

What the hell have we done?

Torn by guilt and sickened by the scene before me, I suddenly wanted very badly to turn tail and run far, far away from here. Yet, I found myself paralyzed by a terror that defied explanation. For the life of me I couldn't tear my eyes away from the grotesque scene, and in the back of my mind I hoped that the third and final werewolf was similarly indisposed.

Whatever it was that Crowley had summoned, it now had the werewolf wrapped tightly in its constantly shifting, incomprehensibly twisted limbs. Again, I tried looking away and failed, entranced as I was by the nauseating rapture of the scene before me.

Suddenly, the violet light engulfed the werewolf all at once, and his screaming stopped. There was a loud *pop*, followed by a tremor that shook the earth. The next moment, the sickly light rapidly retreated downward into the pit. Silence and shadows fell over the clearing like the pall of death itself, leaving nothing behind but an optical after-image super-imposed on the perfect, unbroken darkness.

After I tossed my cookies in front of the pit, I stumbled to the other side where Crowley stood staring into the abyss. As I approached, the wizard turned to address me with a smug, self-satisfied expression.

"Well, that went better than expected. It should be sufficient to secure our—"

I cut him off by punching him square in the face. I didn't hit him as hard as I could because I didn't want to kill him, but I still clobbered him. My restraint was unnecessary, however, as the shadow barrier that constantly swirled across his skin absorbed the brunt of the impact.

"Of all the unholy—" I struggled to find words to express my disgust. "What the fuck was that?"

Crowley staggered before catching his balance. As he righted himself, he rubbed his jaw while meeting my gaze—with surprisingly little animosity in his demeanor.

"*That* was the only way for us to secure passage to Underhill. In her absence, Maeve's demesne has gone quite mad. Neither of us are fae, and we'd surely have been devoured in a similar gruesome fashion the moment we stepped into that pit. Now, we'll be left alone for the duration of our journey to *Ildathach*."

I stared at him, vacillating over whether I should hit him again. "I don't care if it's the only way to hell and back. Don't ever involve me in one of your sick conjuration rituals again."

"'To hell and back'? That's a bit dramatic, don't you

think?" He made an offhand gesture, affecting an air of aloof indifference. "Besides, it's not as though I tricked you. Did the magician not tell you of my plan?"

"Yeah, but—"

"That werewolf would have happily had us for dinner. You should feel no remorse over turning the tables on such a creature."

"Still, that was beyond the pale." I felt my gorge rising just thinking about it. "Aargh, I might be sick again."

"You get used to it after a while. In my view, sacrificing evil supernatural creatures is a bit like lancing a boil—somewhat distasteful, but ultimately quite satisfying."

I massaged my forehead as I waited for the second wave of nausea to pass. "I think I liked the old Crowley better. At least he had the decency to hide the magnitude of his creepiness."

The wizard scowled. "That person was weak, and certainly not up to the task ahead. My transformation was a necessary evil."

"You got that half-right," I muttered, glancing around the clearing. "Wait a minute—where'd the last werewolf go?"

"Never fear, lad—the bitch fled when the necromancer called up Maeve's demesne," Click said as he materialized in front of me. He lit a cigarette, puffing on it as he peered at me through narrowed eyes. "Sure yer' alright? S'not exactly recommended ta' stare at a creature from the seventh dimension. Granted, when they manifest on this plane, yer' not seein' their true form. But translatin' the experience inta' somethin' the mortal brain kin' process s'enough ta' break yer' noggin'."

"I'm fine," I said, more snappishly than I'd intended. "What in the great green googly fuck was that thing?"

"Did I not jest tell ya'? Ya' jest witnessed a planar manifestation o' an entity from the seventh dimension. In truth, Maeve's entire demesne is a reflection o' the same, jest not all focused in one place."

I scratched my head and scowled. "So, when that happened, did the rest of Maeve's demesne vanish or something?"

"Nay, 'twas still there." Click rapped me lightly on my forehead with his knuckles. "Ya' hafta' stop thinkin' in such concrete terms if ya' want ta' master the skill o' travelin' betwixt the planes. That fixed, rigid thinkin'll be the death o' ya' otherwise."

"Sheesh, excuse me for thinking like a lowly mortal." I rubbed a hand over my face in the hopes of wiping away the brain fog I felt after staring into that psychedelic abyss. "And what do you mean, 'travelin' betwixt the planes'? Are you referring to travel between Earth and Underhill?"

Click crossed his arms and tapped his index finger on his lips. "Now that ya' mention it, I am gettin' a bit ahead o' myself. Must have my timelines crossed. Eh, forget I said that, lad."

I was about to protest Click's reticence when Crowley cleared his throat.

"If we might steer this conversation back to the matter at hand? As I said, Maeve's demesne has grown ever more unstable since the Queen retreated to Underhill. We should leave post-haste if we wish to traverse its paths, preferably before it forgets that we made the requisite pre-passage sacrifice."

"Seriously? And what are our odds of making it through before that happens?" I asked.

Crowley shrugged. "I give us a fifty-nine percent chance of navigating to the gateway unharmed."

"Fantastic. Click, can you just portal us there?" I turned to address the trickster, but he was nowhere to be found. "Click? Click!"

"I believe your erstwhile mentor and partner in mischief has departed," Crowley observed in his typical Captain Obvious manner.

"As usual, he leaves when he's needed most." I swept my hand at the dark, foreboding opening to the pit, which looked a hell of a lot more ominous to me after witnessing that sacrifice. "After you."

Crowley raised an eyebrow. "If you're assuming that by allowing me to enter Maeve's demesne first, I'll be eaten while you have time to escape, you're mistaken. The order we enter makes little difference. The thing you saw was merely a focusing of the entity's attention. In truth, it possesses a vast consciousness that encompasses the entirety of the demesne."

"Its body, so to speak," I offered.

"That is as good an analogy as any, although thinking of such an entity in purely three-dimensional terms is a gross oversimplification. As we traverse the depths of Maeve's demesne, it will take time before it notices our presence. Thus, if we are to be consumed by said entity, it's likely that neither of us will be in a position to escape."

I clapped the shadow wizard on the shoulder, resisting the urge to shiver as his shadow magic clung to my skin. "As always, you're a virtual font of sunshine and unicorn farts."

"I fail to see what unicorn flatulence has to do with—ah, you're having a bit of amusement at my expense."

"I'm laughing with you, Crowley, not at you." I stepped to the edge of the hole and peered over into the darkness, then I jumped to a landing a few feet below me. "But if I get eaten by Maeve's mansion, I swear I'll haunt you in the afterlife."

"Haunt me—hah!" Crowley proclaimed as he used his shadow tentacles to descend into Maeve's demesne. "I am a necromancer, druid. If you wish to threaten me, you'll need to do better than that."

"Fine. If it looks like we're going to be eaten, I'm gonna go Hyde-side and kick your ass first."

"Much better," he answered drily. "Although I doubt you'll have time—"

"It was just a joke, Crowley," I replied with a roll of my eyes. "Shit, this is going to be a long trip."

Navigating Maeve's demesne turned out to be an exercise in maintaining one's sanity. I'd walked through the fae queen's mansion many times, but Maeve or one of her subordinates had always guided me. On those occasions, it was weird but tolerable, as the shifting corridors and ever-changing rooms still retained the qualities of a house. Those trips might have been strange, but the interior of the mansion always maintained a sort of familiarity, following at least some rhyme and reason.

But now? It felt like I'd walked into the love child of an LSD-fueled romantic interlude between a Dali painting and an Escher print. After descending the stone stairwell for an indeterminate period, we passed through a baroque-looking wood and iron door, into a cavern painted in psychedelic hues. Then we came to another door, this one a carved stone number that would've given any archeologist a woody. Past that, we ascended a stairwell that spiraled downward through a vast nothingness that reminded me a great deal of the Void.

Again, the stairs seemed to go on forever, until finally we traversed a wall of fog that opened into a steamy, eerily quiet jungle filled with unfamiliar flora. Every plant and tree looked off somehow, and occasionally I'd see something move in my peripheral vision only to find nothing there on searching for the source. I was just about to warn Crowley to keep his head on a swivel when I heard him curse behind me.

"Drat—!" he exclaimed, followed by, "Mrrful-iflle-plifl!"

I spun in a crouch, Dyrnwyn in my right hand and a fireball in my left, only to find the shadow wizard's legs sticking out of the mouth of a two-story-tall Venus flytrap. On instinct, I roasted the stalk with my fireball, aiming just below his feet. When that didn't work, I made to attack it with Dyrnwyn, but the damned sword wasn't lit. Without the magical fire that typically engulfed the blade, it was no better a weapon than any other longsword.

Damned plant must not have enough intelligence to trigger Dyrnwyn's evil detector. Time to do this the druid way.

I changed my breathing pattern almost reflexively, so accustomed had I become to attuning with my nature magic. Then I gathered my internal magic reserves while casting my druid senses outward, both to ensure I didn't suffer the same fate and to make a connection with the flytrap's life force. From what I could tell, the plant wasn't anything natural, but instead the result of typical fae tampering with the natural order via esoteric eldritch enchantments.

If I had the time, I'd unravel their spells and revert the plant back to its native form. However, my companion wouldn't last that long. He was fighting the thing, to be sure, as the two halves of the trap sprouted dark spikes that then turned to tentacles. Those tentacles wrapped around the outside of the plant's "mouth," gaining purchase on the edges in an attempt to open it wide.

Yet, it was clear he'd suffocate before he extricated himself from the trap. Again, acting on instinct, I cast the simplest spell I could think of, which was one that drew every bit of moisture from the plant all at once. One moment it was a green, vibrant, living thing, and the next it turned into a brittle brown shell that drooped and sagged earthward. I hit the stalk with another fireball, cutting it in two. Immediately, the mouth-pod-thing plummeted to the ground, with Crowley still in it.

Before I could assist him further, the shadow tentacles strained again, ripping the pod open with a noise like dry limbs breaking. Crowley rolled out of the desiccated shell of the spiked "mouth" covered in sticky green goo and cursing in an archaic form of the fae language. After a quick visual assessment of his very polluted state, he cast a fire cantrip to burn away the viscous residue that covered him from the top of his head to his knees.

Meanwhile, I stifled a laugh behind my closed fist.

"Feed me, Seymour," I deadpanned.

"What?" Crowley replied with a scowl.

"It's a movie reference." The wizard's scowl deepened. "You alright?"

"I had the situation in hand," he groused as he examined himself for injuries. "I'm perfectly capable of defending myself against an overgrown Dionaea muscipula, after all."

"Yeah, but I figured I'd speed things up by dehydrating it for you." I pointed at a gob of sap he'd missed. "That's a contact poison, by the way."

"I'm well aware. Thus far, it has been deterred by my shadow magic."

"Just don't get it in your eyes or mouth."

He sneered at me, so I left him to his task and kept watch while he vaporized the rest of the poison. "How much longer?"

"I assume you're asking how far it is to the portal?" He zapped a stray bit of sap from his shoulder with a spark of dark energy. The wizard paused to examine himself thoroughly before continuing. "There's no way of gauging distance in this realm. I only know the direction in which we should travel, not how long it will be before we arrive."

"I'm getting a definite 'let's hope the big purple interdimensional monster doesn't notice us before we find the exit' vibe here."

"Indeed. But considering the variety of environs we've traversed, it shan't be too much further now."

He stood to his full height, sprouting a shadow tentacle from his shoulder that morphed into a large, dark eyeball at the end. The thing blinked once, then it arched around behind him, turning as if to examine his backside. A few more minor conflagrations later, and the eye stalk disappeared, reabsorbed into the shadow magic that covered his entire body.

Crowley dusted his hands unnecessarily. "Shall we?" he said as he marched off through the undergrowth.

"Sure," I replied, simultaneously sending out a telepathic signal that put the rest of the plants in this insane jungle on notice.

Master druid coming through. Eat me at your peril.

The plants withdrew from the path ahead, shifting and leaning away from us as we passed. Crowley mumbled something under his breath, too low for me to hear.

"What was that?" I asked a bit too loudly.

"I said, 'I suppose druidry does have its uses.'"

"Everybody needs a little help sometimes, Crowley."

"Yes, and if I should need a gardener, I'll know who to call."

He tromped on ahead with long, ground-eating strides. Meanwhile, I stood in shocked disbelief at his lack of gratitude—and that sardonic comment. By the time I'd thought of a witty comeback, he was too far away for me to respond without looking like an ass by yelling at him.

"Next time, I'll let the plant eat you," I muttered.

3

A short time later, we exited the jungle into a Victorian-era hedge maze that was creepy enough to make me say "Redrum" under my breath. I fully expected the topiary to come to life and chase us through the maze, but surprisingly we made it to the other side without incident. There we found the garden labyrinth abruptly transitioned into the same dark, foreboding cavern we'd passed through on our first field trip to Underhill, more than a year prior in my own timeline.

As I glanced around, I noted the familiar basalt walls and gave an involuntary shudder.

"What was that?" Crowley asked.

"Nothing," I replied. "I just never wanted to see this place, ever again."

"Ah, I'd forgotten how Maeve trapped you here." He cast his gaze around the cavern, taking it all in at a glance. "A pitiable tomb, to be certain."

"I nearly lost my shit here, Crowster—and my life. I'd prefer it if we didn't linger."

"Agreed. However, we'd best be ready when we exit the gateway, as we may encounter unfriendly forces on the other side. I'm about to spend a few moments preparing, and I suggest you do the same."

Crowley sat on the cavern floor, crossing his legs into a lotus position with his forearms resting on his knees. When he closed his eyes, I switched from normal vision to the magical spectrum, more out of curiosity than anything. Rather than being lit up with magical energy, his shadow magic "skin" made him look like a human-shaped black hole, a living door into the shadow realm where the visible light spectrum dare not tread. Spurred by a combination of suspicion and morbid curiosity, I stared for a few seconds until a pair of dark red eyes appeared in all that blackness. They blinked and stared back at me from the center of his chest, tracking me as I walked experimentally left and right.

Just when I thought he couldn't get any freakier, I reflected as I averted my gaze. *Right. Time to see to my own preparations.*

Truth be told, I had already queued up a few spells when we hit the hedge maze. Since I was still in my half-Fomorian form, I had little to do while Crowley did evil shadow wizard stuff. After checking to ensure I had both silver-tipped and iron-enhanced ammo for my Glock, I pulled Dyrnwyn from my Craneskin Bag, figuring it was better than the other, deadlier weapon I carried. As I'd learned from a past run-in with a primary vampire, Le Boucher, *Gáe Dearg* was no more useful against vamps than a mundane spear.

Fire and firearms it is, then.

Rather than looking for remaining signs of my unintentionally extended stay—having already nearly stumbled over a pile of my own petrified poo—I kept my eyes focused on the goal, which was the portal ahead. Something about it wasn't right, but I couldn't quite put my finger on it. I stared at the glassy surface and colorful scene beyond for several seconds before I figured out what was missing.

"Hey, the Treasures are gone!"

Crowley stirred behind me, unfolding himself from the lotus position as he opened his weird, empty but not empty eyes. "Lugh retrieved them early on in the war. Since the Earthbound fae and vampyri were entering Underhill practically at will via transporter spells, The Dagda decided the Treasures would serve the Tuath Dé better if they were close at hand."

A transporter spell was to a magic portal as a moth-eaten parachute was to an elevator. Both provided convenient, nearly instant travel across vast distances and between the planes, but you had about a twenty-percent chance of biting the big one when traveling by transporter spell. They also required massive amounts of magical power to use, which was why portals were the preferred mode of interplanar travel.

The gateway in front of us was one of many permanent portals between Earth and Underhill. After my first visit to the so-called "Land of Youth," on returning I'd used Balor's Eye to fuse four of the most powerful artifacts ever created by the Celtic gods together inside the gateway. That little stunt had caused a system-wide magical feedback loop that sealed every existing portal to Underhill all at once. And, it had pissed Maeve off enough for her to strand me in this cavern, sealing it and leaving me to die. Good times.

After the existing gateways to Underhill were cut off, the Earthbound fae had to find other ways to invade their former home. Where they had gotten the juice to fire up a bunch of transporter spells was a mystery, but one thing was certain—they must have been desperate as hell to do so.

"How'd Lugh manage to retrieve the Treasures?"

"Lugh has the Eye, does he not?"

I side-eyed Crowley, as he'd once stolen Balor's Eye and attempted to use it to increase his power by several magnitudes. His plan had backfired when the Eye rejected him due to his lack of Fomorian DNA. It chose me instead, and I'd ended up carrying the thing inside my head until it turned on me as well.

Eventually, I placed it in a stasis spell in order to defeat its new chosen bearer, and once I got it back, I promptly gave it to Lugh for safekeeping. That whole sordid affair had always stuck in Crowley's craw, and I was ninety-nine percent positive he'd steal it again if given the opportunity.

"I can neither confirm nor deny that statement," I said, poker-faced.

"Oh please," the shadow wizard replied. "How else could he reverse what the Eye had done?"

I ignored his assertion by changing the subject. "Can just anyone come through the gateways now?"

Crowley shot me a dismissive eye roll. "Indeed, although the areas surrounding each are hotly contested territories in the war between the Earthbound Coalition and the Tuath Dé. I only hope the gods still control the other side of this particular portal." He nodded at the sword in my hands. "Dozens of vampires and lesser fae might await us on the other side of this gateway. Keep that sunlight spell you favor ready when you cross."

"Sure," I said with a shrug. "But the spell won't do anything to stop the fae."

Crowley smiled mirthlessly. "Take care of the vampires, and I will handle the fae. If possible, leave a few of the undead intact. I might have need of them, yet."

"That's not creepy at all. But okay."

I took a step toward the gateway, but Crowley stopped me with a hand on my chest. "I'll go through first, casting a barrier of shadow magic ahead of us. Follow closely on my heels and be ready for anything."

"This is your turf. You're the boss."

The shadow wizard frowned, as if he couldn't decide whether I was making fun of him or not. Dismissing my comment with a slight shake of his head, he approached the gateway while summoning an amorphous ball of shadow magic between his hands. Spreading his fingers wide, he pulled his arms apart, pulling the stuff like black taffy. His brow furrowed, then the stuff elongated and flattened until it formed a translucent, man-sized oval that floated in the air in front of him.

"I've seen you do that a lot faster, and with a lot less effort," I remarked.

He gave a short nod. "Yes, but doing it this way allows me to imbue it with quite a bit more durability. A necessity, as I'll need to stretch it even further should we be attacked on the other side."

"Okay, cool. I really have to pee, so can we just go?"

"You should empty your bladder before we engage in battle."

I almost said, *'You're not the boss of me,'* but I thought better of it. Instead, I shrugged. "I'll go after we're out of this cave."

The necromancer stared at me quizzically, then he entered the gateway. Before following Crowley through the portal, I glanced around the cave one last time.

I really hope we don't have to come back this way.

On stepping into the gateway, I immediately knew something was wrong. Having traveled by portal before, via both temporary spell portals and through permanent gateways such as this one, I was familiar with the sensation of instantaneous travel over great distances. Meaning, there was generally little to no sensation at all in most cases, as it was literally like stepping through a doorway—you were *there*, and then you arrived *here*.

Sure, you might feel the shock of moving from one clime to the next or momentarily be overwhelmed by completely new scents and sounds, or be blinded by going from a dark cavern into broad daylight. Except for the time when I'd been involuntarily sent through a transporter spell—basically, a bootleg wormhole tunnel —the transition was always instantaneous. Yet, in this case, my passage from Earth to Underhill seemed to have been drawn out, as if I were walking underwater.

Time seemed to dilate as I passed through the portal as well, which in turn gave me the sensation that I was being drawn out. That feeling of being pulled across space and time persisted for what felt like an eternity. Eventually it seemed as though my entire being had been stretched so thin I might snap like a rubber band, or an overfilled balloon.

Suddenly, I burst through the other side with a *pop*, although I got the impression that the sound existed only in my head. I felt dizzy and nauseous all at once, and my head felt muzzy like I had a bad hangover, except without the usual headache. A weakness over-came me, and I stumbled to my knees. I rolled to my side, clutching my gut.

"The way ahead appears to be clear—strange,"

Crowley said absently from where he stood a few yards ahead.

"I don't feel so hot," I said in a voice that was mine, but not.

Crowley glanced over his shoulder, his strange empty eyes widening in shock at the sight of me. "Oh, this is not good, not at all."

"What?" I asked, pushing myself up to a seated position with my knees pulled up in front of me. "Do I look as bad as I feel?"

Crowley set the oval shadow shield down so that the bottom-most edge touched the ground. Then he spread his arms wide, and the shield expanded to form a ten-foot-tall half-circle around us, until the ends reached the cliff wall behind us where the portal archway stood. Satisfied with the temporary perimeter defenses he'd set up, he walked over and knelt beside me.

"I wouldn't necessarily say you look bad, no. But you most definitely are not yourself, by any stretch of the imagination."

"Meaning?"

He paused, narrowing his eyes in what could have been consternation or concern. "How shall I put this? You appear to be growing younger."

"I what?" I said, reaching for my phone and turning on the camera. I switched to the front-facing lens, gasping as my image appeared on the screen.

Although my biological age was barely enough to allow me to buy alcohol legally, my actual age was somewhere near thirty. If you accounted for all the time I'd spent in the Grove, where time passed differently than it did on the earthly plane, my lifespan was roughly ten years older than my biological age. While I had still retained the youthful appearance of a college-aged male, the mileage had shown in my eyes and bearing, making me seem a lot older than I had any right to look.

But the person looking back at me wasn't the same old prematurely jaded college kid who stared back at me in the mirror every morning. The person on the screen was definitely a familiar face, but someone I hadn't seen in—oh, say four or five years. Instead of twenty-one-year-old me, sixteen-year-old Colin McCool gawked at me from my phone's screen.

"Holy fuck-balls. I've been de-aged."

"Yes, precisely," Crowley said as he grabbed my jaw, turning my face this way and that. "I'm no expert on time magic, but I'd say that you triggered some sort of spell trap when you passed through the gateway."

"You think?" I replied, slapping his hand away. "Shit, this is bad. I can feel myself getting younger, as if the spell is still working."

"Well, the good news is that the effects appear to have slowed considerably since you exited the portal. I'd hazard a guess to say that something interfered with the intended spell velocity. Perhaps your Fomorian DNA is the cause, or the fact that you've dabbled extensively with time magic, or something else entirely." He stroked his chin while examining me like a bug under a magnifying glass. "Fascinating."

I shoved him away, partially because his response was pissing me off, and partially because I needed room to stand. As I pushed myself to my feet, I fought off a wave of disorientation, leaning over with my hands on my knees as it passed. Once I thought I could stand without losing my breakfast—again—I stood to my full height, which happened to be three inches shorter than I'd stood before passing through the gateway.

"Well, shit on a stick and call it a fudgesicle," I said, my voice cracking as I spoke. Then, I yelled at the top of my voice. "Cliiiiiiiiiick!"

I continued ranting while Crowley looked on. "Click, you son of a bitch, you'd better help me fix this—or so help me, I will tell the head of every fucking pantheon that you did this to me before I die."

"No need ta' yell, lad. I'm right here."

I spun around to find the pseudo-god standing right behind me, arms crossed and tapping a finger to his lips.

"I take it this isn't your work?"

"Me? Ya' think I did this ta' ya', an' after all we've been through?" Click made a pearl-clutching gesture. "Right takin' aback, I am by that, an' hurt in no small measure."

"Oh, get over yourself," I growled, although the

crack in my voice diminished the threat somewhat. "Just tell me what the hell happened and fix it."

"And preferably quickly," Crowley added. "The fact that this gateway remains undefended and uncontested bodes ill, I fear. We should move, and soon. While you two discuss this, ah, *unexpected development*, I shall scout ahead."

I caught his eye, acknowledging the wizard with a nod as he passed. Crowley shrouded himself in shadow as he marched toward the forest of tree-sized toadstools that surrounded the gateway clearing. After he'd disappeared into the woods, I turned my attention back to Click.

"Hmm. 'Tis an interestin' spell, ta' be sure," he said, leaning this way and that as peered at me from various angles. "Tight weaves, economic use o' Myrddin's principles—oh, an' that's a nice touch."

"Save the adoration for someone who cares," I groused, "and focus on reversing the spell."

"Hang on," he said as he stood straight once more. I noticed a tightening around his eyes, but that was the only indication of any concern or action on his part. After a few seconds, he threw his arms wide. "Ta-da!"

I didn't feel any different, so I looked at my image in my phone again. Nope, no change whatsoever. "What do you mean, 'ta-da!'? I still look like I'm about to ask Jesse to the prom."

"Not with that acne, yer' not," the immortal wizard

said with some concern. "Witch hazel, ma' boy—trust me on this one."

My frustration finally came to a head, and I snatched Click by his lapels, forcing him to his tiptoes because I wasn't tall enough to lift him off the ground.

"Fix. This. Now."

"Sorry, lad," he said, disappearing and leaving me holding thin air. He reappeared a few feet to my left, arms crossed and leaning against the black basalt cliff next to the gateway. "Best I kin' do is halt the progression o' the spell's effects and prevent further memory loss. At least until the counter-spell fades—but that'll take days."

"Days? You're saying I only have days to live?"

"Aye, but the good news is ya've retained yer' half-Fomorian form. An' ya' still remember who I am. Huzzah!"

Growling loudly, I rubbed a hand over my face. "Can you at least tell me what happened?"

"Nasty bit o' time magic, god-level stuff and keyed specifically ta' anyone bearin' the mark o' druid magic. They cast it on the gateway, likely figurin' ya'd walk through it eventually. Powered the spell with energy from the portal itself—fairly ingenious, if I do say so ma'self."

My pants had become quite loose around my waist, so I cinched up my belt before plopping down on a nearby boulder. "Wait, you're saying one of the gods did this?"

"Obviously," he replied as he shook a cigarette from the pack he always kept. Click pointed the unlit cigarette at me. "Not one who knows ya' well, howe'er, as they didna' account fer' the effects o' yer' Fomorian blood. Lucky thing ya'd shifted before passin' through that gateway, else we'd be wipin' yer' fanny an' fittin' ya' fer' nappies 'bout now."

Click's observation reminded me of a case I'd worked years prior that involved quite a bit of necromancy. Finnegas had been surprised that I wasn't affected by a necromantic circle we'd found and blamed it on my "curse." That was long before I knew I was half-Fomorian, although the old man knew full well about my heritage at the time. Thinking of how he kept that secret from me for years made me chuckle, even though it still pissed me off.

Ornery old bastard.

"So, my natural Fomorian magic resistance slowed the spell down. Do you think if I shifted completely, it'd reverse it?"

Click lit his cancer stick, puffing on it and blowing smoke out his nostrils as he shook his head. "Too risky, lad. Ya've been aged in reverse, meanin' that certain skills ya' had before might've been lost in the process. If ya' try ta' shift, there's no tellin' what could happen. Ya' might turn back ta' full human an' accelerate the spell's effects again. Naw, yer' better off stayin' in yer' current form, till we figure out how ta' reverse it fer' good."

"Great." Then, something horrible occurred to me,

and I stood to my feet. "Oh, hell. When I was this age, I could barely cast a simple cantrip. What if I can't use druid magic anymore?"

The pseudo-deity cupped his chin, allowing the cigarette to dangle from his lips as he replied. "S'quite possible. Only one way ta' find out."

Wiping my sweaty palms on my now oversized jeans, I thought of the easiest bit of advanced magic I could cast. I finally settled on the sunlight spell I kept queued up almost constantly these days. Licking my lips nervously, I raised my hand above my head, then I spoke the trigger word for the spell.

"*Solas.*" Nothing happened. "Man, I am so fucked."

4

"Now what?" I asked Click. "I can't go back through the portal, because I don't want to risk getting hit with that whammy again. I can't stay here, because without my magic I'll get trounced by the first large group of fae or vamps we meet. And I can't go back to—well, you know where—because I have unfinished business here."

Click rubbed his smooth, boyish chin as he considered the situation. Or maybe he was contemplating opening a pizza parlor on Mars. The guy was a mystery to me, and more than a little crazy. For the life of me, I could never predict if he would be fully mentally present at any given moment.

"Truth be told, ya' could do any or all o' those things. But what did the culprit *want* ya' ta' do?"

"Obviously, they wanted to kill me."

Click shook his head slowly. "Nay, lad. If they'd have

wanted ta' kill ya' they'd have waited here ta' ambush ya' once the spell did its work. Let's assume the individual in question knew 'bout yer' Fomorian blood after all. Might be they set this trap ta' prevent ya' from moving forward with yer' plan. Mayhaps they wanted ya' ta' pack up an' head home."

"But why would a god want me to fail? Everything I'm doing here benefits the Celtic pantheon. If I beat the Vampire Nations, they'll likely withdraw their support for the rebel fae. That'll end their invasion into Underhill, for sure. It just doesn't make sense to sabotage me right now."

"Ah, but what if it wasn't a god or goddess from the Celtic pantheon?" Click said as he pointed skyward in 'eureka' fashion. "Even better—what if said deity were settlin' a personal beef?"

"How would that be better?"

A frown flashed across Click's face, only to be immediately replaced with his usual, self-assured grin. "Point taken, but it fits ma' theory, does it not?"

"It's definitely not out of the realm of possibility, considering all the enemies I've made recently."

Click nodded enthusiastically. "Egg-zactly, lad. Why, ye've been slayin' deities an' demigods right an' left of late. Could be any o' at least a half-dozen potential culprits."

"Yeah, but which of them could cast a spell like this?" I said as I took a seat on a boulder. "It's not just any god or goddess who'd mess with time magic, after all."

"Meanin', t'were someone desperate or with very little ta' lose." He took a final puff from his cigarette before discarding it and crushing it under foot with an air of finality. "Yep, I definitely need ta' look inta' this further."

A shimmering seven-foot-tall oval appeared in the air behind Click, through which I saw a tall mountain range with pine-covered foothills along its base. Winged humanoids circled in the skies at a distance, and the slate-gray peaks didn't belong to any terrain I recognized.

"Wait a minute—you're leaving me here?"

Click gave a dismissive wave over his shoulder as he turned to enter the portal. "Pfah, ye'll be fine. That necromancer yer' runnin' with is a right handful. Besides, I'll send someone ta' babysit ya' till I return."

"Hah, very funny," I replied with a scowl.

"Listen, I know this is difficult, but hormones are all a part o' puberty," Click quipped over his shoulder as he entered the portal. "So relax, lad—a bit o' acne cream'll clear that right up."

I flipped him off as the portal disappeared in a blip of magical energy. Despite his casual attitude toward my predicament, Click was right about one thing—the entire situation was frustrating beyond belief. I'd already been underpowered for the tasks ahead before coming to Underhill. Now, things had gotten much, much worse.

No sense crying over spilled milk. Time to take a personal inventory, so I can figure out how to salvage this mess.

On the plus side, I was still in my half-Fomorian form. That meant I was more than a match for any single vamp or common fae. And I still had Dyrnwyn, Gáe Dearg, and Orna, although the latter sword was much too large for me to wield effectively in this form. All the firearms, special ammunition, and munitions I'd had on me were still in my possession, and I still had all the fighting skills I'd possessed as well.

Or did I?

On a whim, I drew Dyrnwyn and stood, moving farther into the clearing to give myself more space. After taking a deep, calming breath, I began to flow through several fencing drills and forms that I'd learned over the years. I started with the Celtic style Finnegas and Maureen had taught me, moving into Filipino and HEMA systems I'd picked up in later years, and finally ending by attempting some of the tengu *kenjutsu* techniques I'd learned from Hideie in recent months.

My movements felt *off* at first, until I adjusted for my shorter stature. Despite that, everything worked—right up until I tried to recall what Hideie had taught me. It was weird, because I definitely remembered training with him, but the skills I'd picked up were just gone.

That wasn't all bad, though, as it indicated that the

retrograde aging of my body had happened much faster than the deterioration of my memory. If I could pinpoint exactly how far back the mental de-aging process went, I'd have a pretty good idea regarding which skills remained.

Since I couldn't cast my sunlight spell, that meant I'd been mentally set back to sometime before my first trip to the Hellpocalypse. During that period, I'd possessed at least a basic knowledge of druidry. Meaning, I must be capable of minor cantrips, as well as a few more impressive feats of magic that required more time and mental preparation to execute.

Let's figure out where I stand.

Sheathing Dyrnwyn, I shook my arms out and cracked my neck. First, I tried to summon a fireball, then a lightning spell. No dice. Next, I cast my flash-bang spell, and it went off like a charm. After that, I cast a spell I used to use to beef up my personal wards, back before I began to rely on my Fomorian DNA to do the same work in battle. It also worked flawlessly.

Finally, I sat down cross-legged, slowing my breathing to enter a druid trance. It took much more effort than it had previously, and I had to go through several breathing cycles before I was able to connect with the magic in my surroundings. However, I *could* still directly connect with nature via my use of druidry. That was something, at least.

Scratching my head, I considered where that left me, power-wise. Back on Earth, I could manage against your average human hunter or mage, or even a supernatural creature like any run-of-the-mill vampire, 'thrope, or fae. But in Underhill?

Fucked. So very fucked.

Here I was as likely to run into a deity as I was to meet one of the ancient fae. I'd be hard-pressed to survive against a god or demigod in this state, and even an entity like Peg Powler would pose serious issues. Yeah, I was good and rightly fucked, but at least I knew what I was working with now.

———

So, looks like I'm doing this the old-fashioned way—by sneaking around and staying under the radar. I sighed, realizing that I could no longer cast a chameleon spell. Then I remembered that I still had Gunnarson's invisibility cloak. Frantically, I rummaged around in my Bag until I found the damned thing. *Oh, sweet mercy, it's still here. Alright, this I can work with.*

By the time Crowley returned from scouting the area, I'd switched around my kit to maximize the odds that I'd survive a trip across Underhill. Thankfully, I never tossed anything away since I could just throw stuff in my Craneskin Bag and forget about it. I could blame it on laziness, but the truth was, after Jesse's death I could never bring myself to part with anything that reminded me of our time together. Besides, most thrift shops frowned on donations of tactical equipment. That meant I still had all the gear I used to wear back when I was hunting with Jesse in high school—gear that actually fit my current, smaller frame.

Score one for my sentimental hoarder instincts. Yay, me.

As for clothing and armor, I'd switched out of my jeans and light combat boots for a pair of my old Kevlar motorcycle pants and steel-toed riding boots. Topside I strapped on a tactical plate carrier that had stab-proof level IIIA soft plates protecting me on the sides and back, and a swimmer's cut level IV plate in the front that offered mobility while sacrificing some coverage.

Across the front of the plate carrier, I'd made good use of the MOLLE system to strap four thirty-round magazines for the 5.56 caliber short-barreled M4 that I'd dug out of my Bag. Two mags were loaded with silver-tipped ammo, and the other two were loaded with iron-tipped, while the mag that was loaded in the SBR alternated between the two types of rounds. I'd just have to remember to double-tap targets until I switched mags, which was probably a good policy anyway.

As for optics, I was running a Trijicon 4x32 ACOG, mostly due to the battery-free illumination and bullet-proof design. I had the rifle slung on a one-point for maneuverability, allowing for quick transitions from rifle to sidearm, to close combat weapons. In a pinch, I could snap the rifle off the sling to get it out of the way, as it was a bitch to fight with a sword while your rifle was swinging around getting in the way.

Speaking of close combat, I'd rigged Dyrnwyn in a breakaway shoulder scabbard, situating it for an awkward but necessary over the shoulder draw. My Glock 17 sat on my right hip, again loaded with a nineteen-round magazine consisting of alternating silver and iron-tipped ammo. I carried two more extended magazines for the Glock on my left hip, one filled with silver and the other with iron-tipped rounds.

Topping my kit off was my silver-plated Bowie knife, carried handle down on the left side of my plate carrier for easy access with either hand. Inside my Bag, I'd rearranged the contents so that Gunnarson's cloak of invisibility and Diarmuid's Red Spear sat within easy reach. The two magical artifacts were my nuclear options, so to speak, and I planned to keep them inside the Bag until I really needed them, and for good reason.

Gáe Dearg would draw too much attention, and besides, Aengus likely still possessed its counterpart in this timeline. Thus, being seen with it would be a dead giveaway that I'd come here using forbidden magic, and that's the last thing I needed. As for Gunnarson's cloak, the damned thing was fickle, and I was afraid that it might not accept me as its bearer in my current, weakened form. Hopefully, I wouldn't need it before I found the Dagda.

One can hope.

When Crowley entered the clearing, he glanced at the new look and harrumphed. "I take it this means I'll be casting most of the magic during this trip."

"Suffice it to say that my body wasn't the only part of me affected by that reverse aging spell."

He gave me a more thorough visual assessment, finishing with a grunt. "No matter. It appears you still know what you're about, based on your chosen weaponry and setup. As for me, I am accustomed to operating in a mage-hunter team, having done so during my tenure with The Cold Iron Circle."

"With Bells, you mean."

A dark look flashed across his features—darker than usual, that was. "That is correct."

"I'm sorry, Crowley. I didn't mean to bring up bad memories."

"On the contrary, they are among the most cherished memories I possess. Thank you for reminding me why we're here." He glanced over his shoulder at the mushroom forest from whence he'd recently returned. "Speaking of, there's something you should see. Come."

Crowley abruptly spun around and headed back into the forest with me following close on his heels. On entering the shadows created by the tall, gently swaying toadstool trees, he motioned for silence by placing a finger to his lips. Within a few steps, we came to a thick wall of ferns that obscured the view ahead, and he motioned for me to kneel as he did the same.

Once I complied, he cloaked us in shadow before gently parting the ferns to reveal a scene that was both shockingly gory and hauntingly familiar. As I swung my gaze back and forth, it was all I could do to resist gasping at the destruction ahead.

Hole-lee shee-it.

A combination of fae and vampire bodies, both whole and dismembered, were strewn all over the forest glade ahead. Various body parts hung from trees that I knew were not indigenous to this area of Underhill, oaks and willows that would be more at home in my native Texas. Many corpses remained in a more or less complete state. Of those, most were bound to the ground by grass or strung up by vines in the canopy above.

Here and there, I spotted a vampire that had been impaled by large, thick thorns. Elsewhere, signs that the fae and vamps had fought back were evident. Large circular burn marks dotted the trees, along with jagged char marks that were indicative of lightning blasts. The forest floor was littered with limbs and vines that had been torn or chopped away, some still clinging to the dead.

Considering that the damage to the plants appeared minimal, I had a hunch that they were regenerating rapidly. As proof of my suspicion, a large oak tree healed itself before my eyes, partially replacing scorched bark and severed limbs over the course of perhaps a minute. During that time, I continued to assess the scene, wishing to make certain I knew exactly who or what was responsible for the carnage I'd witnessed. After I was satisfied with my assessment, I got Crowley's attention and signaled for him to follow me back to the gateway clearing.

"I counted at least three dozen dead back there," he said as we exited the forest. "I've never seen the like in all my time in Underhill. Moreover, the predatory plant life we encountered was most certainly foreign to this plane. Any clue what might have done such a thing?"

I gave a short nod as I sat on a large rock. "I've seen destruction like that before—just not on that level."

"Whatever it was, it tore into them with a rage I've rarely seen," he remarked. "It almost looked like it was carrying out a personal vendetta."

"If I'm right, it was. I'm fairly certain that was the work of a druid oak."

The shadow wizard raised an eyebrow at me. "A druid oak, or *your* druid oak?"

I scratched my nose with a knuckle. "Unless the Dagda has been planting more of them, there's only one in this timeline as far as I know. And to my knowledge, mine is the only druid oak in history that's completely autonomous and mobile."

"Mobile, meaning..."

"My Oak can teleport."

"Ah. That explains it, then."

I furrowed my brow as I fixed him with a hard stare. "That's not common knowledge, so if you could keep it to yourself, I'd appreciate it."

"Of course. But now I see why you're so eager to bond with the oak in this timeline. Egads, but what a tactical advantage control of such an entity must provide. And the utter destructive power of the thing—" He shook his head in apparent disbelief. "It almost leads one to believe that you have been holding back."

"Not entirely, and not in this timeline or my own. Even after a druid bonds with an oak and assumes control of a grove, it takes decades, and sometimes even centuries, for them to truly master that power. I, um, took a shortcut to druid mastery in my own timeline, and I still hadn't tapped a fraction of my Oak's power there."

"Oh?" Crowley sat on another boulder, so he faced both me and the forest beyond. "Do tell."

"Let's just say I used the ultimate cheat code and leave it at that. It was a one-time thing, and not something I can repeat here. That is, not unless Finnegas were alive in this timeline, and he's not."

"How do you know that the Seer is dead?"

"I came across some graves at the junkyard in Austin. At the time, I didn't want to admit who they belonged to, but now?" I shook my head slowly. "If Finnegas was alive, he'd have found me already."

"You seem quite unaffected by that revelation," Crowley observed. "I take it your mentor had also expired in your own timeline?"

"Yep." The memories were still raw, and I felt the old man's absence just as acutely here. But I'd learned to cope with those feelings since his passing, so my expression remained neutral as I *tsked* away the matter.

"Bottom line is that we can't count on help from that quarter. We need to find the Dagda."

"Meaning, nothing has changed, despite your recently altered state. Except that one more obstacle now lies in our path to deific assistance."

"Oh yeah?"

"We've not been accosted since we left the gateway. Have you wondered why?" He swept a hand at the vast forest of mushroom trees that lay beyond the clearing. "That verdant killing field runs in a wide swathe around this entire hillock and clearing. It seems that the Vampyri and rebel fae had captured this gateway before they ran afoul of your would-be vegetal familiar."

"Are you saying the Oak's magic is blocking our way out of here?"

"Precisely," he replied with just the slightest hint of condescension in his voice.

"I'm pretty sure that won't be an issue. C'mon." I slapped my hands on my thighs and stood, marching toward the tree line without looking back to see if he followed.

5

I stopped at the edge of the forest, taking a moment to enter a druid trance so I could extend my senses ahead. After a few breathing cycles, I cautiously pushed my awareness outward through the mushroom trees and to the killing field beyond. At first, I merely probed the edges of the area—partially to verify that it did indeed surround us, and also to get a feel for the semi-intelligent plant life that the Oak had left behind.

As I gently investigated the killer flora that occupied the area, I was assured beyond a doubt that it was the Oak's work. After living with it—or rather, in it—for one Earth year and perhaps the equivalent of a decade in Grove years, I'd recognize that magical signature anywhere. No doubt about it: this was the work of the Druid Oak.

Now that I'm certain of that, let's run a little test.

I extended my awareness even further, all the way

into the heart of the glen and into the midst of the deadly trees and vines that had slaughtered a platoon of vampires and fae. Once there, I chose one of the willow trees at random and touched it with my mind. Instantly, the willow's branches began to shake and thrash in agitation, as if the thing were casting about to determine the location of a hidden intruder. Before the tree could alert other plants around it—and potentially place us in danger—I projected my image to the willow, imprinting my own unique druidic signature to it telepathically.

As quickly as it had erupted into movement, the willow tree settled down until it was calmly swaying back and forth in the breeze. Since we had to pass through the killing field, I contacted each plant and tree in the area in turn, getting similar reactions at first contact and upon identifying myself. When I had calmed a swathe of the killing field approximately ten yards wide, I opened my eyes and gave Crowley a nod.

"We're good. They won't harm us now."

"Are you sure?" he asked as he arched an eyebrow.

"As sure as a druid can be when communicating telepathically with semi-sentient plants. It's not an exact science, you know."

I walked ahead, pushing through the ferns without looking to see if Crowley had followed. Outwardly, I maintained a calm demeanor, but I kept a nervous watch on the foliage all around. Once I reached the approximate middle of the patch of deadly vegetation, I turned and spread my arms wide.

"See? They're perfectly docile now."

The ferns parted and Crowley's head poked through. "For a moment I'd thought your druidic magic had completely abandoned you, but wonders never—"

The shadow wizard was cut off mid-sentence when a thick, thorny vine shot out from the undergrowth, wrapping itself around his neck. Before I could react, the plants and trees nearest to Crowley came to life, thrashing, flaying, and grabbing at him from every direction.

To his credit, the wizard did a fine job of responding to the threats. Almost instantly, he sprouted several shadow appendages of his own in an attempt to fight the various vines, tree limbs, and grasses that were accosting his person. Then, twin fireballs appeared above his hands, and I knew things were about to get out of control.

"Wait, stop!" I cried aloud, simultaneously sending a general mental broadcast to the nearby plant life. "He's a friend."

Just as suddenly as the attack had started, the plants and trees withdrew, although one vine stubbornly held onto Crowley's torso. The wizard gestured with one hand as if he were about to release his fireball. I waved my hands back and forth in response.

"Don't do that," I whispered sotto voce. "If you attack them with fire, I don't think I'll be able to convince them you're friendly."

The wizard scowled, then the fireballs disappeared. However, that last vine reluctantly held onto Crowley.

"Hey, c'mon now—let him go." The vine rustled in protest. "I mean it. Let go."

Slowly, like a child caught with their hand in the cookie jar, the vine unwrapped itself from around Crowley's chest. Then, it slunk back off into the undergrowth from whence it came. Just to be certain, I sent out another mental broadcast declaring Crowley as an ally, then turned my gaze on my companion.

The shadow wizard drew himself up indignantly, crossing his arms and staring down his nose at me. "I thought you were certain that the plant life would not attack?"

"So I forgot to tell them you were with me. Big deal. You're still in one piece, mostly," I said with a smile. "Good thing you had a gardener around, eh?"

Crowley continued to stare at me imperiously, not moving a muscle. I pointed to where a leaf and some twigs had lodged in the shadow wizard's hair. A small, thin shadow tentacle detached itself from his back, whipping up to snatch the detritus from his head.

"There's still one, um, over there," I said, straight-faced. The shadow limb moved to the right side of his head. "Nope, other side. Yep, that's it—right there. I think that's all of it."

The shadow tentacle held the remaining leaf over Crowley's head. A second later, the leaf was consumed by a sickly yellow fire until it shriveled up and turned to ash. After the dust had blown away into the wind, the shadow wizard uncrossed his arms before marching past me in a huff.

"I should never have helped him," he muttered under his breath. "No good ever comes of assisting Colin McCool. Oh sure, the druid can fall into a muddy pig sty and come up smelling like a rose. Meanwhile, everyone around him steps in pig waste."

I stifled a laugh, which caused Crowley to pause and glance over his shoulder. As he caught sight of me in his peripheral vision, I covered my mouth behind my hand, diverting my attention to a nearby oak. The wizard merely shook his head, then he resumed his march in what I assumed was a northward direction, based on what I remembered from our last jaunt here.

I allowed him to go on ahead, waiting until he had disappeared behind another willow tree before following. Before I could catch up, Crowley's voice echoed from up ahead.

"Ah, druid—I think we have another problem."

Rather than walking around the willow tree, I chose to duck and dodge under and through its drooping branches. It was harmless to me now, and even with my current diminished druidic powers, I doubted any plant native to Earth would present a serious threat. My eyes were on the ground as I dipped underneath the whip-like strands on the other side of the tree's drip line, entering into the small clearing ahead.

"Crowley, it's like I said—just leave the plants alone and they'll leave you alone—" I suddenly found myself quite speechless as I exited the willow's foliage and saw what stood beyond. "Oh."

Crowley stood in front of another oak tree, but it wasn't just any oak tree—it was the Oak, my Oak. As I emerged into view, I had the sense it was measuring me, and the tree's presence felt quite ominous and foreboding for several long seconds. Thankfully the shadow wizard had the good sense to stand still and appear nonthreatening, and instinctively I did the same.

After a time, the Oak seemed to physically relax, and the threatening feeling was replaced by the familiar calm I normally felt in the tree's presence. Since it seemed to recognize me, I attempted to communicate with it directly.

Hey, it's me, Colin McCool. Remember?

After a brief pause, the Oak sent a series of images to me. The first was of me as an adult, perhaps with fewer of the faint worry lines I'd gained over the previous year. The next was a vision of the junkyard, lit up by a bright light, followed by the appearance of a mushroom cloud in the distance. The last was an image of the graves I'd found at the junkyard when I passed through Austin.

Did those belong to Finnegas and Maureen?

I received only an intense feeling of sadness in reply, which I took as a yes.

I saw you back on Earth, didn't I?

The Oak sent back several images of me protecting Anna and the children, freeze-frame stills of events that had happened since my return to the Hellpocalypse.

You've been watching me for some time, then. Why didn't you approach me or make contact?

An image flashed in my mind of a gray, amorphous humanoid figure that warped and shifted into a perfect facsimile of me.

Ah, you thought I was a doppelganger. That makes sense. How'd you know it was really me?

Again, images flashed through my mind, this time of me communicating with the plants and trees in the killing field.

I suppose that's proof enough. With Finnegas gone, I'm the only druid left.

The same sense of sadness emanated from the Oak that I'd felt earlier, but less pronounced.

I miss him too—well, both of them. I'm here all alone now, just like you, and I could really use your help.

The Oak failed to respond, which wasn't unusual, as it rarely engaged in spontaneous conversation. Yet I sensed something through our mental connection, a vague feeling that was not quite distrust. Hesitation, maybe? Or fear.

I'm not going to hurt you—I could never do that. I just need to bond with you so I can access my full powers.

In response, the Oak's limbs and leaves shivered and lashed about.

"Druid, I assume you're communicating with that great hulking bulk of chlorophyll and wood pulp," Crowley said. "But if you're going to anger it, please wait until I've vacated the thin strip of forest it has claimed."

I ignored Crowley's protests, because I didn't want to lose the connection with the Oak.

Did I say something wrong?

The Oak sent me an image of a rabbit caught in a snare.

No, I don't mean you any harm. I just want us to connect—

The Oak cut off the communication abruptly, and it disappeared in a swirl of dead leaves and grass. Despite my attempts to contact it again, I sensed that the Oak had traveled far, far away, and that it was refusing to respond to my telepathic overtures. Stunned, I stood there with my mouth agape for several seconds, wondering what had just happened.

"Well, at least it didn't tear us limb from limb," Crowley remarked as he turned to face me. "That is something, at least."

I shook my head, still disbelieving that the Oak—my Oak—would shun me like that. "I honestly don't know what happened. We were communicating just fine, it recognized me, and then I told it that I wanted to bond with it."

"And then?"

"That's when it took off."

"Ah."

I frowned in consternation. "Ah, what?"

"Perhaps you would be more familiar with this sort of thing than I, considering your current state of being. It seems, to me at least, that your great green familiar is going through a rebellious stage."

"You mean it's acting like a teenager."

"Well, yes—although I didn't want to come right out and say it, as such."

"Gee thanks," I replied saltily. "I normally wouldn't expect so much tact from you."

"This," he said as he made a grand gesture that covered me from head to foot, "is exactly what I'm referring to. Have you not noticed that you've been acting somewhat, oh, shall we say, *hormonal* since you exited the gateway?"

"I am not acting hormonal," I shouted, throwing my hands in the air. "So get off my back!" Crowley merely gazed at me with a knowing, self-satisfied look on his face. I took a few deep breaths, ending with one final, long exhalation. "Okay, so maybe you have a point. But I can't help it if my body is doing things I don't want it to do."

"Perhaps the same goes for your familiar," he said, raising an index finger in the air. "Consider that it thought you were dead. It, being a relatively young creature, suddenly found itself alone in a nightmare world where its entire purpose for living had been utterly and completely erased from existence. Since your counterpart's death, and that of your mentor in this timeline, it has been fending for itself."

"And taking revenge where it could."

Crowley narrowed his weird, empty eyes. "And for an entity not normally given to violence, that would indicate it had experienced quite a bit of trauma, wouldn't you say? Picture a recently orphaned teenage child, who, on finding herself bereft of family and home, struck out into the great wide world alone. Now, imagine that she was forced to fend for herself for months on end."

"Go on."

"Think of how that child would feel, after essentially being abandoned by her parents—"

"Through no fault of my own," I interjected.

"—and surviving for months alone, only to find out that her father was still alive. Having somewhat successfully fended for herself and done fine without a father figure to protect her, would she want to give up her newfound freedom in order to regain that which was lost?"

I sighed and scratched my head. "Look, I get what you're saying here, but it doesn't make sense. For one, a druid oak can't survive without a druid master, at least not according to Finnegas. It's a symbiotic creature, and it'll just wither away and die without a druidic bond to nourish it. Besides, why would the Oak be mad at me? It's not like the other me meant to die in a nuclear holocaust."

"Certainly, but that's inconsequential. The feelings of abandonment and subsequent resentment and anger would still remain. And in a relatively immature mind, those feelings could be distorted to such an extent that the need for family would be replaced by a desire to avoid being hurt by a similar loss again."

I rubbed a hand down my face as I considered Crowley's theory. "Wow. Honestly, that makes a lot of sense. Since when did you get all Dr. Phil and stuff?"

"I had been studying literature and research on human attachment and emotional bonding, before Belladonna's passing."

"Oh."

Crowley stared off into space for several moments, then he turned his gaze on me again. "Standing here isn't going to get you any closer to regaining that thing's trust, nor will it help you discover how to force a bond on it that it may not be willing to accept. It appears that now, more than ever, you require the Dagda's knowledge and assistance." He inclined his head in the general direction we'd been traveling. "Shall we, then?"

I pretty much agreed with everything Crowley had said, especially his assertion that I needed the Dagda's help now more than ever. But something was nagging at me about the Oak's sudden exit that I couldn't quite put my finger on.

"You go on ahead, I'll be right there."

As Crowley picked his way through the giant mushroom stalks ahead, I knelt to search the forest floor.

Sifting through the grasses and ferns at my feet, I finally found it—a single, brown, curled oak leaf.

I was right; it is dying. And the more power it uses, the faster it'll age and speed along to its death.

I had no idea how long it would take for the Oak to wither and die, and I really didn't want to find out. We needed to track down the Dagda, and fast, so I could save my Oak and get my powers back. And we needed to do that before Click's counter-spell wore off—and I was de-aged out of existence.

No pressure, Colin. No pressure at all.

6

We exited the toadstool forest after perhaps a half-day's march, pausing at the shadowed edge of the outlying thickets to survey the landscape ahead. Time and space worked differently here, and while we'd traveled in the same general direction as last time, the terrain ahead looked quite unfamiliar. I took a knee to ensure I stayed hidden as I stared at the scene before us.

These woods were supposed to lead directly to the Dagda's bountiful fields, and past that, his cottage and homestead. Instead of rolling hills covered in neat rows of summer wheat, oats, and rye, the land ahead was barren and scorched. Where nature's bounty was concerned, nothing but cracked earth, dust, and a few sparse tufts of dead grass lay ahead for as far as the eye could see. Here and there, craters dotted the fields and gentle slopes, scarring the earth in blackened pock-marks twenty to thirty feet across.

There'd been killing done here, that was a fact, but the bodies had since been picked over by carrion feeders, leaving nothing but sun-bleached bones, rotting leather armor, and patinaed buckles and fittings. As I surveyed the land, I spotted the odd dented shield, broken spear shaft, or bent bronze sword poking up from or lying haphazardly in the dirt. Off in the distance, a tattered and faded green banner swayed with tired indifference from a shaft that had been thrust at an odd angle into the dry soil atop a low rise.

All-in-all, it reminded me a hell of a lot of Tethra's killing fields.

"What do you think happened here?"

Crowley squatted beside me, brow knit in contemplation. "A battle, the likes of which Underhill has never seen." He shaded his eyes with one hand, casting his gaze slowly back and forth across the horizon. "It goes on for miles, seemingly."

"And no sign of the Dagda's farm. Destruction like this had to involve more than just a few fae and some vamps."

He gave a grim nod. "This was a clash of the gods, no doubt." He stood and strolled to the edge of the forest, where the undergrowth abruptly gave way to scorched earth. "And look here," he said, kneeling to run his fingers through the dry soil. "The earth has been salted.

Who else but a god or goddess would spite the Dagda so?"

"I can't see how he'd allow for that to happen. Not unless—" I grimaced, not wanting to say it. "You don't think the Dagda's dead, do you?"

Crowley stared off into the distance. "I'm not sure, and I think it's best we refrain from jumping to any hasty conclusions."

"I distinctly heard a 'but' in that sentence."

He stood, allowing the salted, parched dust to sift from his hand. "But this bodes ill for the master of these lands, nonetheless."

"Right." I scanned the landscape again, searching for any sign of danger. Then, I turned my attention to the skies, pointing at some specks that circled in the distance. "You see that?"

"Carrion birds, either feeding or spying for their master."

"Badb, you think?"

He hissed through his teeth. "Or one of the other Morrígna. Nemain in particular would revel in slaughter of this sort."

"I have a hard time seeing Macha involved in something like this."

"Oh?" Crowley said with genuine surprise in his voice as he turned his gaze on me.

"I've had some dealings with her in the past. She seems the type to scheme from the shadows rather than confront her enemies openly."

The shadow wizard gave a short, barking laugh. "Do not fool yourself, druid. Macha is as much a Phantom Queen of Battle as her sisters."

"I'm sure, but she's helped me on more than one occasion." I nodded at the black birds circling ahead. "Think we should check that out?"

"I do not care for the prospect of traveling any distance in Underhill exposed. However, it might take us days to go around this vast barren landscape, and there's no way to tell where that detour may lead. We could easily end up in the territory of one of the Tuath Dé who stands in opposition to the Dagda and his allies."

"You really think some of the Celtic gods and goddesses teamed up with the vamps and Earthbound fae to oppose the Dagda?"

He gestured at the parched, salted land. "The answer lies before you."

I let out a low whistle. "That's messed up. Besides, I don't see what they'd get out of it. Back in my own time-line, Badb and Aengus were angling for some sort of return to their former glory on Earth. I got the impression they wanted to be worshipped again by humans, and on a grand scale. I fail to see how handing the Earth over to the Vampire Nations would accomplish that."

"Not unless they intended to wipe the slate clean and start over anew." Crowley's shadow-filled eyes swirled as he fixed me with his dark gaze. "Imagine a scenario where humans have been nearly wiped out by the undead. Should some god or gods swoop in to vanquish their oppressors, how could the remaining population *not* fall to their knees in adulation of their saviors?"

"A double-double cross. First Badb and company turn on their own kind, then they turn on the Vampyri who helped defeat them." I gave a forlorn shake of my head. "Damn it if it doesn't make a hell of a lot of sense, and it's exactly the sort of thing I'd expect from Badb. No wonder Macha opposes them."

Crowley tsked. "It is all conjecture until we speak with the Dagda." He inclined his head at the birds circling over the rolling, desolate plain in the distance. "Come, let us see what awaits us in this vast graveyard."

Crowley and I trotted across the barren landscape, doing our best to cross the vast distance of open space before any enemy forces that might be lurking about spotted us. Although it appeared that nothing living was present for miles around, this was Underhill, after all. When you were dealing with high Fae and Celtic gods, illusions and invisibility were not beyond the scope of possibility.

Moving at the limit of my Fomorian speed, Crowley was hard-pressed to keep up with me, even while loping along on his shadow magic tentacles. When I noticed that he was no longer at my side, I glanced over my shoulder and found him straggling several hundred yards back. I slowed my pace without commenting on his inability to match my own.

Thus, we maintained a speed that I estimated to be in the realm of forty miles per hour, certainly much faster than any human could travel on foot. The birds had been circling at a distance that I estimated to be at least five miles, perhaps more. Yet Underhill fooled us again, as it was well over an hour before we drew close enough to identify them as battle crows.

"Have they seen us yet?" I asked.

"Oh, most certainly. I would assume that we drew their attention long ago. If they do indeed answer to one of the Morrígna, I would expect her to be along shortly.

"That is, if they recognize us. The way you look right now, you could easily be one of the unseelie Fae. And as for me, the only thing that moves at this speed carrying this much firepower is a member of a Vampyri hit squad. Unless the birds are in direct mental communication with Badb or Nemain, I doubt very seriously we would be much cause for concern."

As we drew closer to our destination, cries of battle and the clash of metal weapons rang out over the rolling plain from up ahead. The wizard and I shared a look, and I kept pace as he poured on as much speed as he could manage. If another battle was raging, we might find the Dagda there—all the more reason to cross the distance and see what was going on.

Crowley frowned as we crested a low rise, which allowed us to achieve a high enough vantage point to see what had drawn the crows' attention. "Indeed, it seems they have concerns enough of their own."

Below us in a long, relatively flat valley between a pair of low ridges, approximately two thousand fae and vampires were engaged in battle. At first it was difficult to tell which side was which, because from where I stood it looked to be just one huge, broiling mass of combatants. I then realized that half of them wore modern tactical gear and clothing similar to my own, while their opponents sported a wide variety of Bronze Age and medieval armor and weapons.

The battle had apparently been raging for some time, probably since the early morning hours when Crowley and I were first emerging from the gateway. Serving as proof, hundreds of corpses lay strewn across the field of battle, echoing the scene that had first greeted us at the edge of the toadstool forest.

"Do you recognize anyone down there?" I asked.

"Not yet," Crowley replied as he observed the battle's ebb and flow. "Neither do I recognize the livery and standard borne by the troops native to Underhill."

With no small amount of chagrin, I realized that the side I'd marked for Underhill's team were mostly bedecked in various shades of green. I kept that oversight to myself as I tried to make some sense of which was the losing side.

"I don't see any of the Celtic gods either." Something caught my eye just then, a seemingly familiar form amidst the chaos. I squinted, shielding my eyes from the false sun above as I attempted to make out more detail. Cursing, I cast a cantrip to enhance my already superior Fomorian eyesight.

"What do you see, Druid?"

"I'm not sure, but I think that might be Jesse down there." I pointed to the center of the primary skirmish line, where a green pennant fluttered in the soft breeze that blew through the valley. "See there? The brunette in the pale green robe, fighting with a short sword and a shillelagh."

He spoke a few words in an obscure fae dialect, and the swirling mass of shadow in his eye sockets coalesced into sharp, fine points of blackness. Contrasted with his pale skin, it made him look like a cartoon character from one of those old Saturday morning comic strips. I'd have laughed if it weren't for the fight raging below and my current messed-up predicament.

"It seems she's shed her dryad persona," he remarked.

"Maybe the Dagda did something about it in this timeline? Or had the other me already bonded with the Oak? Ah, hell, all this dual timeline shit gets me confused."

"Regardless, if that is indeed your former paramour, we had best lend her side whatever aid we can offer." Crowley's eyes returned to their new normal—spooky and fucked up, versus funny and fucked up—as he pointed at the valley floor. "See there? The tide is turning in favor of the vampires and rebels."

Crowley was right. The bad guys seemed to be rallying around a central leader, a female vamp wielding a huge two-handed sword. She knew what she was about, and she was quickly cutting a path of destruction through the Underhill army's lines toward Jesse's position.

"Aw, shit." I looked at Crowley, and he waved me off toward the battle.

"Go. I will do what I can from up here before joining you below."

"Just don't get killed," I said as I sped off down the hill, shouldering my rifle at a run.

I lost sight of Jesse and the female vampire, so I kept my eyes on the pennant and headed in that general direction. As I ran, I popped off rounds at random vamps and rebel fae, alternating my targets based on how I'd stacked my ammo in the magazine. There was no way I could've pulled it off in my fully human form, but my Fomorian dexterity allowed me to score several headshots, dropping leeches and fae like flies as I approached.

Once I hit the edges of the battlefield, I found it was all I could do to pick my way through the corpses while staying on my feet. Dead bodies littered the ground for a good fifty yards around the area where the living and undead were currently engaged. That sea of corpses offered little in the way of firm footing, and even those bodies that had succumbed to rigor mortis shifted sickeningly underfoot. The patches of bare ground I found were little better, the soil soaked and turned to thick, cloying mud with the lifeblood of hundreds of dead fae.

Oh, the smell—ugh.

I'd been in battles before, most notably fighting large groups of zombies and ghouls, but never had I engaged in close quarters combat on a large scale like this. The lesser undead stank, but this was something else entirely. The scents of fresh and spoilt blood mixed with piss and shit created an entirely natural yet absolutely *wrong* bouquet that turned my stomach.

And the sounds. Some of the bodies I passed weren't yet dead. Mixed in with the clash of metal and the sounds of flesh being sliced and ripped apart were moans and groans that chilled me to the bone. I hated the fae—always had, always would. But until you heard one of the *fear dearg* or a buggane crying for their mother as they tried desperately to shove their intestines back into their gut—well, you didn't really know how deep that hate went, or where it might give way to reluctant sympathy.

I didn't have time for any mercy killings, so I kicked away the odd hand that reached out to snag my leg as I passed, keeping my eyes on the battle ahead. Steering for the spot where I thought I'd be closest to Jesse, I unslung the rifle and tossed it in my Bag, as it'd only get in the way now. Once my hands were free, I pulled Dyrnwyn from its sheath, smiling with grim satisfaction as the blade flared to life with a heat and light brighter than the sun.

I guess all these fuckers are evil in their own way. Figures.

By then, I'd reached the outer edge of the active battlefield. Taking one last look around to get my bearings, I made a wild guess as to Jesse's position in relation to mine, then I dove into the fray. Slashing at some random vampire's neck, I cut loose with a battle cry.

"For the Dagda!" I screamed as I laid about with Dyrnwyn. "The Dagda!"

The shout was as much to identify myself to Jesse's side as it was to overcome the nervous tension that had built in me on the way down. I was dressed like the vamps and Earthbound fae, and hell if I wanted to get killed by friendly fire. It'd be pretty freaking dumb to get ganked by the side I was trying to help, after all.

Soon nearby fae who were dressed in green took up the call as well, echoing it across the field of battle and assuaging my friendly-fire fears. But once I was deep in the fray, there was little time to worry about such matters. The battle was absolute chaos, and it was all I could do to cut my way through the rabble before me. Most of the combatants were low-level vampires and fae, and they fell beneath the wrath of the legendary blade I carried just as easily as any human would fall when cleaved by three feet of cold steel.

As for the Fair Folk, the armies on either side consisted of your typical red caps, glaistigs, leanan sídhe, clurichans, and the like, with the odd buggane and ogre thrown in for good measure. Basically, they were the kinds of fae I might run into at Rocko's trailer park or hanging out at the Bloody Fedora during happy hour. As for the vamps who bolstered the rebel fae's ranks, they appeared to be relatively young for the most part, if the speed at which they moved was any indication.

As I progressed toward my goal, I caught two vamps off guard, beheading the first and chopping the second off at the knees before they knew what hit them. Then I found myself in the midst of the enemy, realizing only then that the flaming, white-hot sword I held and the fact I was screaming the Dagda's name kind of marked me out as a target. At that point, it was pure survival.

A dark-haired, goateed male fae in tan cargo pants and a matching plate carrier came at me from the right, swinging a nasty-looking mace with a spiked brass ball at the end. He was splattered in blood from head to toe and had the bedraggled look of someone who'd been fighting for his life for hours. As he swung that mace down at my head, I parried to the outside, redirecting the blow with a hard chopping motion as I turned to face him.

Dyrnwyn did the work for me, however, blazing with a fury I'd rarely seen as it responded to the mass of evil beings that surrounded me. As I turned the parry into a redirection, the blade cut through the wooden shaft of the mace like butter. Following through with the motion, the burning sword severed through the fae's left forearm, lopping his hand off at an angle, just past the elbow. Knowing that the sword's heat had likely cauterized the wound, I took no chances, as he was still a threat. A quick thrust to the throat finished the job, and I barely registered the look of shock in his eyes as he fell to his knees before me.

Step by step, I cut down those who stood in my way, slicing a path through the skirmishers toward my intended goal. Every so often I'd see a patch of pale green cloth whipping in the wind, and I altered my course each time as I fought my way closer to it. Finally, I made it through the thickest part of the fighting, emerging into a smallish clearing that had spontaneously cropped up around Jesse and her vampire counterpart.

7

J ust as I forced my way through the skirmish line that surrounded Jesse and the female vampire, my ex-girlfriend's voice rose up above the clamor of battle as she challenged the female vampire to single combat.

"You and me, you two-bit, 'roided up leech," she said as she pointed her short sword across the small clearing at the vamp. "It's high time you and I had it out, Cessily. Single combat, winner take all."

I glanced from where Jesse stood on one side of the clearing to the female vampire standing on the other side. Cessily stood at least six and a half feet tall, a giant compared to me in my current condition. The vampire was built like one of those Scandinavian cross fitness athletes, with a powerlifter's thighs and a broad, muscular upper body. Adding to the Viking war goddess look, her light blonde hair was pulled back into a thick braid that kept it out of her steel-blue eyes and away from her square-jawed, pert-nosed, high cheek-boned face.

Huh, Chalk one up for the Vampyri's willingness to buck convention.

Typically, master vampires chose their progeny based on their supermodel looks first, and their utility second. In this case however, it seemed her maker chose her primarily for the latter, as Cessily was more "super-hero" than "supermodel." She *was* pretty, but she definitely had a road warrior, apocalyptic warlord look going rather than a social media fitness influencer kind of thing.

As evidence, I noted the necklace of severed ears and fingers that hung around her neck, as well as the extensive gore that covered the black motorcycle leathers she wore from head to toe. Fresh blood on her face and hair glistened in the false sunlight, and when she licked away a speck on her upper lip, it made her look that much more sinister.

Oh yeah, she's a bad one.

"You sure you want this, Princess?" the vampire crooned in a high, feminine voice that contrasted with her stature. "Because I don't think you're up to the challenge."

"Wouldn't have offered if I didn't," Jesse sneered.

"Fine," Cessily replied, planting the tip of her longsword in the mud at her feet. "How's this going to work?"

"If I lose, my troops will surrender their arms and quit the field. You agree to let them go peacefully after they disarm. And if I win, your side does the same."

Cessily wiped a stray bit of gore from her cheek with a knuckle as she considered the terms. "I'm good with that. Just give me a second to talk it over with my lieutenants."

As Cessily conferred with a short, dark-haired female fae and a dark-skinned male vamp in hushed tones, Jesse relaxed and stretched, working the kinks out of her neck and shoulders. As she did, I noted she wore leather armor under the loose, pale green tunic I'd spotted from atop the hill. Her upper legs were bare, but she had matching leather greaves covering her lower legs, tucked into sturdy ankle high boots with a low heel and bronze caps at the toes.

The leaf-shaped sword she held thrummed through the air as she flourished it in lazy circles while she waited. I was almost certain the blade had magical properties, and the fact that it had been forged of steel and not bronze told me it was a more recent creation. Yet the shillelagh in her other hand seemed to have no particular enchantments placed upon it. That said, it bore nothing in the way of nicks and scratches from the day's battle, so I was more than certain it hid tricks of its own.

"Are we doing this or what, Giganta?" Jesse said with a sigh and an affected, impatient scowl. "Because I have vampires to kill and places to be."

Hah! She stole that line from me. Or did I steal it from her?

"Oh, we're doing this, cupcake," Cessily replied, glancing over her shoulder at Jesse. The female fae smirked and the male vamp had an expression of grim satisfaction as they returned to their places at the edges of the circle behind their commander. Cessily casually turned to face Jesse once more, snatching her longsword up almost lazily. "Whenever you're ready, Cordelia, say when."

Jesse's eyes narrowed as a smile played at the corners of her mouth. Keeping her eyes on Cessily, she shouted over her shoulder. "Fergus, sound the horn."

Behind Jesse, a tall, lean male fae with fine features and dark hair waved Underhill's battle standard back and forth in response. Then, with one gloved hand he grabbed a brass coronet hanging from a sling across his chest, bringing the ivory mouthpiece to his lips to blow a short staccato tune. The bugler played the same short song over and over again, until the sounds of battle subsided all around and warriors from either side turned to see what the fuss was about.

So, Jess is in charge. Go figure.

Seeing my old flame up close tugged at my heartstrings a bit, but I dismissed the sentiment for the sake of staying on mission. Although I mentally commanded Dyrnwyn to extinguish its fire, I kept it in hand just in case. Then, I took a moment to get a better look at Jesse using my mage sight, to see if she really had shed her dryad persona as she had in my timeline. She definitely still possessed some druid magic, or it possessed her, but not near the levels I'd seen when she was hopped up on the Oak's power after the tree's birth.

Let's hope she has enough left to deal with the giant, scary vampire chick, because she's gonna be pissed if I jump in to save her.

The thought was interrupted as I got jostled from the side. I almost stabbed the offender—a squat, red-bearded dwarf in a green tunic that matched Jesse's. When he backed off with his hands in the air, I relaxed and lowered my blade. I noted that his helmet had been lacquered a deep red color, and I wondered if he was related to Rocko or Sal.

"Easy now, lad," the dwarf said in lilting English. He inclined his head at the combatants facing off in the clearing. "Show's startin', and I'm just tryin' ta' get a decent view."

A quick glance around us revealed that eyes on either side were now locked on Jesse and Cessily. I turned my attention back to the red cap. "You been fighting for her long?"

He shrugged as he adjusted his thick leather breast plate with one hand, slinging blood off his cleaver with the other. "Aye, since she took over. The coldblooded scab yonder's been harassing us fer' weeks, sendin' assassination squads after our commander at night, killing our pickets an' the like. Commander had enough, called her out ta' do battle, an' now we'll se toothed twat get her just desserts."

A buggane on the other side of the dwarf cle throat loudly before spitting phlegm and blood ๛ the ground. He wore no colors to speak of, except for the blood-matted coat of fur that covered him from head to toe. "Eh, the Dagda's pet rat'll fall a'fore ol' Cess, mark my word."

With a twinkle in his eye, the red cap tilted his head as he met the buggane's gaze. "Care ta' wager on that? Say, five ton that the dead cunt meets her final end at ma' lady's hand?"

"Shoor as eggs is eggs, I'll take that bet." The buggane pressed a nostril closed with his thumb and blew snot on the ground. "Trout inna' hand, I say."

The dwarf suppressed a smile behind his thick beard and mustache as they shook on it. Then, he crossed his arms and nudged me with an elbow. "Day's lookin' up, it seems—p'raps I have ya' ta' thank? Stay close, then. If yer' ma' lucky charm, I don't want'cha ta' get killed an' break the spell."

"Gee, thanks," I replied sourly as I wondered what happened to Crowley. "You wouldn't happen to have seen a necromancer roaming around, would you? Dark hair, smoky eyes, pale and creepy as fuck?"

"Can't say I have, lad," the dwarf replied. I opened my mouth to say something else, but he placed a finger to his lips. "Hush now, they're 'bout ta' begin."

Now that the red cap was ignoring me, I had no choice but to focus on the fight brewing in front of us. Was I concerned about Jesse? Sure, but I figured she hadn't lasted through weeks of fighting in Underhill on her good looks alone. She'd always been canny and tough, and I figured she had some tricks up her sleeve for dear Miss Cessily.

Jesse sure didn't look worried as she and the vampire began circling each other in the makeshift ring. She moved with a confidence I recognized, a cocksure awareness that she had everything under control and the enemy was right where she wanted them. As the two commanders stalked each other, a susurrus arose among the fighters gathered all around, punctuated here and there with a few crass calls for bloodletting.

Apparently the red cap isn't the only one who wanted to see this match happen.

"Rip her fucking head off, Cess!" a female voice screamed from across the ring. The shout was met with similar cries for wanton bloodshed on either side, escalating to a collective roar as the vampire sprang into action.

Cessily crossed the ring with speed that no one her size should possess, swinging her greatsword at Jesse's neck faster than any human eye could track. Seeing such a large person move so quickly reminded me that vampires were more than simple undead creatures.

Even the youngest of them possessed magic of their own —mostly subtle, understated powers that allowed them to move with an alacrity that defied common sense and physics. Despite that, Jess danced nimbly away with a dancer's grace and a fighter's skill, not even bothering to block the attack.

She moves quick. Not vampire quick, but definitely super-human. Huh.

That was all well and good, but what had me worried was that she was facing a taller, stronger opponent who could move with even greater speed. Additionally, Cessily wielded a weapon that gave her a considerable reach advantage against Jesse's short sword and shillelagh. All told, it added up to a considerable disadvantage for my former girlfriend, unless she evened the odds somehow.

As I considered how the fight was weighted in the vampire's favor, she proved me right by blitzing forward with a middle forehand slash while Jesse had her back to the "wall" of warriors encircling the ring. When fencing with lighter swords, you might block such a blow in quarte or prime. However, against a greatsword attack with all that mass and vampire strength behind it, Jesse's defense needed to be rock solid.

C'mon, Jess—show this vamp what you've got.

I held my breath as Jesse blocked the stroke using both weapons, bracing her body by bending her lead leg and nearly locking her back leg. As the clang of steel on steel rang out across the clearing, the force of the cut drove Jess back a good six inches. She dug in with her toes, keeping her heel from catching so she could give ground to absorb the ferocity of the blow.

Good girl, but watch the...

Quick as a wink, Cessily used the rebound action of the clash to bring her blade around for another cut to Jesse's head. Jesse was positioned on the inside, where she could parry and strike with the shillelagh. But that move would be risky for Jess as well, since the Celtic-style short sword lacked a decent cross guard. Meaning, unless she'd achieved a bind on the block, Cessily could simply slide her blade down Jesse's and slice a few fingers off.

Thankfully, it didn't seem like Cessily was much of a fencer. Like a lot of younger vampires, she wasn't classically trained in weaponry, and relied mostly on her superior physical attributes to win fights. So, she had done the obvious thing, which was to quickly cut the opposite direction, and without any angular footwork to give her a positional advantage on that second cut.

Amateur.

I fully expected Jesse to block laterally with both weapons again while moving further to the inside where she'd have the advantage of shorter weaponry. However, she surprised me and Cessily both by squatting ass to heels while slamming the butt of the shillelagh on the ground, burying it a good three inches in the blood-soaked ground. As the vampire's sword whistled through the air overhead, she nimbly shoulder-rolled past on the vamp's right, slicing Cessily's thigh on the way out.

Then, three things happened fast. First, Cessily pivoted clockwise and chopped straight down at Jesse's backside as she rolled away. Second, Cessily's right knee buckled as she shifted much of her weight to that leg. And third, the shillelagh sprouted branches, leaves, and vines from the head and shaft that instantly wrapped around the vampire's limbs and torso.

I'd been right about Jesse's sword. Vampire flesh was tough, and Cessily was wearing thick leathers. Yet even though it had been a glancing cut, Jesse's sword had sliced through the muscles on the front of the vamp's right thigh like butter. That took a lot of the heat out of that downward cut, because as soon as Cessily felt her leg give, she instinctively pulled the attack to shift weight to her left leg again.

Thing is, it didn't matter. The leafy vines and branches that had entwined the vampire's body and arms yanked back on the vamp with such force, there was no way she could've completed that final downward swing. In short, the vampire was trapped.

You'd think that a vampire with Cessily's size and strength could just bull her way out of it, either pulling the club from the ground or tearing the vines in two. Yet the smooth, blackthorn stick was rooted to the earth like it had been set in concrete. The vines also had the advantage of using the vamp's momentum to pull her off balance, since she was already shifting weight in that direction. As the tall, muscular vampire was yanked backward, she fell toward the stick, the tip of which had elongated into a needle-sharp spike.

When Cessily tumbled backward toward the shillelagh, the vines and branches shortened to speed her along. The vampire let out a surprised gasp as the spiked tip of the stick entered her torso just under the ribcage on the left side of her back. Gravity and momentum drove her down the smooth blackthorn shaft a good six inches, even as she fumbled and clawed behind her in an attempt to remove the magicked stake from her back. Despite the vamp's best efforts, the vines finished the job, constricting with one final pull until the tip of the spine exited Cessily's chest, piercing her leathers just left of her breastbone.

Ooh—Ouchtown, population you, bro. Now, where in the fuck is Crowley?

8

As the vampire commander's struggles subsided, I glanced around the circle to gauge the reaction of the crowd. Would the fighting cease now that the rebel leader had been vanquished? Or would the rebel side choose to continue the battle?

Regarding the outcome of the fight, I'd only seen it coming at the last second when Jesse planted that stick, and only because I'd used similar tactics before myself. I doubted that the rebel side had expected things to go as they did, and based on the collective gasp that rose from their side when it happened, I was right. The lot of them looked stunned by the outcome, and I heard plenty of muttering about her use of magic to defeat their leader.

As for the Underhill troops, they seemed to be waiting for something, whether it be for the other side to lay down arms or a cue from their leader to attack. That is, except my red cap friend, who chuckled with sinister, self-satisfied glee as he turned to address the buggane.

"Pay up, sucker," he said as he extended his hand, palm-up.

"Ain't payin' nothin'," the buggane protested. "The human cheated, she did. Bet's off."

The red cap affected nonchalance, but I noticed his grip tighten on his cleaver as he studied the larger fae beneath hooded eyes. "Izzat so? Well then, I s'pose there's nothin' ta' be done fer' it."

As I watched this little vignette unfold before me, I casually glanced around to assess the overall situation. The rebel side's soldiers continued to cast about in a dazed state of disbelief and uncertainty. Meanwhile, Jesse's troops fingered their weapons, eyes darting about warily as they watched to see what the enemy might do. The tension in the air was palpable, layered as it was atop the cloying battlefield stench of blood, offal, and waste.

At the edge of the clearing, Jesse grabbed Cessily's hair with her left hand as she lopped the vamp's head off with one clean, downward cut from her short sword. She raised her gory prize overhead, spinning slowly in place as her fierce, determined gaze swept across the field of combatants.

"Lay down your arms!" she commanded. Her voice echoed across the valley floor, evidence she'd imbued it with magic to add a bit of "oomph" to the imperative.

"Your commander is dead, and the victory is mine by rights. I will not say it again."

It seemed as though some of the rebels were ready to surrender as a few of them began to lower their weapons in resignation. Just then, I caught movement out of the corner of my eye. Bringing my weapon to guard, I turned around, only to find that the red cap had decided to act unilaterally in defense of fair play.

"Cheat me, will ya'?" he hissed as he leapt at the buggane. "Nobody cheats ol' Tommy Shelby!"

Really? Do all these fuckers mimic crooks from TV and cinema?

Jesse's head snapped around, her gaze searching for the source of the commotion. Her eyes skated over me then back again, lingering long enough to convey a moment of shocked recognition before skipping past to the red cap.

"Tommy, no!" Jesse warned, a moment too late.

The red cap known as Tommy Shelby—if that was his real name—took the buggane unaware, causing the larger creature to stumble and shy away from the furious little fae's onslaught. The *fear dearg* obviously expected this, being the practiced little cutthroat that he was—that all red caps were, in fact. His kind were thugs, brigands, and murderers, every last one, each well-practiced in the low arts of subterfuge, ambush, and violence of action in same.

A moment's hesitation was all Tommy needed. He took full advantage by darting between the hairy brute's knees, slicing left with his cleaver and right with a straight razor as he passed. As the dwarf came out the other side, thick dark liquid spurted from the deep, clean incisions his blades had made, spilling down the buggane's thighs and soaking the already blood-stained ground.

Tommy knew his work well, and it was only a moment's passing before the welshing monster sagged to his knees from rapid blood loss. The red cap turned on a dime, coming up behind the buggane and kicking him forward so he could march up his back and bury his chopper in the hirsute fae's skull. With a grunt and a mighty tug, he yanked the blade free, standing triumphantly atop the buggane's corpse as he raised the bloody cleaver in the air.

"Fer' the Dagda!" he shouted.

Across the clearing, I saw Jesse mouth *fuck* as she spared Tommy a passing look of utter and complete acrimony. She tossed Cessily's decapitated head away, snatching her shillelagh from the ground in the same smooth motion. As soon as her hand touched the dark, glossy surface of the wood, the magically grown foliage withered and crumbled to dust, freeing the weapon so she could wield it once more.

Behind her the standard bearer sounded three notes on his horn, and a call rose up from somewhere in the mass of combatants. "To arms, to arms!"

It looked like things were about to go straight to hell in a barbed wire handbasket, so I lit Dyrnwyn up again as I cast about for someone to kill. Just as I picked out my first victim, a shout rang out behind me from back where I'd entered the fray.

"Necromancer! 'Ware the necromancer!"

Immediately, I spun around to see what was happening, but I was too damned short to see over the milling mass of fae and vamps. Cursing my current condition, I shoved Tommy off the buggane's back, then I jumped up there myself to gain a better view.

"Hey, now," the red cap complained. "No need fer' that."

I growled and thrust the white-hot tip of my sword in his face, then I turned my gaze toward the rise. At the edges of the crowd, vampires were fleeing left and right, darting and zipping this way and that as another group of soldiers marched in formation down the slope. I squinted, shielding my eyes from the glare of false sunlight above as I cast a vision-enhancing cantrip.

Nope, not soldiers. Zombies.

Crowley strode at the forefront of the phalanx, tossing necromantic balls of magic this way and that into the crowd. Wherever they struck, vampires froze in place, turning to pillars of ash before their remains crumbled and blew away in the wind. A few of the older vamps seemed to be able to resist his magic, and in those cases the wizard's spell acted more like acid or fire, eating away at their flesh and leaving huge gaping holes behind.

On witnessing Crowley's approaching wrath, the

vampires began to scatter. After that, it was a full-on rout. None of the undead wanted to face a master necromancer. Once the vampires broke ranks, the rebel fae realized their numbers were too diminished to put up a decent struggle. Soon they laid down their weapons and raised their hands in the air, and Jesse's troops began rounding them up.

As for Crowley, he was not to be deterred. Using his shadow tentacles, he hopped on the back of a zombie ogre, directing it to chase after the fleeing vampires as he threw balls of sickly green death magic after them. Unfortunately for the necromancer, the vamps proved to be much faster than his undead steed. The wizard soon gave up and turned back, garnering more than a few unfriendly stares from the Underhill fae as he approached.

"Crowley, you son of a bitch," I said, flashing him a broad grin as I shouldered my way to the edge of the crowd. "How'd you know things were about to get ugly?"

Using his shadow tentacles, he dismounted from the undead ogre with a dismissive shrug. "I got here as quickly as I could, with little thought to the timing of my arrival. In all honestly, it simply took that long to raise a sufficient number of undead to turn the tide of the battle."

When I realized that the fucker wasn't even worried about the fact that I'd charged into a battlefield full of vampires and fae, all I could do was shake my head and laugh.

"What?" he asked, his brow knit with confusion.

"Nothing," I said as I clapped a hand on his shoulder.

"You seem to be none the worse for the wear," he observed drily. "Perhaps in need of a bath, but it appears the effects of the curse have not diminished your ability to defend yourself."

"About that," Jesse said from somewhere behind me. "What are you two doing in Underhill, and what the hell happened to you?"

Turning to greet her, I smiled broadly. "Good to see you too. Jesse this is—"

She cut me off with backhanded flick of her hand. "I know who he is—everyone in Underhill does. The question is why you're both here. Especially since one of you is supposed to be dead."

"How much time do you have?"

Jesse grimaced at me, only shifting her gaze away when something or someone behind me drew her attention. "Tomás! Stop right there, you stupid piece of shit."

"General?" a small, sheepish voice replied.

"Don't act all innocent—you know you fucked up. They were about to surrender until you knifed that buggane."

"He welshed on our wager," the speaker said with a bit more conviction. "What was I s'posed ta' do?"

Recognizing the voice, I turned around—more out of self-preservation than respect. I might be friendly with the Syndicate red caps back home, but here I was just another human. Flaming sword or no, it was definitely not a good idea to turn your back on one of those shifty little fuckers.

Recognition showed in the red cap's eyes, then he scowled and crossed his arms over his chest. "Looky 'ere, it's the cunt that shoved me earlier."

"Hey," Jesse protested. "What did I tell you about using that word around me?"

"Sorry, ma' lady," Tommy said as he lowered his gaze. "T'won't happen again." He stole a glance at me, mouthing the word *twat* behind his hand.

"Don't bite off more than you can chew, Tommy," Jesse warned as she gave a rueful shake of her head. "He might look like Howdy-Doody, but trust me—you do not want that fight. Anyway, you don't have time for starting more shit, seeing as how I'm putting you on K.P. duty for the next week."

"Jest fer' a wee bit o' cursin'?"

"No, for fucking up my plan. You're dismissed." Jesse kept her eyes on the dwarf as he retreated—she was no fool. It was only after he'd gone that she addressed us again. "If this is going to be a long story, I'm not going to hear the whole damned thing while I'm covered in guts and blood. Besides, I have to make sure my people don't kill the captives—not until they've been questioned, at least. Crowley, do you know how to get to the Dagda's cottage?"

"I know the way, yes."

"That's where we're encamped. Head there and wait

for me at the command tent—I'll catch up when I'm done here," she said, pursing her lips as she added a final directive. "And don't kill any of my people on your way there."

"I make no promises," I said as she marched away to deal with her troops. If she'd heard me, she gave no indication.

"Can we trust her? That is to say, this version of her?" Crowley asked.

"I'm not sure," I said. "But do we have a choice?"

Crowley and I left the battlefield and the cries of the wounded and dying behind, heading toward the army's encampment near the Dagda's farm with his undead army in tow. The terrain remained relatively familiar for a few miles, consisting of gently rolling hills that had been ravaged by magical warfare, much the same as the lands we had passed on our way here. Eventually that landscape gave way to sparse woodlands. This wasn't like the toadstool forests that grew around the gateway, but an Earthly forest, populated with species of trees I recognized—poplar, oak, elm, and maple.

I shot Crowley a quizzical look. "Does any of this look familiar to you?"

Crowley gave a slow shake of his head. "Not in the slightest. However, Underhill is fickle and prone to change its environs to suit its moods. The Dagda's absence or the massive battles that have taken place here may have influenced these lands in some way. If so, what we're seeing would be a direct response to that influence."

"If you say so," I replied with a shrug. "These are your stomping grounds, so I'll defer to your judgment."

Crowley seemed satisfied at that, and we continued on. Soon the forest thickened, and we found ourselves having to pick our way through thick undergrowth and foliage. I worked a little druidic magic, nothing major but enough to ease our path through the thick brush. Before long, we exited a tangled wall of brambles only to find a wide, bubbling stream blocking our path.

I frowned and scratched my head. "This definitely wasn't here the last time. Are you sure we aren't lost?"

"Again, traveling in Underhill is an uncertain undertaking. Sometimes you reach your destination in short order, and on other occasions you might travel for days to cover what before was a short distance."

"So, what you're saying is, we're basically at Underhill's mercy."

He replied with a terse nod as his gaze swept left and right, high and low, obviously searching for whatever dangers might lurk ahead. I noted uncertainty in his expression, which was unusual for any version of Crowley—especially so for the grim, post-apocalyptic iteration this timeline had produced.

"You see something?" I asked.

"Nothing yet, but I am experiencing the unsettling sensation that we are being watched."

"Well, that's not cliché at all, is it? We find ourselves walking through a spooky, unfamiliar forest, and suddenly you start to get the heebie-jeebies." Suppressing a smirk, I punched his shoulder as I headed toward the bank ahead. "If you spot any fetishes hanging in the trees, be sure to let me know, alright?"

Crowley dismissed my comment with a grunt. "This is a land made whole cloth from magic, in which anything and everything might be trying to kill you at any given moment. Be on your guard."

"Advice taken," I said, reaching into my Bag to pull out the M4 and reattach it to the one-point harness that sat around my neck and shoulders. "So, do you think I should load for vampires, or Fae?"

"Both. Come, let us cross the stream and exit this forest as quickly as possible. I am in need of rest and sustenance."

"Yeah, yeah—my dogs are barking, too," I said as I picked my way toward the water's edge below. On reaching the bank, I turned my gaze ahead to find the best path across, only to be stunned by the scene before me.

The wide, shallow stream was nearly broad enough to be called a river, although it was hardly deep enough to be classified as such. Crystal-clear waters revealed a rock-lined bed of smooth, multi-hued stones a few feet below the surface that stretched from shore to shore.

Broad oaks and willows lined the banks, casting soft shadows that reached far out over the water's edge, sheltering small schools of darting silvery fish from the bright, pinkish-purple skies above.

In the center of the stream where the current was faster, jutting boulders caused the water to froth as the waters parted around them, only for it to resolve into the same glassy surface a few yards past. Sweeping my gaze further downstream, I followed the stream's lazy, meandering path to a placid pool where large, iridescent dragonflies hovered above the surface. There, a trout broke the dappled surface with a flick of its tail, gulping down one hapless insect before hitting the water with a loud splash, disappearing after into the water's depths.

Taking a deep breath, I allowed myself an instant to take it all in, because moments of beauty like these had been rare over the last few months. The irony was not lost on me that I would find a moment of peace here in Underhill, of all places. It was a reminder that *Tír na nÓg* was a real-life fairytale kingdom, albeit one that might try to kill you at any given moment.

Time was, I'd have given my left nut to experience this— but those days are long past.

In the early days, shortly after I was introduced to The World Beneath, I'd been enamored of it, perceiving the supernatural with the naive, boyish fascination only a child—or teenager—could experience. But that was then. The last few years had been hell on me, and along the way I'd lost my sense of wonder and no small amount of innocence. It was a shame, really, but the truth was I could do without it all—the magic, druidry, time travel, everything—just for a chance at living a normal life.

No sense in wishing for what isn't. If life serves you a shit sandwich, you don't scrape off the middle—you get used to eating the crust.

While I gaped and gawked at the scenery, Crowley was obviously in no mood to loiter. On descending the bank, he immediately began crossing to the other side, using his tentacles to keep him well above the water's surface. The undead he'd raised followed close behind, trudging into the water, oblivious to the fact they were getting soaked. A few lost their footing and were swept away downstream, only to sink below the surface once the current took them to deeper sections of the brook.

"Are you going to retrieve those?" I asked, pointing to a zombie that had just sunk like a stone, leaving only a trail of bubbles behind to mark its passing.

"As we've seen, at present there's no shortage of corpses in Underhill," Crowley replied, keeping his gaze firmly fixed on the far bank. "If it happens to find its way to shore, it will be along presently. If not, the fish will sup well this day."

"Litterbug," I muttered as I began traversing the stream by hopping from boulder to boulder. The wizard and his troop of zombies were just ahead, and I was roughly a third of the way across when I heard a rumbling in the distance. "Yo, Crowster—do you hear that?"

Crowley turned to face me, his tentacles twisting like black licorice whips beneath him. "My ears are not as sharp as yours, Druid. Therefore, the answer is—"

The shadow wizard cut his retort off mid-sentence as he tilted his head toward the ominous sound. Presently, the rumbling grew louder, becoming audible even to his fully human ears. When he quickly untwisted his shadow limbs, corkscrewing his body to face the shore, I knew we were in trouble.

"Run," was all he said before he began scrambling toward the bank.

I couldn't identify the threat by the sound, but for all I knew, a herd of angry *fuaths* or a couple of vicious *fachen* were coming to rip us to shreds. Taking Crowley's advice, I began leaping my way across, jumping between the largest boulders in an attempt to get to the other side quickly. I was halfway across the stream and Crowley was most of the way there when the threat came into view upstream—a tidal wave of floodwater twenty feet high, rushing toward us with all the speed and fury of an oncoming train.

I froze for a split second, staring dumbstruck at the coming onslaught of frothing water, mud, branches, and stones. Then the water hit us, and everything after that was chaos. I had never really been a strong swimmer, but in this form it didn't matter because I could hold my breath for an extended period of time. Crowley, on the other hand, could not, and as I was buffeted along underneath the water, I worried that he would not survive the flood.

But soon I could only concern myself with my own survival, as my attention was wholly occupied by keeping myself alive. Over and over again, I was smashed against rocks, struck by tree limbs, and tossed head over heels until I didn't know which direction was up. Every so often I'd spot a ray of sunlight through the muddy, debris-strewn maelstrom, and I'd attempt to kick my way to the surface, only to get tossed and turned around and slammed back to the rocky river bottom again.

Each time I was forced back to the bottom, the impact threatened to knock the air from my lungs. At times it almost felt as though the water was trying to force its way into my mouth, like it had a will of its own. It was a struggle just to keep from exhaling stale air and sucking water into my chest. After what seemed like an eternity underwater, I found myself fighting the urge to do exactly that.

Just when I thought I couldn't hold my breath a second longer, the flood waters passed, and I spotted daylight above. I kicked my way toward the light like a man possessed, sputtering and gasping for breath as I broke the surface. *Underhill's sickly-sweet atmosphere never tasted so good,* I reflected as I wiped my eyes and searched for the shoreline. I spotted a sandbar island in the middle of what now was more a river than a stream and swam toward it as hard and as fast as I could.

Although the flood surge had passed, the water level seemed to have risen considerably due to the flood, and the current was much stronger than before. In my current state, it was all I could do to reach the sandbar, crawl my way up a few feet, and flop down on my back, exhausted. I took a minute to catch my breath and recover, then I sat up and took an inventory of my gear.

Rifle, half my magazines, and my pistol, all gone. Well, shit. At least my Bag is still here. I have more guns and ammo, but what I don't have more of is—

A cold chill went down my spine, causing me to fumble and feel over my shoulder. Thankfully, Dyrnwyn was still sheathed there, presumably staying put of its own, semi-sentient volition. With a sigh of relief, I drew the sword to dry it off, turning the sheath upside down to drain it of water. When that was done, I examined the Bag for signs of damage, turning it upside down as I had Dyrnwyn's sheath. Unsurprisingly, not a single drop of water came out of it, and the ugly patchwork leather carryall was as dry as the Mojave Desert. Fae magic was weird.

Time to start searching for Gomez.

"Crowley!" I yelled, cupping my hands to my mouth. "Speak up if you're out there!"

The guy might be an uppity, creepy pain in the ass, but right now he was the only friend I had—and my best chance for finding Lugh and making it back to

Earth alive. I frantically searched up and down the river's edges, hoping to find some sign of life amidst the debris that had been left behind by the flood. For several minutes I continued to call out to him as I walked the length of the sandbar island, until eventually I heard a response further downstream.

"I'm here," a weak voice cried from a pile of detritus on the north side of the river.

A large, jagged-edged tree trunk fell off the top of the pile, then a long, shadowy, cephalopodic appendage emerged from amidst the remaining debris. Soon three more tentacles appeared, moving branches, stones, and logs out of the way. After the pile had been reduced by half, Crowley's wet, bedraggled form crawled out, looking like a drowned rat. His face was scratched, bloodied, and bruised, but he was moving and apparently in one piece.

"You alright there, Crowster?" I called across the water.

"Indeterminate, but I am alive."

"We'll call that a win, then," I replied with relief in my voice.

"Only just," he said. "When I realized I would not escape the rushing waters, I enclosed myself in a bubble formed of shadow magic. It allowed me to breathe whilst protecting me from being smashed against the rocks and debris. That was, until the bubble burst."

He made as if to push himself to his feet, but his trembling arms gave way and he fell flat on his face.

Wisely, he gave up on the idea, instead rolling over on his back to recover.

"Whoa there, dude. Just relax and let me come to you."

The water level continued to subside, and soon I was able to pick my way across by jumping between rocks until I reached Crowley's location. He lay there with an arm covering his eyes, his chest heaving. A stray trickle of blood ran down his cheek, but I doubted he even realized he was bleeding, what with how soaked we both were. Absently, I noted that his blood had a definite oily cast to it, but I kept the observation to myself.

"Did you notice anything weird about that flood?" I asked as I plopped down on the shore next to him.

"That it appeared out of nowhere, with nary a cloud in the sky? That a placid forest stream turned into a raging river in a matter of seconds? Or are you referring to the face that appeared amongst all that frothing water and debris, just as it overtook us?"

"Really? I didn't see that."

Crowley gave a grim nod. "Just so. A woman's face, laughing as it swept us away."

"Some sort of water spirit, maybe? Could be we've pissed something off by trespassing on its territory."

"I don't think so," Crowley said as he slowly pushed himself to a seated position. "Whatever caused that flood, it is more powerful than any water spirit I've seen. An entity with enough power to call up a torrent like that would not have escaped the Dagda's notice. I doubt he would allow such a creature to dwell here. Gods and ancient fae are nothing if not territorial."

"Whatever it was, it's gone now. And if it was trying to kill us, it didn't do a very thorough job," I said as I suppressed a ragged smile. "The bad news is it looks like your zombies are a *wash*."

Crowley fixed me with a look of disgust. "Perhaps I should have drowned. It would certainly be better than suffering your juvenile humor."

"Admit it, that was an excellent dad joke."

"Pfah." The shadow wizard flicked a waterlogged lock of hair from his eyes, then he stood on shaky legs. "Even when I was young, I was never given over to such puerility."

"Sorry you had it so rough, Crowley," I said, meaning it.

He cleared his throat, sweeping his gaze further up the riverbank and into the woods beyond. "We should probably make ourselves scarce before our unknown adversary sends another tsunami our way."

"Yeah, Jesse's probably already waiting for us anyway."

Proud bastard that he was, he stumbled only slightly as he headed up the slope on his own two feet. I allowed him to take the lead up the bank, observing him for signs of hidden injuries and sticking close to make sure he didn't fall. As we entered the woods, I maintained a rear guard, keeping a careful watch behind to ensure that nothing followed after us.

9

Hours later, we arrived at the Underhill army's encampment, located on a hill overlooking the ruins of the Dagda's farm. The camp itself was set up in a radial fashion, with tents and pavilions arrayed in a spoked pattern around the command tent and a central, circular clearing. The camp was neat and orderly, free from the trash and clutter one might expect to see with this many fae living in close quarters.

That stood in sharp contrast to the Dagda's farm, which had been burned and razed. Sadly, there was nothing left but blackened stumps and charred beams to mark where his orchards and cabin once stood. As for his livestock and perpetually roasting hog, they were nowhere to be seen.

Damned shame. I could totally destroy a giant ham sandwich right about now.

When we reached the center of camp, Crowley said

he needed time to meditate and tend to his injuries, using who knew what sort of magic. While he was doing creepy shadow wizard stuff, I laid out on a bench to grab some much-needed shut-eye. It seemed like only minutes had passed when I was awakened by the not-so-gentle nudge of a boot on my shoulder.

"There are better places to sleep than on that hard-ass bench," Jesse said.

"Like where?" I yawned as I forced open eyes that had been glued shut by tear salt, mud, and exhaustion.

"Like on a cot in one of these tents, for example."

"Nobody offered," I said as I sat up, stretching and yawping. "Besides, you get sleep when you can. Isn't that what Maureen and the old man taught us?"

"True, true," she conceded. "Follow me, sleepyhead. I need to get this grime off me, and you need to fill me in on how you became the real-life version of Honey I Shrunk the Druid."

After I grabbed my gear, Crowley and I followed Jesse to a smaller tent behind the command pavilion. When she noticed the shadow wizard had come along, she shot him a warning look before meeting my gaze.

"You can come in," she said to me. "But Fuamnach's lackey stays outside."

"I haven't been her 'lackey' for some time," Crowley countered icily. "Believe me when I say I want my adoptive mother dead just as much as you. Nevertheless, I do not follow where I am not wanted. Druid," he said, inclining his head before he turned on heel and strode away.

After he'd gone, I gave Jesse a put-upon look. "He's not so bad once you get to know him."

"Whatever," Jesse muttered as she ducked under the tent flap. "Once a slave to the Tuath Dé, always a slave to them."

Rather than pointing out the obvious, I held my tongue and followed her inside. The space within was roughly twelve by twelve, with a ceiling elevation of about eight feet at the edges, peaking to about twelve feet at the center pole above our heads. It had been appointed with rugs, a small divan, a cot, and little else save for assorted weaponry, a chamber pot, and a bowl and pitcher, presumably to be used for hygienic purposes.

Immediately on entering, Jesse unbuckled her belt, placing her sword and shillelagh on a rack before shrugging out of her blood-stained tunic. I looked on as she filled the basin, using the clean, clear water to rinse the blood from her hands, arms, and face in silence. The fact that she wasn't bothering to speak was more than a little unnerving, but I resisted the urge to fill the silence with idle chatter.

To be honest, I wasn't sure what to say to this version of Jesse, or how to open this conversation. For starters, I had no idea what her standing had been with the other version of me in this timeline. Because of that uncertainty, I was concerned that I might have stepped into a minefield by running into her here in Underhill. After a couple of minutes of uncomfortable silence, impatience won out over my better judgement.

"So, what's new?" I said with what I hoped was enough casual joviality to cover the nervousness in my voice. It was only after a long, pregnant pause that she replied, speaking so softly she might have been talking to herself.

"What's new? A lot has gone on since the last time I saw you, Colin. Where do I start?" Suddenly she turned on me, hands clenched at her sides and her brow knitted in anger. "Oh, I know—where the hell have you been? After the bombs fell, you disappeared, and the Oak went into a panic. You freaking abandoned me, damn it."

Water dripped down her face in pink rivulets as she stared at me with hurt in her eyes. I reached in my Bag for an old, more or less clean t-shirt and handed it to her.

"I'm sorry, Jesse. I honestly didn't know where you were."

"You didn't know? Colin, I was magically connected to the Druid Oak you planted, and it was at the junkyard when the bombs fell." She snatched the shirt from my hand, shooting daggers at me with her eyes while she wiped herself off. "What if the Oak had been destroyed? Did you even bother checking afterward?"

"I checked," I half-lied. "The junkyard had been abandoned."

"Must've been after I was rescued," she spat. "When things went sideways, the tree freaked out and split, you were nowhere to be found, and as for Maureen and Finnegas..." Her voice trailed off before continuing in a near whisper. "The wards around the junkyard trapped me there, alone and near death without the Oak's magical sustenance, but unable to die because of what had been done to me. If it hadn't been for the Dagda showing up, I would've been stuck in that rusting metal graveyard forever."

Ah, so the other me and Jesse didn't consummate their union. Meaning, he didn't bond with the oak. Phew.

"Jess, I went into survival mode after everything went down, just like everyone else. If I had known you were out there, alone, I would've come looking for you. You know that."

She shot me an annoyed glance out of the corner of her eye. "I thought you were dead, you twerp—everyone did. And you let me think that."

If you only knew.

"I had to go into hiding. In the days after the bombs fell, it quickly became clear that there had been an orchestrated effort to wipe out all the human magic-users. The Cold Iron Circle, the witches' covens, and the hedge wizards? All gone. With me being one of the last druids and all that, I thought it was best to let everyone think they'd killed me." Another half-truth, but plausible. "Since then, I've been running all over Texas, trying to find a way to defeat the vampires and save what's left of humanity. You do remember there are humans dying back on Earth, don't you?"

I tried to say it with as little venom as possible. Yet I couldn't help but feel as though Jesse had gone native here in Underhill, forsaking her own people to fight a war for the Tuath Dé.

"Oh, you think I don't know that?" she countered as she loosened a few straps on her breastplate. "I was there, Colin. I saw the destruction, and I wasn't able to do a damned thing about it."

"So did I. But I didn't leave—I stayed to fight."

Rather, I got back there as soon as I could.

Jesse turned on me, her slumped shoulders and resigned tone conveying that her anger had transitioned into frustration and regret. "It's not like I had any choice in the matter. For weeks I laid there in the yard hovering between life and death, unable to move or cast any magic, but still in tune with the Earth enough to feel sickened by the radiation and death that ravaged the city. Mercifully, at some point the Dagda showed up, and he swept me away to Underhill. Even if I'd wanted to, I was too weak to resist."

"He was the one who made you human again?"

"Mostly human, anyway. He worked on me for what seemed like an eternity, salvaging what was left of my humanity so I could survive without the Oak's magic. When I was strong enough, he taught me how to survive here in Underhill. If it wasn't for him, I'd be dead."

"I noticed you still have some magic," I remarked. "Did he teach you that?"

"He left a little nature magic in me, saying I'd need it to protect myself. Also, I'm pretty sure there wasn't enough of the human side left of me to make a whole being without it." She pursed her lips and snorted a soft laugh. "As much as I resent him for ensorcelling my ghost into that damned Oak, I owe him everything. The least I can do is defend his lands in his absence."

———

That little revelation threw me for a loop. In my time-line, Jesse had conspired with the Dagda, readily agreeing to merge with the acorn to help him enact his plan. She had admitted as much to me during our ill-fated trip to Big Bend. I wondered, what else had been changed in this timeline after I'd failed to stop the Vampyri from piercing the Veil?

"Yeah, I kind of had a bone to pick with him over that, too," I said, lowering my gaze and shaking my head to hide my surprise. "Typical manipulation of the gods. He needed me to nurture and bond with the Oak. Obviously, he figured the best way to ensure that was to make you a part of it."

She dried her hair and face with my shirt again before tossing it back to me. "Too bad for the Dagda, he had no idea you'd already moved on, eh?"

I said nothing, because there was nothing I could say

that would alleviate the discomfort we both felt regarding that topic. Jesse turned away as she fumbled with the hindmost straps on her leather cuirass. Failing in the attempt, she groaned in exasperation before turning to me with a pleading look.

"Can you please help me with this?"

Sheepishly, I approached her and undid the last buckle, at which point she pulled the breastplate off over her head, flinging it into the corner with the rest of her gear. Underneath, she wore nothing but a sweat-soaked muslin shift that left absolutely nothing to the imagination. I stood right behind her, close enough to feel her body's heat and brush against her as she adjusted the shift. She smelled of blood and sweat and female musk, a scent I knew well from the days when we'd hunted together as teenagers.

Before I knew it, unbidden memories of the frenzied, amateurish, groping sex we used to have ran through my mind. In those days we'd drive home after finishing a job, pumped up on adrenaline, caffeine, and hormones, high on the thrill of the hunt. Being teenagers, we thought the best way to burn off all that nervous energy was to pull over on some lonely country road and screw each other's brains out.

While I didn't regret any of those memories, that was the last thing I wanted to be thinking about at the moment. As I looked away, I felt a familiar warmth in my nether regions, the result of an instinctive but defi-nitely unwelcome response. My body was responding in ways that my mind protested, and I found myself blushing furiously as I turned aside, clasping my hands at my waist to hide the result.

Jesse pivoted to face me again, tugging her shift to air it out and making a face as she sniffed her pits. "Ugh, what I wouldn't do for a hot shower about now."

I continued to look away, trying to act casual but failing in the attempt. After all, it was hard to be subtle when you had your hands cupped over your crotch. And if the heat in my face was any indication, I was pretty sure I was blushing up a storm.

Jesse raised an eyebrow at me, then she started laughing. "Oh my gosh, Colin—did you just get a woody?"

"No," I protested. "At least, not on purpose."

Despite the awkward silence we'd endured just moments before, Jesse couldn't help but find amusement in my current condition. After a few stifled chuckles, she soon burst out laughing, and not in that delicate, hand-over-mouth giggling thing some girls do when an attractive guy is present. No, she fell into full-on, side-splitting, rip-roaring laughter that lasted for what felt like an eternity.

Meanwhile, I stood there thinking of baseball with my hands over my crotch. A strategy which, I might add, didn't work in my sophomore geometry class when Ms. Krause bent over in front of me to pick up the eraser, and it didn't work now. Mercifully, after a time Jesse's laughter subsided enough for her to speak again.

"Oh, don't bother hiding it," she said, wiping her eyes. "It's not like it's anything I haven't seen before."

I let my hands drop to my sides. "It's not my fault, alright?"

She affected false seriousness as she laid a hand on my shoulder. "Now, now, no need to feel ashamed. It's a natural response that everyone goes through during puberty."

"Go ahead and laugh, but this is no laughing matter. I have hormones raging through my body like I haven't felt since high school. I mean, look at my forehead— when was the last time you've had this many zits?"

"Not recently. I don't get zits anymore, not since the Dagda put me back together. Incidentally, I remember our high school days well, Grabby McGraberson."

"What can I say?" I growled as I crossed my arms and stared off into space. "I was a horny kid."

"Yes, you were. Oh man, did I need a laugh. Thanks for that." Jesse chuckled and wiped her eyes again while I continued to fume. "Relax, Slugger. I'll give it a rest, since you're *obviously* in a great deal of distress. Speaking of, Colin—how *did* you get like this?"

"I kind of got cursed when I came through the gateway to Underhill."

Jesse rolled her eyes. "Yeah, I can see that. But how, and why?"

"You mean, who did I piss off this time?"

"Pretty much. It must have been a god or goddess, right? Because Colin McCool can't just settle for pissing off run-of-the-mill wizards and witches and fae. No, you have to step in the deepest pile of shit you can, every single time. So, tell me, who is it now?"

"Honestly I have no idea. Sure, I've had some recent run-ins with a few of the Celtic gods. But honestly, I don't know how any of them could've tracked me here."

"You mean here in Underhill? Seriously? Colin, this place is full of Celtic gods and goddesses."

"Oh, right. I meant, tracked me from *Earth*," I said, hemming and hawing around as I tried to recover from my faux pas. "I was in hiding, remember? Nobody knew I was coming to Underhill, so how did they know to lay that trap for me in the gateway?"

Jesse flashed me a crooked grin. "There's more to this, isn't there?"

"Nothing important," I replied. *Time to change the subject.* "You've been talking about the Dagda like he isn't here anymore. Considering the condition of his demesne, I've been fearing the worst. Tell me, what gives?"

Her eyes narrowed as she pressed her lips into a grim, hard line. "He was killed, Colin, by Nemain. She and her husband—that is, the war god Neit what's-his-face. They came to the Dagda requesting terms of parley, under the false pretense of offering to help drive the rebel faction out of Underhill. They caught him off guard and turned on him, and while he wounded Nemain and killed Neit, that hatchet-faced bitch still managed to finish the job."

"Seriously? Are you sure he's dead?"

"Colin, I'm the one who found him."

I sat on the cot, dropping bonelessly onto the hard, unyielding surface. It was what I'd suspected all along, but having my suspicions substantiated was still a punch in the gut.

"I can't believe they killed the Dagda. I thought he was invincible."

"Guess not. And since he passed, me and this ragtag band of fae have been the only thing keeping the invaders from occupying the Dagda's lands."

"Is this the only place the battle is being fought?"

Jesse barked a short cynical laugh. "Not even close. To the east on the seaward side of Underhill, Niamh and her father Manannán mac Lir war along the coast and the oceans, where he reigns supreme. To the north of us, Lugh's fighting a one-god war against the forces that have invaded his lands. And to the south, Aengus Óg leads a larger contingent of troops against any rebel forces that come through the gateways. In fact, if it weren't for Aengus we'd have been overrun. That pretty boy can fight."

"Oh, so Maeve did survive—that's good to know. But Aengus, seriously? I honestly can't believe he sided with the good guys."

"After they killed the Dagda, that was a foregone conclusion. Aengus might not have gotten along with his father, but they loved each other, and the Dagda's assassination was something that Aengus could not stand for. Thank goodness too, because his leadership went a long way toward uniting the various factions in Underhill against the invading forces."

"Well, piss." I leaned forward and covered my face with my hands. Despite our recent differences over my slaying of his son—or at least, my part in it—my heart was heavy at hearing the news. Wiping a stray tear from my eye, I looked up and met Jesse's gaze. "Damned shame about the Dagda, but I guess there's nothing for it. Thing is, I really needed his help."

Jesse looked at me askance. "You're hoping to bond with the Oak, aren't you?"

"In fact, I am. I need its power to defeat the vampires that took over Texas back home. I made the mistake of going after their leader on his home turf, and he almost killed me."

"What in the heck made you want to do that?"

"Luther was being held as a political prisoner, and I wanted to free him. If it wasn't for Crowley showing up when he did, I wouldn't be here right now."

Jesse rolled her eyes. "I guess they know you're not dead now."

"Yep. You know Bells is gone, right?"

"I heard," Jesse said, her voice neutral.

Belladonna had never been her favorite person, and I was pretty sure the feeling was mutual. Bells had been my rebound girlfriend back when I was getting over Jesse's death, years before her rebirth via the Druid Oak.

Yet I doubted that Jesse wanted her dead, despite any jealousy she might have once felt.

"I found some graves at the junkyard. Any idea who they belong to?"

Jesse looked crestfallen, her shoulders slumping as her gaze shifted to the floor. "You know who—Finnegas and Maureen. I insisted the Dagda bury them before he brought me to Underhill."

Yet another guess proven to be true. Shit.

I released a frustrated sigh. "What was it the big purple guy said? 'This day extracts a heavy toll.'"

"What big purple guy? That thing on *Sesame Street*, or the one from the old Mickey D's kid's meals?"

Oops, guess I'm getting my timelines mixed up.

"Never mind," I said, dismissing the slip with a wave of my hand. "All I'm saying is, it's a real shock to find out the Dagda is dead—and to have my suspicions confirmed about Maureen and Finnegas."

"This whole flipping thing has been hard on everyone, Colin. And how the hell did it happen, anyway? One day things were normal, I was living in the junkyard with the Oak, and then the next—poof! Nuclear war."

"I'm still figuring that whole puzzle out. If there's one thing I'm certain of, the vampire nations are at the heart of it."

"You think?" Jesse replied sarcastically.

"I know it's obvious, but there's more to it than what you've seen. They had a plan going into this—a long-term plan, something they'd been putting together for years. And they didn't do it alone."

"Oh?"

"They had help from the Earthbound fae, and probably from Badb and Nemain. I still don't see what the Celtic gods and goddesses get out of it, but I have a strong hunch they're trying to return to their former glory on Earth."

Jesse crossed her arms and scowled. "How are they gonna do that when all the humans are dead? It's going to be really lonely back there without any worshipers to make them feel all important and godly."

"You have to remember that they don't think like we do. They're immortals, or the closest thing to it. The gods and goddesses, the more powerful and ancient fae, the primaries who lead the vampires—they all think in centuries and millennia, not in days and months like humans. Hell, the Vampyri Council might have been planning this for decades, putting their Renfields in positions of power and cutting deals with influential fae and Tuath Dé, just waiting for the right time to put it all in motion."

Jesse uncrossed her arms and placed her hands on her hips. "So, what are you going to do about it?"

"First, I have to find a way to bond with the Oak. Problem is, I tried communicating with it and it ran scared at the first mention of bonding. It's like the thing's gone crazy, and I don't know how to fix it. That druid oak is the last of its kind, and with the Dagda gone, if it dies that's it—no more druid oaks or groves. And potentially, no more druids."

In this timeline, at least.

Jesse threw her arm over my shoulder as she sat down next to me on the cot. "The Dagda might have created druidry, but you know he's not the only druid among the Celtic Pantheon, right?"

I shot her a sideways glance as I responded with incredulity in my voice. "What you mean he's not the only druid? I thought druidry was the Dagda's thing—something he created to give humankind a way of balancing the scales between us, the supernatural races and the gods."

Jesse shook her head. "You never did pay attention to Finnegas' history lessons, did you?"

"Obviously not, but can you blame me? Whenever the old man started in on 'the early years of the Druids,' or 'the heyday of the Druids,' or 'back when the Druids were a force to be reckoned with, ma' boy,' that was my cue to zone out." I gave a rueful chuckle. "Thing is, I'd do anything to have to sit through one of those lectures now."

Jesse squeezed my shoulder before placing her hands in her lap. "I know exactly what you mean. I haven't lost just one mentor since all this crap happened; I've lost two. But I do have some good news. There someone who can help you bond with the druid oak, Colin. That is, if you can find Lugh."

10

We left the camp with haste, knowing that we didn't have much time to find Lugh and enlist his help in getting me back to my full, druid-master strength. According to Jesse, if I had any hope of saving the Oak, Lugh was it. That made sense, considering that Lugh had a reputation in Celtic mythology for being a sort of Jack of all trades. As the legends had it, he was the most gifted of the gods, basically good at everything he put his hand to—or so it was said. And according to Jesse, those talents included druidry.

What Jesse didn't know was that Lugh was my half-brother on my mother's side, a fact I'd only recently discovered. Finnegas' geas had suppressed any and all knowledge of Mom's Fomorian heritage from me, until he released me from it at the time of his death. If not for that geas, it would have been easy to put it all together because the clues had been there all along.

Dad used to call Mom Ellen, even though everyone else knew her as Leanne. While my young ears heard "Ellen," he was actually saying "Ethlinn" with a soft "th" sound. Ethlinn was another name for "Ethniu," Lugh's mother... and mine.

My being a demigod—or rather, a demi-titan—made a lot more sense than my *ríastrad* being the result of a curse cast on me by Fuamnach, which was what I'd been led to believe after it first emerged. And who else in Celtic mythology suffered from the so-called warp-spasm? None other than Cú Chulainn, Lugh's son. Like I said, the clues were there, which was why Finnegas had spelled away my memories in the first place.

All that deception, just to keep me secret and safe.

I figured I could count on Lugh for help, as he'd been proven to have a soft spot for me in the past, likely due to our shared parentage. But from what Jesse told me, Lugh was a very hard individual to find at present. My big brother wasn't just another of the minor deities in the Celtic Pantheon, but one of the big boys and girls. I was almost positive that if he wanted to remain hidden, hidden he would stay.

It could take some time to track him down—or to get him to notice us—which was why we were heading to Lugh's lands with all due haste. Crowley claimed the roads in Underhill were a bit more permanent and predictable to travel than going overland. Thus, we took the main road that led away from the Dagda's farm, knowing it would be the quickest route to our next destination.

Currently we strolled down a cobbled pathway that was roughly the width of a two-lane road. In the hours since we left Jesse's camp, the terrain surrounding the road had gradually transitioned from gently rolling hills and fields to a dark, forbidding forest. Although we'd left the stench of the battlefield far behind, it had been replaced by an oppressive humidity and the earthy, methane funk that indicated we were traveling close to Underhill's swamplands.

True to form, the woods on either side of the road consisted of twisted, anthropomorphic trees and a thick, mossy canopy that blocked out the false sun above. The sparse sunlight piercing the woven archway of foliage over our heads barely illuminated the forest floor bordering the road for more than a dozen yards. Shadows grew deep beyond that point, and I heard things lurking and skittering out there in the darkness.

While the roadway remained clear of debris and undergrowth, it felt more like we were walking through a cave than a forest. At times I had the distinct sensation we were traveling down the gullet of some massive, antediluvian creature. I fully expected a bevy of giant, semi-intelligent spiders to ambush us from overhead at any given moment. Yet I had to admit that it was preferable to traveling overland, especially under these conditions.

"I'd hate to be walking through that," I said, letting

my gaze wander into the sinister-looking thicket that boxed us in on both sides. "Tell me again why we didn't stick to the roads the first time?"

"I was under the impression that we were engaging in a bit of subterfuge," the wizard replied as he casually swept his gaze left and right. "You were cursed when you exited the gateway, and we were working under the assumption that there were Celtic gods searching for you, possibly to end your existence on this plane. It only made sense for us to take the indirect route while maintaining as much anonymity as possible."

"It would've been nice to have discussed that beforehand, but okay. Next time don't just make assumptions unilaterally. Include me in the decision-making process."

Crowley crossed his arms as he considered my request. "Hmm, yes. I suppose it never occurred to me to discuss such measures with you. I merely assumed you'd be smart enough to want to remain hidden from those trying to kill you. Next time I will not be so quick to presume intelligence on your part, and instead I'll take your predilection for poor decision-making into account."

I scratched at a bug bite on my arm as I counted to ten. "I'm going to let that slide. Any idea how we might find Lugh or draw him out?"

"Not really. I may be able to recruit a bit of help in that regard," Crowley said. "But it will require a slight detour."

"Let me guess—we're going to visit Peg Powler."

"Precisely," Crowley said. "Not only is Peg a minor power in Underhill, but she maintains a rather robust surveillance network so she can keep tabs on Fuamnach and other entities that she might find herself at odds with at any given time."

"A surveillance network as in human intelligence? Or rather, fae intelligence?"

Crowley shook his head. "Neither. She mostly gathers information via spell work."

"So, she knows stuff. What makes you think she'll help us?"

The wizard rubbed his stubbled chin before answering. "She has proven helpful in the past, has she not? She also hates Fuamnach with a passion, and that alone should be reason enough for her to provide assistance."

"Let's hope."

"Indeed," he replied as he pulled to a stop. We'd reached a fork in the road, with either choice leading off toward another tunneling path through the gray, shadowed forest.

"Which way from here?" I asked as I slapped at a quarter-sized mosquito that had landed on my arm.

Crowley spared a quick glance at my forearms, which were now covered in bites. "You're still a druid, are you not? Don't you possess knowledge of a cantrip or something to keep small insects at bay?"

"I did, but I can't remember it now," I said as I

tongued a molar. "I don't see them bothering you. How are you doing that?"

He tapped a finger on his chin as he considered our choices. "They don't like the shadow. Or rather, they can't sense any life beneath it. Now, be quiet and let me think."

I waited roughly thirty seconds before speaking. "You're lost."

The wince was almost imperceptible, such was his self-control, but it was there. "I am not lost; I am merely temporarily perplexed. It seems that Underhill has shifted since last I traveled this way, and I wish to avoid taking us along the wrong route."

"When you say 'wrong,' are we talking wrong direction, or wrong neighborhood?"

He raised his chin to sniff the air, as if he were a sommelier choosing between two wines based on the bouquet alone. "Either path should take us to Peg, but I'm fairly certain one is more dangerous than the other."

I cocked my head sideways and gave him the brow. "You figured that out by smell alone?"

The shadow wizard swiveled his head toward me, an amused grin on his face. "It's Peg's magic I'm tracking, not any mundane scent. My senses may not be keen enough to track a doe through the forest, but I was trained to recognize a fae's magical signature by scent alone."

"And what does Peg's magic smell like?"

He turned his gaze back to the pathways ahead,

staring down each for a time before responding to my question. "Like longing, decay, and death."

"Peachy," I said under my breath.

Crowley transitioned from stillness to action all at once, strolling toward the left-hand branch of the road with haste. "Come, Peg's cottage isn't far now. There we can rest, and hopefully she'll have some plan to share for locating Lugh Samildánach."

Casting a wistful glance down the other pathway, I scurried after the necromancer, wondering if he'd made an informed decision or an arbitrary choice spurred by fear of perceived incompetence.

———

We made good time down the path Crowley chose, and soon we entered the swamps that bordered Fuamnach's lands. Those boggy, marsh-filled forests had been Crowley's playground when he was a child, or at least as much of a playground as you could possibly find in Underhill. And they were the undisputed territory of the unseelie miscreation known as Peg Powler.

Somehow during the shadow wizard's tragic childhood, Peg had become a nanny of sorts to Crowley, although I really didn't understand how that relationship had developed. Peg's reputation was that of a typical predatory water hag, a fae entity that existed solely for the purpose of drowning innocent people, and in some cases, abducting and eating children. Why they established their relationship, and how it had been nurtured to its present form, was beyond me. Mysterious wizard that he was, Crowley had never deigned to elaborate on the topic.

The shadow wizard pointed off the trail to our left. "There's a path hidden back there, or at least there was when last I came this way. If we follow it, it should take us to Peg's cottage forthwith."

"'Forthwith' would be great right now," I said as I swatted away a cloud of gnats. "I could use a break."

"Is fatigue catching up with you? I would think your Fomorian vigor would be sufficient to sustain you for the journey," Crowley remarked, barely hiding the disdain in his voice.

"I'm only Fomorian underneath the skin. Everything on the surface is pretty much human."

"I still don't understand—"

I cut Crowley off with a growl. "I've got chafing going on, all right? That combined with the bug bites is driving me nuts."

"I'm sure Peg can whip up a poultice or an ointment that would take care of that in a snap—not to mention those pustules on your face," he said bemusedly. "Although, if you hadn't lost your ability to cast druidic magic, you might be able to take care of that situation without Peg's intervention."

"We both know those spells were wiped from my memory when I got de-aged. And as for Peg's 'intervention,' I'm not so sure I want to slap something made from eye of newt and bat wings all over my face."

Never one to miss an opportunity to get his digs in, Crowley ignored the jibe I'd directed at his mentor. "Such minor incantations are first-year material. You should have learned those spells when you were still in high school."

"If you're trying to upset me by insinuating that I was not the best student of druidry, don't bother. The fact that I neglected my magical studies was not exactly a secret." I gestured toward the swamp. "Now, can we just drop it and focus on finding Peg's cottage?"

"Oh, by all means," Crowley replied smugly as he led the way into the swamp.

I followed him down the path, muttering under my breath all the while. "Everybody just *has* to kick the druid when he's down. Just because I'm suddenly a teenager, it doesn't give everyone license to crap all over me. Honestly, how many times have I saved the world? Or at least saved Austin? Do I get credit for that? Do I get any respect? Noooo, of course not. They're all like, 'Don't show Colin any love for what he did in the past—instead, let's give him shit for the stuff he's dealing with today.'"

Crowley glanced over his shoulder to flash me an amused grin. "Come now, druid. You must realize I've been waiting for this moment for some time. It's not every day my former rival receives a comeuppance of this nature. And while it does rather inconvenience my plans for destroying the vampires, you can't expect me to pass on the opportunity to milk it for all it's worth."

"Whatever," I said, flipping him the bird as I glared off into the distance. Out on the water, something popped above the surface. It almost looked like a turtle's shell, but it had black moss all over it. At the same moment, the swamp grew deathly silent. "Um, why did everything get quiet all of a sudden?"

Crowley's self-satisfied grin faded from his face, only to be replaced by a look of grim concern. "I can think of any number of reasons. Be on your guard."

"Don't have to tell me twice," I said as I drew Dyrnwyn.

Suitably armed, I turned my attention back to the turtle for lack of anything better to focus on. No sooner did my eyes lock on it again than I could swear its ass blinked at me. Then it disappeared beneath the water with a soft *bloop*, leaving me wondering if I'd seen anything at all.

I nudged Crowley with my elbow, raising my chin in that direction.

"Hey, did you see that?"

"See what? Acknowledgement requires descriptive language. Use your words."

"Hell, I don't know what it was. I thought it was a turtle, then its ass blinked."

"Beg pardon?"

"I didn't see a head, so I figured it was pointing away from me, right? Then, its ass blinked. Or rather, it had eyes on its ass that blinked. I've never seen a turtle with eyes on its ass, so that's why I was asking if you saw it."

"It could've been anything," he said with a shrug. "The swamp is full of wildlife, some magical, some not. Although much of it is harmful, even predatory, there's little here for us to worry about—" Suddenly, Crowley stopped directly in front of me. "Druid, we have company."

I looked over his shoulder, searching the undergrowth and the murky waters to either side of the path for the threat. It took me a moment to identify it, because the thing blended so well with the waters in which it remained mostly hidden. When I did finally make it out, the shape was unmistakable—that of a humanoid head, with mottled green skin, brownish black hair, pointed ears, and big black eyes, poking up just high enough out of the water to observe us from where it was submerged in the swamp.

"Ah, right. Not a turtle."

"It's a grindylow," he said. "And where you find one, you find many."

"It doesn't look like much to me," I said. "Looks kinda small. With a noggin that size, it can't be more than three feet tall."

"Yes, but they hunt in packs," Crowley replied as four tentacles sprouted from his back. "A lone grindylow would definitely be of no concern to us. But in large numbers, they can be quite deadly."

"Define 'large numbers.'"

"Dozens. And they are vicious. They have no trouble surviving beneath the surface of the water, and when they attack, they feed in a frenzy not unlike the piranhas of South America."

"Well, that's just great. You think we can outrun them?"

Crowley shook his head, casting his gaze to the left and right as he did so. "It's too late for that. Look around you, and you'll find we are already surrounded."

I did just as Crowley indicated, realizing that what I had taken for tree stumps, rocks—and yes, turtles—were actually more grindylows, watching us from the water. A high 'chirp' echoed nearby, similar to a frog's mating call, but much more ominous in tone. Soon, others answered all around us, and dozens more of them popped their heads out of the water. As I turned in a slow circle, I spotted dozens of pairs of dark, hungry eyes staring back at us from the murky waters.

"Ruh-roh, Raggy," I muttered under my breath as blue flames began to flicker up and down Dyrnwyn's blade. "Do they always attack when they gather like this?"

"Indeed. When they reveal their presence in these numbers, they are not showing up for midmorning tea."

I gave a curt nod. "Alrighty then. Now that I know the score, I can work with that."

Switching Dyrnwyn to my left hand, I drew my Glock. Taking aim at the first head, I pulled the trigger, double tapping for good measure. The rounds hit cleanly, bursting the thing's head open and sending pieces of skull, green skin, black hair, and gray matter flying off into the water. I didn't wait to see if the grindylow was dead, choosing instead to swing the sights to the next head, firing at it as well. Within the span of five seconds, I managed to clip two more, evening the odds slightly before they all ducked under the water.

"Well, now you've done it," Crowley chided. "They'll hide themselves from here on out, then come at us when we least expect it."

"You mean I didn't scare them off?"

"You don't scare grindylows off. Once they attack, the best you can do is fight a running battle and hope to survive."

"If that's the case, then might I suggest that we run?"

Crowley's shadow tentacles lengthened, anchoring to the ground and lifting him several feet above the muddy trail. "That, my dear druid, is an excellent suggestion."

The shadow wizard was gone almost before I realized he had fled, those long shadow limbs propelling him at speed by latching to and swinging off tree limbs and hanging vines. I responded in kind, taking pot shots at any little green heads I saw as I ran. Even though Crowley was moving at a decent clip through the trees, if I had been in the lead, I would've already left him behind. Instead, I pulled rear guard, knowing that I had a much better chance of surviving a grindylow dogpile than he did.

As we fled, every so often I would notice little splashes in the water, letting me know the grindylows were keeping pace with us as we sped along the muddy trail. We'd only gone a quarter mile or so when a baker's dozen of the things leapt out of the water to attack.

Two of them were directly in my line of sight, and I was able to get a good look as they flew through the air at us. They were short and thin, roughly three to four feet tall, with spindly, muscular arms and legs that ended in clawed fingers and toes. Their scaly skin was dark green on their face, limbs, and back, fading to a lighter green and then a pale yellow on their bloated, distended stomachs. As they leapt, they opened their mouths wide, screeching like demonic four-year-old children with lips curled back in a snarl to display a mouthful of crooked, razor-sharp teeth.

Ah, hell. Where's Tim Allen when you need him?

11

The pair of grindylows ahead of me had leapt out of the water straight at us, so I had to assume most of the rest had done the same. As I calculated the parabolic arcs of homicidal, supernaturally strong toddlers, Crowley used his shadow tentacles to good effect by climbing into the canopy above, well out of the immediate reach of our enemies.

Meanwhile I had roughly thirteen of those rabid little fuckers flying at me, and little time to react.

Thirteen—how'd I know that? Druidry?

No time to consider it now. All I did know was that I had a sort of map inside my mind that told me where every single one of those things were, like a mental radar system or something. And right now, it was telling me I was about to get dog-piled by hell's own offspring.

Move, Colin—or you're going to be gator food.

I cast my old reliable flash-bang spell above me in

the air, closing my eyes and dive-rolling away from the scrum as it went off. My timing was near perfect. As I ducked out of the way, all thirteen of those things collided with each other in mid-air, right where I had been standing. As I rolled to my feet with Dyrnwyn in hand, I spun to assess how the lot of them had faired.

A few of the miniature swamp things lay dazed in the muddy surface of the trail, either out cold or rubbing contusions they'd sustained in the collision. Others were picking themselves up off the ground, and more still were engaged in fighting their brethren in minor squabbles that had resulted from bumping into each other. Only about half of them were in any shape to attack at present, and I for one didn't intend to give them time to regroup and come at me in force.

I was just about to wade in and start laying about with Dyrnwyn when I heard Crowley's voice overhead. "Spell incoming!"

Glancing up, I caught the leading edge of a massive fireball out of the corner of my eye. It tracked across my field of vision, landing in the middle of the pack of grindylows where it exploded in a conflagration of fire and heat. I shielded my eyes and face with my left arm, turning away from the explosion in time to catch a trio of the little bastards sneaking up on me.

"Not today, chumps," I said, sweeping Dyrnwyn in a wide arc as I spun to face them.

Smoldering chunks of their fellow grindylows flew past as I stepped toward the new threat. I was about to say something witty when an odd bit of grindylow shrapnel struck me in the back of the head at speed. The fireball spell that Crowley cast must've been a doozy, because the force of the impact was enough to stagger me, knocking me straight into the three terror-istic amphibians.

Seeing the opportunity of a lifetime—I was meal enough for six of the cannibalistic crayon eaters—they pounced as I stumbled to one knee. Dazed as I was, I barely managed to raise my blade in time to skewer one through the chest. The other two simultaneously landed on my shoulders, sinking their sharp little claws into my human skin and Fomorian flesh, chomping down on my neck on one side and my biceps on the other.

"Yee-owww!" was pretty much all I managed to get out of my mouth as the pain of dozens of needle-sharp teeth cut through the haze of my minor concussion.

Knowing I needed to get up and toss the things off, I pushed off the ground with my free hand. However, those bloodthirsty little fart-goblins were fast. No sooner had I taken a three-point stance than a half-dozen more leapt on me, latching onto my legs, arms, and back. Wherever they landed, they sank their razor-sharp claws into my flesh and immediately began chomping down on yours truly.

"Ah, bloody hell!" I growled, channeling my inner Brit as I kicked one of the rancorous ankle-biters back into the swamp.

Immediately I set about grabbing and tossing them

off me, which was a feat unto itself. Those miniature maulers were strong for their size and peeling them off took quite a bit of work, despite my Fomorian strength. Thing was, every time I managed to pick one off and launch it into the swamp, two more would appear to take its place.

Once I realized I was fighting a losing battle with that approach, I started slicing at them with Dyrnwyn. It was risky business, because the blade glowed white-hot now that so many of the grindylows were upon me. I made decent progress for the span of several seconds, swiping the blade as close to my legs and torso as I dared, severing scaly green heads, arms, and legs in the process.

Then the fuckers latched onto my sword arm, hampering my ability to attack with Dyrnwyn. Out of desperation, I glanced up to see if I could count on an assist from the necromancer, but he was busy scampering through the trees as two-dozen scaly green swamp toddlers followed in hot pursuit. I opened my mouth to yell at him, figuring if he saw how bad off I was he might toss a spell my way.

That's when one of those minuscule monstrosities climbed his way up my frontside. Once he reached my chest, he climbed higher, latching onto my head like an alien facehugger so he could chomp down on my scalp. The unfortunate part of that maneuver—if any aspect of it could be deemed fortunate—was that the little bastard mashed his junk right in my face.

Oh, the humanity. Wait a minute, is he...?

Yep, the tiny green creep started humping my head.

"Alright, that does it!" I screamed, although it came out more like, "Arribbbit, zat dozzimph!" because I had a grindylow doing the watusi on my face. The fact that I had my teeth clenched and lips pursed to avoid getting orally violated probably didn't help matters any, either. However, having somewhat suitably given voice to my outrage, it was time to go about actually ameliorating the situation.

I had at least a dozen of those angry, vicious little turds clinging to me, ripping at my flesh with their teeth and claws like the piranha that Crowley had likened them to earlier. And while they'd have a much harder time rending my Fomorian flesh underneath, the little shits were doing a fine job of flensing me from head to toe. Blood was pouring from my wounds in streams, and while they hadn't hit an artery yet, it was only a matter of time.

Having retained at least some ability to move, I began spinning around in circles in hopes of flinging the grindylows off. However, I had two or three on each leg, and it was all I could do to remain standing to prevent more of them from climbing on with their fellow cannibals. When that didn't work, I had to get more creative, because I was about to literally suffer death from one-thousand cuts.

What a punk-ass way to go, brought low by a couple dozen nightmarish kindergartners, and getting skull-fucked in the process. How humiliating.

I could see the epitaph now. "Here lies Colin McCool, who suffered a death most cruel, having been bitten and bled dry, only to die while being humped in the eye." It wasn't Shakespeare, but it was all I could manage while being tea-bagged by a horny swamp kobold.

Nope, not going down like that.

Although I was bound and determined to escape said embarrassing and disgraceful fate, my options were limited. Fighting against this number of small, super-naturally strong and fast creatures had proven to be futile, because once they got in close, I lost my advantage of size and strength. As for magic, I'd used what was pretty much the only spell I could instacast back when I was at this stage in my magical education.

Wait a minute—maybe there's a better way to use that spell.

The flash-bang spell essentially worked on two principles, the conservation of energy and combustion. To cast it, I simply excited the air molecules around my hand, instantaneously creating enough energy to create a significant amount of heat and light. Real flash-bangs used ammonium nitrate, releasing all the energy in one instantaneous explosion all at once. The trick with my spell was compressing and superheating the air such that the oxygen and hydrogen present would combust, creating a similar effect.

I'd only ever practiced casting it with my hands, but in theory the spell wasn't limited to that point of detonation. Which led me to wonder, could I create the same effect over a larger area?

Only one way to find out.

Knowing I had one shot at this, I turned my focus and attention inward to prepare the spell. This feat of mental concentration was unspeakably difficult, considering that I had a dozen or more grindylows shredding my skin, and one very horny little shit-head thrusting away like a miniature Magic Mike at my forehead. Adding insult to injury, I was starting to get woozy from blood loss, which meant that my Fomorian healing factor was lagging behind my injuries.

Out-fucking-standing.

Despite those distractions, I managed to center myself, achieving a semblance of a druid trance while breathing mostly through my nose for obvious reasons. Once I'd reached a nominal state of focus, I began gathering the nearby air to me, using druid magic to concentrate the oxygen and hydrogen in a thin layer all over my body. This took precious seconds to accomplish, mostly because I lost control twice and had to start all over again.

Once I had a sufficient layer of compressed, flammable gas around my body, it was time to begin step two. I began agitating the gas molecules, using what little magic I possessed to compress them further while speeding them up and causing them to collide with each other. Mentally, I felt myself beginning to fade, so I used my last bit of consciousness to force those molecules to greater and great activity, until...

Fa-floooom!

The spell ignited, instantly lighting up all around my body with all the force of my normal flash-bang spell, but also releasing quite a bit of heat energy as well. It was much like releasing a fireball spell, except I'd had the wherewithal to direct the heat and explosive force outward—most of it, anyway. The desired effect had been achieved, namely that I'd released a great deal of heat and light all at once.

What I hadn't expected, however, was the effect it had on those ferocious little marsh munchers. Apparently, they didn't like heat and flame so much, being amphibious, water-dwelling creatures. As the spell detonated, it seared and scorched their flesh wherever they were touching my skin—or what was left of it. In most cases, this meant that the superheated gas went straight down their gullets, frying their lungs while charring and blistering the insides of their respiratory passageways.

Or in the case of the one that had been trying to blind me with his Junior Johnson, he suffered third-degree burns to his twig and chuckleberries. The lot of them fell away from me immediately, most dropping to the marshy ground clutching their throats, or rolling about in a vain attempt to extinguish the searing pain that bone-deep burns create. None of them lasted more than a few seconds, because getting your alveoli sautéed was not conducive to continued existence on the prime material plane, apparently.

In the case of the horniest little grindylow, he leapt off me like the Jersey Devil—and I knew what that looked like because I'd actually met the real deal. The lascivious little reprobate danced and hopped about, hands on what was left of his weiner as he shrieked like a banshee. As his compadres went through their final, agonized death throes all around, that creep ran and leapt into waist deep water, splashing it at his groin as if that was going to heal his charred equipment.

"Hah, serves you right, you pint-sized, perverted peckerwood," I muttered, swaying back and forth as I dripped blood onto the muddy ground all around me.

As I observed the destruction I had wrought, I likewise took notice of the black spots that had appeared at the edges of my vision. Glancing down at the ruin the grindylows had made of my arms and torso, I realized that what I had thought were shreds of fabric were actually pieces of my own skin. Absently, I noted that the remainder of the grindylow pack had fled in all directions into the swamp.

"That's right—run," I whispered as my eyelids sagged and my vision dimmed.

While I was busy bleeding out, the randy little turd who'd gone to funkytown on my head had given up on relieving his pain, choosing instead to swim off into the murky waters where presumably he'd hole up and heal.

Not so fast, you little shit.

I followed his progress with my gaze, fumbling for my pistol so I could take the little bastard out in a final act of vengeance. By the time my hand finally found the grip, I was struggling to remain conscious in the face of hypovolemic shock. As I drew my Glock, a female figure in a white, toga-like dress rose up from the water in front of the grindylow, who stopped on a dime to cower away from her in response.

The woman was beautiful—a pale, luminous vision of female perfection with flowing dark hair, resplendent green eyes, and facial features straight from an ancient Roman sculpture. Floating there like the Lady of the Lake, she paused in stillness in front of the grindylow, ignoring him as she locked eyes with me across the water. She flashed me a quirky, crooked smile, maintaining my gaze as she snatched the grindylow out of the water.

The last thing I saw before blacking out—and it might very well have been a mirage or hallucination created by my oxygen-deprived brain—was her delicate ivory hands effortlessly ripping the grindylow's head from its neck. Once that was done, she discarded the pieces while keeping her gaze locked on mine. As the creature's black blood spread over the waters like oil from the Deepwater Horizon, the woman slowly sank back into the depths of the swamp, disappearing with nary a splash or wake to mark her passing.

I awoke an indeterminate amount of time later, my head pounding and my ears ringing like I'd tied one on the night before. My eyes were glued shut, whether with crusted blood or eye boogers, it was hard to tell. I reached up experimentally to rub my face and assure myself that my nose and ears were still attached.

"Ugh, I feel like I got hit by a train."

"So, the young druid awakes," a wheezy, gurgling female voice said from somewhere nearby. I recognized that voice immediately. I had heard it a couple of years prior on our first visit to Underhill.

"Peg Powler, I presume?" I said as I pried my eyes open and sat up, casting about for the source of the voice. Failing to locate her, I looked around to see if Crowley was present. When he proved to be absent, I turned my attention instead to assessing my current state.

As my blurred vision cleared and my eyes adjusted to the gloom of the deep swamp, I did a quick visual survey of my person. Although my clothing had been ripped to shreds by those toothy little bastards, the skin and flesh underneath looked to be perfectly intact. However, those places where I had been bitten were covered in a slimy, greenish brown paste that was quickly drying to a flaky, muddy crust on my skin.

Experimentally, I lifted my arm to my nose and took a whiff. The smell was exactly what I expected, a combination of swamp gas, rotting vegetation, and a vaguely medicinal, iodine note.

"Don't you be wiping that stuff off yet, young demi-human. Your ability to heal might be the equal to that of some of the gods, but you'll be needing ol' Peg's magic to put you right as rain, and that's a fact."

I nodded, as much to acknowledge her wisdom as to assure myself it was the proper course of action. "Obviously, I'm in no position to argue. Incidentally, your efforts to help me have been noted."

"I suppose that's as close to thanks that ol' Peg'll get, even though she's not a fae-born creature—no, not at all. T'wasn't Peg's fault she was cursed twice and then once more, first when her children drowned, and again when she went mad with grief, and the final time when that old fae witch turned her into what she is now."

Wisely I remained silent, as it seemed Peg's intentions were not so much to explain herself to me, as they were to simply reflect on the past. I knew a little of her origin story, although that version differed quite a bit from what she had just shared. Supposedly, she had drowned her own children—whether due to insanity or wickedness, I had no idea.

As these legends often go, when Peg realized what

she had done she went mad with grief and drowned herself in the same bog, intending to spend eternity in a watery grave next to her children. But due to divine intervention, or that of some fae spirit playing the world's cruelest prank, she was not allowed to die. Instead, she was magically transformed into the unnatural thing that spoke to me from the murk of the swamp.

Speaking of, I continued to cast my gaze about in an attempt to locate where Peg might be hidden. However, I might as well have been looking for the invisible man, or Click, for that matter. Peg was a ghost.

"Where's Crowley?" I asked as I gave up, choosing instead to locate my gear and Craneskin Bag.

"Your things are nearby, stacked neatly over there by the wall of the hut. And as for the boy, he prowls the swamp searching for the remainder of the bog children who nearly laid you low."

The mention of the grindylows brought to mind the last thing I'd seen before I passed out. That being the lady in white who had ripped that horny little swamp chomper's head off.

"I saw something out there—or I think I did. I don't know whether it was my imagination, or real."

"Aye, you saw something, something that doesn't belong in my swamp. Wasn't your imagination, and your eyes didn't deceive you. Crowley searches for her as well."

"Don't suppose you care to tell me what 'she' is?"

Silence. "Right, then answer me this—why aren't you out there searching with him?"

She cackled, her laughter echoing off the surrounding mangrove and cypress trees until it trailed off into wheezing breaths. "Peg doesn't need to leave her island to know what's in her swamp. Told the boy as much, little good that it did. Thinks he's protecting ol' Peg now that he's come into his own. Forgets who it was that showed him his true power in the first place."

I considered that tidbit of information, tucking it away before moving on. "He's somewhat in awe of you, you know. And he's defended your integrity on more than one occasion. Although he never has explained how you and he met."

"What you mean is, he hasn't told you why I never ate him," Peg replied smugly.

"I didn't want to come right out and say it, but yeah."

The old water hag chuckled softly, her low laughter playing counterpoint to the cicadas and frogs that sang out in the swamp. "Mayhap's ol' Peg ain't what you think she is. Leastwise, not anymore."

"Honestly, I didn't mean to offend, only to understand."

"Been around nigh on a thousand years, druid. You're as likely to understand me as you are to decipher what the wind says to the Earth as it passes o'er."

Silence grew between us, and I let it be. Sometimes it was better to avoid pressing immortal creatures, as they could be fickle and cantankerous. After pushing myself to my feet I marched over to my Bag, digging around in it for clothing to replace what I was currently wearing. Figuring that Peg could watch me no matter where I was on her island, I disrobed and changed out the open. With some reluctance, I chose to leave the foul-smelling flakes of dried poultice in place, despite my better judgment.

"The boy told me why you came here, and what you seek," Peg said after I'd dressed.

"I need to find Lugh to regain my powers and save my Oak. Do you know how we can find him?"

"Hmm, a worthy quest, no doubt." She seemed to chew on my question in silence for the span of many heartbeats. "Consider, druid—p'raps the better question to ask is, how can you get Lugh to find you?"

12

Before I could ask what Peg Powler meant, a horn sounded in the distance. "What the hell? Did Jesse's army follow us here?"

Peg hissed before replying. "Your ol' love remains in the Dagda's lands, bound by debt and honor to defend same. Nay, 'tis Herne and his Hunt, come ta' finish what the goddess started when ya' walked through the gateway."

"Wait, what goddess?"

"No time ta' explain, druid. You've little chance of survivin' against Herne the Hunter. Now, grab your belongings and move!"

Off to my left, a pathway opened in the undergrowth just past Peg's cottage, the thick vegetation receding to reveal a dirt trail that led down to the water. It didn't escape my notice that the trail pointed in the opposite direction from which we'd heard the hunting horn's call.

After tossing my Bag over my shoulder, I snagged Dyrnwyn as well.

The horn sounded once more, closer this time. I ran down the trail, pulling to a halt at the water's edge. "What next? Am I supposed to swim across? Because I've seen what inhabits your swamp, and I am not eager to go skinny dipping with that menagerie."

"Hush now, my pets may hear and take offense. Your path lies ahead, and you only need have faith to walk it."

Before my eyes, slick round stones rose from the swamp's murky depths. The muddy, irregular hemispheres floated just above the water's surface a few feet apart, creating a steppingstone path that led off into the mists. After shaking off a momentary flashback to the grindylow attack, I reached out to tap the first rock experimentally with the tip of my boot.

Rather than proving a solid, immovable surface, it dipped slightly before rebounding and bobbing in the drink. On the other side of the stone, a brownish-green head rose from the water on a wrinkled, serpentine neck. It craned around slowly, revealing itself to be a turtle's head, complete with a snapper's beak and dark, beady eyes that regarded me with mild disdain.

"I'm not stepping on that," I said.

"You'll do as you're told, and gather up my lad in the process," Peg's voice hissed. "Either that, or you'll find yourself in Herne's pot a'fore daybreak tomorrow."

"Eh, right," I muttered. Then I leapt on the first

turtle, landing with both feet and catching my balance before hopping to the next.

"Can ya' move any faster?" Peg groused. "I've raised a fog, but that'll only deter them for so long."

"Fine, fine, I'm going," I replied as I began leaping hopscotch style across the swamp. After the first several jumps, I picked up steam, until I was fairly sprinting across the water.

Somewhere to my right, a long, sinuous shadow snaked its way through the water, just far enough below the surface to conceal its identity. Whatever it was, it was easily large enough to swallow me whole. I was reminded of the giant dragon turtle I'd seen Peg riding at the battle of Mag Mell, and for a moment I wondered just how deep the swamp went.

Perhaps because I allowed myself to become distracted, I nearly found out when I misstepped on the next turtle in line. My boot slipped off the mud and algae-slicked side of the turtle's shell, and I barely recovered by planting my trailing foot firmly on the poor animal's back. Just then the horn sounded closer still somewhere behind me, and I thought I heard hounds baying in response on either side.

After wobbling and swaying back and forth for a few seconds, I caught my balance and continued on, deeper into Peg's demesne. "How much farther?"

"Not much, druid," the hag's disembodied voice replied. "There's an island up ahead, upon which a trail begins that will lead on for several leagues. At the end,

Crowley awaits your arrival. He'll know the way from there."

"What if I get lost? This place is huge. There are no landmarks to follow, and no sun or stars in the sky to guide my way."

"You won't, so long as you trust the trail. Heed me, druid. Once your feet touch soil I'll have ta' leave you so I can lead the Hunt astray."

"Right." A few leaps later, my feet landed on the soft, muddy bank of the isle. I didn't see a trail ahead, so I called out to the water hag. "Peg?"

"What is it, druid? Hurry and speak your piece, as I'll not see the Shade-cursed perish for the sake of your need to be coddled."

"Thanks," I said, taking a risk that somehow felt right in the moment.

All I heard for several seconds was the plopping noise of dozens of turtles submerging back into the water behind me. After the span of several heartbeats, Peg spoke. "See the changeling safely out of the swamp, druid, and you'll be welcome at my hearth after and always. Now, no more talk, as Herne's hounds can hear for miles. Be well, McCool, until next we meet."

Another trail appeared in the undergrowth ahead, the plant life parting to reveal a path covered in thick moss. I heard the hounds bark and bay closer still to my right, left, and behind, answering a bugle call that sounded like it was only a few hundred yards behind me. Wasting no time, I sprinted down the path, noting that the moss gave and rebounded beneath my feet, and that the vegetation closed back again behind me as I passed.

Heedless of where the trail might lead, I ran on, picking up speed until I fairly flew through the swamp. Occasionally I crossed waterways on partially submerged logs, giving way to narrow fingers of earth shored up by mangrove and cypress roots, or soft, sandy soil that I was almost certain would swallow me whole like Buttercup and Wesley. During one stretch I ran for half a mile on a thick carpet of floating vegetation that gave and rebounded with my every step.

Eventually the bugle's call and the hounds' cries faded in the distance, at which point the trail came to an abrupt halt at a large, football field-wide flowing bayou, with a small island in the center not far from where I stood. The water was less opaque here, allowing me to see several feet down to the undisturbed bottom. While there were no apparent dangers lurking below, there was certainly no clear way across and no path around, either. I waited for a minute or so in silence, then my impatience won out over my better judgement.

"Crowley," I stage whispered, cupping my hands around my mouth to direct my voice away from the direction I'd come. "Crowley, are you there?"

"I'm here," he answered, his voice coming from the island fifty-ish yards across the water.

As I strained to see where he hid amongst the thicket of swamp rose, buttonbush, and young willow trees that covered the island, I realized the small land mass was slowly getting closer. Like many things in Peg's swamp, it seemed Crowley's hideout was not what it appeared to be.

The "island" stopped its progress roughly twenty feet from shore. Although silt had been kicked up along the bottom of the bayou, I made out at least one stump-like testudinal leg below the water's surface. An area of deep shadow at the center of the island receded, and soon Crowley stepped out of the brush to greet me.

"Honestly, man—how many giant turtles does Peg have?"

"I don't think it can be rightly said that she owns them," he replied. "Only that she's befriended them."

"I only know of two ways to make friends with wild animals. Feeding them and communing with them. Which method does Peg use?"

"You don't want to know the answer to that question," he said. "Incidentally, this is our ride across this lake. Unless you want me to grab you with my tentacles, you'll need to swim over here."

"That water might be clearer than it is around Powler's island, but it still smells like ass. Thanks, but I'll jump."

"Suit yourself."

I backed up and took a running leap, misjudging the distance and landing on at the spot where the shell curved steeply down to the water. As I began to fall backwards, I frantically waved my arms in circles in an attempt to catch my balance. Just as I was about to fall into the water, Crowley snagged my shirt with one of his shadow tentacles.

Instinctively, I reached for it, hanging on as he pulled me forward. The thing felt exactly as I'd imagined, like calamari covered in a mixture of road tar and motor oil. Once he'd dragged me up to the relatively flat portion where he stood, I pushed the tentacle away from me, frowning with disgust.

"Ugh. No offense, but that is nasty."

"You get used to it," he said as a smile played around the corners of his mouth. "And it can't be much worse than being grinded on by a grindylow."

I looked off to the side, sour-faced. "You, uh, saw that, eh?"

"I caught a glimpse or two, yes, as I scrambled through the treetops with the remainder of the grindylow pack in pursuit. Sadly, I did not have time to enjoy the full show. Although, you appeared to have gotten the, *ahem*, thrust of it."

"Laugh it up, why don't you," I said, crossing my arms over my chest. "It's not like I haven't been humiliated enough since we arrived here."

He chuckled good-humoredly. "It's really not your

fault. Peg seemed to think it was attracted by the hormones coursing through your system."

"You *told* her?" I asked with incredulity in my voice.

"How could I not? She needed to know the nature of your wounds before they could be properly treated. Incidentally, she said you'd acquired a nasty case of the pox in your eye, which she remedied while you were unconscious."

"'The pox?'"

"Syphilis, or gonorrhea, take your pick."

I glared at Crowley in silence. "Now you're just fucking with me."

"Oh no," he replied, shaking his head. "I am deadly serious."

Remembering how sticky and gooey my eyes had been when I woke up beside Peg's hut, I hung my head and covered my face with one hand. "Just wait, Crowley. Someday you're going to be the one with egg on your face, and I am going to be merciless."

"As I understand it, it wasn't egg that you had on your face." My silence must've conveyed that he was treading on thin ice, because he raised his hands in supplication. "Alright, alright—I've had my fun now, and I will allow you a reprieve."

"If you tell anyone about it, I swear I'll strangle you with your own shadow tentacles."

"Impossible, but I take your meaning fully." He took a moment to stare off in the direction of Peg's cottage, tearing his eyes away with a short shake of his head.

"She'll be fine, Crowley. Not even the Master of the Wild Hunt could fuck with a witch as powerful as Peg in her own territory."

When he turned to face me again, his mouth was set in a grim line. "I was merely wondering if she'd managed to drown one of them yet."

"Kinda hard to drown a god, I would think. But it'd be funny if she did."

"Hmm, yes—I'd like to see that. However, we need to reach the far shore as quickly as possible."

"Why's it so important we get over there?" I asked as I peered at the other side of the bayou, which was slowly getting closer. "As far as I can tell, it's just more marshland."

"Yes, but this slow-moving river divides Peg's swamp from Lugh's lands. I doubt very seriously that Herne would follow us there."

"I thought that the Dagda's lands bordered on Lugh's. Isn't that how we got there last time?"

Crowley's smile was almost imperceptible. "This is Underhill, where the rules of time and space are flexible. As you know, each territory takes on characteristics of its master. A side effect of that transformation is that lands belonging to allied gods and fae often connect in some fashion."

"Two questions. First, how did Lugh's lands end up being so damned miserable when he's supposed to represent the best of the Tuath Dé and Fomorians? And second, Peg's allied with Lugh?"

"The real Lugh is a darker and more troubled figure than the man-myths make him out to be," Crowley replied.

I thought about my mother and our strained relationship. "Gee, I can't imagine why."

"'Gee,' indeed. And in answer to your second question, consider it a politically neutral relationship."

"Kind of like, I dunno, the United States and Brazil or something. Not close allies, but they don't hate each other, either."

"Just so," he said as he headed for the other side of the turtle's back. "Come. Lugh's castle shouldn't be far now, and if we're to find him that would be a good place to look."

After we disembarked from "turtle island," we picked our way through terrain that was slightly more forgiving than what we'd left behind, eventually finding a wide, well-worn path to follow. While Peg's lands reminded me of a full-on Louisiana swamp, Lugh's demesne bore characteristics of the riparian wetlands found in East Texas. The landscape consisted of marshy, boggy soil rife with sedge ponds and small, slow-moving streams, with most of the land covered by an old-growth forest of alders, dogwoods, willows, and oaks.

Thankfully, the air here was cleaner and less oppressive, although I was still plagued by large, bloodsucking insects that would put any Texas mosquito or sand fly to shame. While the remnants of Peg's poultice partially protected me, the damned things managed to find exposed skin just the same. Eventually I found a patch of lemon balm, or at least something that smelled like a close relative, which I crushed and rubbed over my arms, face, and neck.

"That should improve the odor of Peg's poultices considerably," Crowley observed as we walked side-by-side down a tree-lined path.

"Meh, the smell faded hours ago. Guess my olfactory nerves finally gave up the ghost."

"Mine haven't," he replied dourly.

"Hey, at least it doesn't smell like ass here. Peg's whole demesne reeks. Honestly, how could you stand hanging out there so much, back when you were a kid?"

"I was never a child. And as for the general hospitality of Peg's swamp, I found it to be quite preferable to the cold, lonely corridors of Fuamnach's castle."

"Ah, right." The discussion of Peg's swamp reminded me of what I'd seen back there. "By the way, Peg mentioned you were out looking for something while I was down. Did you find anything?"

"You're asking if I found any sign of the woman in white. No, I did not. Furthermore, I didn't manage to get a good enough look to identify who she was."

"A lake maiden, maybe? Might explain why so many grindylows gathered to attack us at once."

He dismissed my suggestion with an offhanded

wave. "Grindylows might be base creatures, but they are not so easily controlled. While it's just as likely that we happened to be in the wrong place at the wrong time, if something did compel them to attack us, it would be more powerful than a mere *gwraig annwn*."

"Whatever she was, the way she ripped that little bastard's head off said she was pissed that they failed."

"Hmm, yes. I believe that one was their chieftain—which, incidentally, was why he was so intent on showing dominance over you. Perhaps she killed him to make a point."

"Think she was the one that sent the flood after us?"

Crowley's eyes narrowed. "I'd speculate that it's more than just a coincidence."

Somewhere in the woods to my right, a twig snapped. Instantly, a ball of sickly, greenish balefire coalesced above Crowley's right hand. I dropped into a crouch, reaching to draw Dyrnwyn as I went back-to-back with the shadow wizard.

"Think she's come back for thirds?" I whispered over my shoulder.

"Perhaps," he replied in a low voice. "Be vigilant."

"When am I not vigilant?" I hissed.

"Shall I make a list? Now, hush, so we can determine what stalks us."

Even though it rankled me to be shushed by the wizard, I bit back a retort, choosing instead to focus on pinpointing whatever was moving through the trees. Calming myself, I took several deep breaths before dropping into a light druid trance so I could extend my senses outward. While I couldn't find any small animals that would mind-meld with me, I got an impression of the general location of the thing by tracking the reactions of the local fauna.

Whatever the thing was, it was large, and it moved quickly. Once I had a lock on it, I opened my eyes so I could visually verify what my druid senses told me. Soon I caught a flash of gray fur through the trees at head level. I shuffled through my mental files for a creature that was over six feet tall, furry, and gray, and all I came up with was a 'thrope, or maybe a buggane.

Neither of those options worried me much, but I sure in the hell didn't want to be ambushed by one of them, either. I nudged Crowley, inclining my head to draw his attention to the thing's current position.

"It's moving toward us, slowly," I whispered. "Get ready."

Crowley pivoted around so he stood shoulder-to-shoulder with me, but at a ninety-degree angle. That way, we could cover 270 degrees of surrounding forest, reducing the odds of being flanked. My druid senses told me the creature was within ten yards of us, although I saw nothing to indicate its presence through the thick foliage ahead. One thing I did know was that Dyrnwyn hadn't lit up, which meant the creature wasn't evil, or it wasn't intelligent enough to have any sort of moral compass.

Huh.

"Hey, Crowley," I whispered. "Hold off for a sec—"

Before I could finish that request, a giant hound burst out of the highest branches of the tree canopy directly in front of us. He was long and lean, and built like a greyhound, but with a shaggier coat of grey fur and a broader, more robust snout, jaws, and skull. Although the dog was easily eight feet high at the withers, he hadn't leapt off the forest floor—I'd have heard or seen it. Which meant that the dog had snuck through the treetops to get in position to attack.

While my mind was working on that mental math, Crowley loosed his attack. Two three-foot wide balls of balefire—basically, fireballs made from death magic—struck the hound in the snout and the chest. I'd seen the effects of that sort of offensive spell before, and generally it wasn't pretty. Balefire would cause plant life to shrivel and die on contact, and as for living flesh, it would rot and slough off on contact.

Yet the dog shrugged the death magic off like water. Or, more precisely, the balefire burst on impact, dissipating and fading from sight as if it had been countered with an anti-magic spell. Thus, the spell did little if anything to slow the hound, and the arc of his trajectory would end with him landing on us both.

Dyrnwyn still remained inert in my hands, and I had to make a split-second decision whether to fight or see where this led. My gut told me that the animal was merely acting on instinct, either defending its territory or protecting a litter of pups nearby. Regardless, I was a sucker for dogs, 110 percent, and there was no way I was going to kill an animal that was just protecting its home.

Better hope I'm right, because if not, I'm about to be puppy chow.

Just before the hound landed, I lowered my blade and pushed Crowley well out of the way with a Fomorian-powered shove.

13

The dog pushed me to the ground with one massive paw, pinning me without crushing my chest. It was the size of a Kodiak bear, but taller at the shoulder due to its longer legs, and I had to marvel at what a feat of control it must've been to hold me down without caving my ribs into my spine. He turned his head to the side, growling at Crowley before swinging his Clydesdale-sized muzzle toward me.

With his lips pulled back in a snarl to expose his long, dagger-like canines and shorter, but equally sharp incisors, the dog sized me up with gold-flecked, silver eyes. I met his gaze for an instant, acknowledging the massive hound without indicating any threat. Lowering my eyes to stare at his muzzle, I spoke in calming tones, even as a low growl rumbled in the dog's massive throat.

"Easy there, boy," I said as I lowered Dyrnwyn to the

ground beside me. "We don't mean any harm." Crowley must've stirred or made some threatening gesture, because the dog looked to its right and growled again. "Crowley, whatever you're doing, stop before this thing bites my face off."

"If I don't do anything, he might still," the wizard replied in a low voice.

"Naw," I said. "He's a good boy. He just doesn't know if we're friend or foe."

In response to my calm tone, the dog swiveled his head back to me with a less fierce and more curious look in his eyes. He tilted his head sideways, first one way, then another. Then he leaned in closer, allowing me to get a lungful of his dog breath, which wasn't too bad, but he did have some flesh stuck between his teeth that was starting to rot. I kept my eyes lowered and my mouth closed and waited patiently as the dog sniffed at my chest, neck, and face.

I could almost feel Crowley tensing as the dog let out a low, short whine. Suddenly it licked my face with its rough tongue—once, twice, three times—whining and barking as if it had found a long-lost friend. I laughed because it tickled, scratching behind his ears as I attempted to wrestle him away.

"Okay, okay, stop, you big lug," I said in a tone of mock protest. "I get it, we're friends now."

The dog gave a short, sharp bark as he bounced off me. As I pushed myself up to a seated position, he laid his chest on the ground, bowing and stretching his front legs out before him while keeping his hindquarters in the air. He wiggled his rump and swung his tail back and forth, obviously inviting me to play.

"It appears he likes you," Crowley said.

Something clicked then, and I thought back to what I remembered of Lugh from Celtic mythology. "Didn't Lugh own a magic greyhound or something?"

"Failinis was the hound's name, and he passed through several owners over the centuries, back in the heyday of the gods. Lugh took ownership of him from clan Tuireann, by way of *éraic* for the death of his father, Cian. Another legend claims the hound ran with MacCumhaill's fianna, only to be slain by them when it killed one of their number." The dog growled at that, and Crowley had the good grace to look abashed. "Or so the legends say."

When I pushed myself to my feet the dog stood as well, lowering his head to my height and panting contentedly, tail wagging. I reached up and scratched him behind the ears again, rubbing his jowls and patting his neck. The dog seemed to enjoy this, leaning into the rub I gave him hard enough to push me off balance.

"Failinis. Is that your name, boy?" I asked. The great grey hound pricked his ears at that, which I found to be hilarious. He continued looking at me, head tilted and mouth slightly open, like he was waiting for me to continue. "So, you're Lugh's dog, eh? Can you take us to him?"

Failinis barked again, then he scratched the ground once with a forepaw before bounding off into the forest. Crowley and I exchanged a look.

"I guess we'd better follow him," I said. "Let's hope we can keep up."

As it turned out, keeping up wasn't an issue. Failinis would run down a trail, then he'd come bounding back again, panting and carrying on as if to say, "Hurry up, humans!" I kept a pace that I thought Crowley could maintain, but as for the dog, he had no fatigue in him, and he proceeded to run off and then come back to fetch us for the length of the trip.

We ran like that for a good ten miles before the dog stopped, finally laying down in front of a wall of dense thicket. I slowed to a walk as I neared where the dog lay, stopping and listening while I waited for Crowley to catch up.

"You hear that?" I said as he pulled up beside me.

"Your ears are better than mine, but it sounds like battle."

"Exactly." I walked up to the thicket, scratching the dog between the ears as I walked by. Parting the foliage with my hands, I peered through a screen of leaves and branches to see what lay on the other side. "Good boy, Failinis."

Crowley took up a position beside me. "Are we there? Has the hound led us to Lugh's castle?"

"Yeah, but we're not home-free yet," I replied. "See for yourself."

I stepped aside, and Crowley took my place so he could peer through the thicket as I had. Although he rarely showed emotion, his shoulders slumped just enough to tell me his assessment matched mine.

"There must be thousands of them," he said as he stepped away from the thicket wall.

No doubt, the scene beyond was the last thing either of us expected. Failinis had led us to Lugh's castle, alright, right to the edge of the forest surrounding the immediate grounds. Unfortunately, in the three-hundred yards or so of cleared land between the marshy forest and the castle moat, an army was encamped—one that easily numbered five thousand or more.

As I surveyed the encampment, I spotted pale banshees and their sisters, the cloven-hoofed baobhan sith of Scottish legend. There were entire cavalry brigades made up of bloodthirsty fuathan, including the satyr-like ùruisg and the skinless horses known as the nuckelavee. Shellycoats and other water fae rode them, bearing wicked-looking weapons of hooked and serrated bone. Here and there among the gathered troops, giant fachen towered above them, launching boulders at the fortress like living, moving artillery machines.

Beyond that I saw battalions of leprechauns and glaistigs, fear dearg and merrowfolk, along with their fairer cousins, the gancanagh and leanan sidhe, arrayed in formations and geared up for battle. Amongst the fae sat platoon-sized units consisting of human-looking soldiers in modern garb. Runners moving at supernatural speed flitted between those camps, sometimes reporting to fae, and at other times sticking to their own. These were vampires, obviously, probably trained to act as rapid response strike teams should the army breach the walls of the castle.

Never had I seen this many fae and vamps gathered in one place. Obviously, they deemed Lugh's castle to hold some military and strategic significance, or perhaps they merely wanted the owner dead. For whatever reason, they'd convened in force and were standing directly between us and our objective.

I ran a hand through my hair before gesturing offhandedly at the massive encampment and castle. "Well, at least we know where Lugh is now."

Crowley and I had been arguing for the better part of an hour about our next steps. He wanted to sneak past the army and enter the castle. I thought it was suicide, which it was. I was about to say so for the hundredth time when I noticed that the dog was standing erect with his ears perked up, facing the direction from which we'd come.

When Failinis started growling, I knew something was up. Meanwhile, Crowley was still caught up in arguing his position.

"I can easily conceal us under cover of darkness, and then all we need to do is cross the moat and scale the castle walls."

I held a finger to my lips, silencing him. "Hang on a sec, I think the dog hears something." I cocked an ear in the general direction of Peg's swamp and listened intently for several seconds. "Nope, nothing. False alarm, I—"

At that very moment, a horn sounded in the distance.

"Well, fuck."

The dog's growling grew deeper, and his hackles raised on the back of his neck. Crowley and I shared a look, mine questioning and his concerned.

"We need to move, druid," he said, in the most serious tone I'd ever heard him use. And hell if Crowley wasn't usually one serious motherfucker.

"What's the deal with this Herne dude, anyway? From what I understand, he was just some sucker who got cursed by the fae. Am I wrong about that?"

"Dead wrong, I'm afraid. He is of the old gods, and a power unto his own. The Gauls once worshiped him as Cernunnos, the Romans as Silvanus. Every tale of the Wild Hunt across Europe goes back to Herne the Hunter, leading his hounds in pursuit of whomever he chooses. And these days, he hires himself out in mercenary fashion to any god who'll pay his price."

"Great. How the hell did he track us here? Especially with Peg working her voodoo to lead him astray."

Crowley frowned and cast a worried glance in the direction of the swamp. "While Peg's magic is substantial, he is not called the Hunter for nothing."

Howls echoed from the south, southwest, and west, indicating the Hunt had already nearly surrounded us. To the east was Lugh's castle and the rebel army, leaving us only one direction to go. The horn sounded again, and Failinis took off to the west, presumably to defend his master's lands.

"Shit, I hope he'll be alright," I said as I watched his tail disappear into the forest.

"If we're lucky, he'll lead them off our trail," Crowley replied. He pointed to the forest north of us. "Now run!"

"Why is this starting to feel like a recurring theme for this trip?" I asked as I took off in the direction he suggested, barreling through the trees and undergrowth like a spooked deer.

The horn trumpeted again behind us, closer now, and if the barking and baying noises were any indication, the hounds were closing in as well. I let Crowley take the lead since he was slower than me, although running was a hard pill to swallow. It soon became clear that Crowley could not outrun Herne and his Hunt, which led me to determine that we might have to stand and fight after all.

"What's the plan?" I asked, calling ahead to the shadow wizard.

"The plan," he panted over his shoulder as he swung from tree to tree on his shadow tentacles, "is to not get caught."

"I don't think that's an option," I replied, glancing to my left and behind us. I saw flashes of brown and black fur through the trees, maybe twenty-five yards off. "They're catching up fast and hemming us in to boot."

"We can handle his pack—they're merely oversized *cú sídhe*. But Herne is another matter."

I said nothing, because I was intently watching and waiting for one of those faery hounds to leap out of the bush at us. As well, the forest was thinning out now, revealing our position to our pursuers and theirs to us in turn. Although I was only able to snatch the odd glance over my shoulder while running at this speed, I counted at least a half dozen cú sídhe and cŵn annwn following us.

What was worse was that they appeared to be herding us in a specific direction. It was disconcerting to say the least, and I almost wished we'd taken our chances with the army that was attacking the castle. At least then Lugh might have portalled out, snagged us, and portalled back into his castle again. Maybe.

As I lamented that we hadn't taken that option, a large black ball of fur and teeth leapt out of the woods at me, taking me by surprise. I had no weapon at the ready because sprinting through the forest with a longsword in your hand was just asking to lose an eye. I drew my fist back to cuff it across its snout, hoping it would give me sufficient reprieve to arm myself.

Before I delivered the blow, an even larger gray ball of fur and teeth flew over my head, plowing into the cú sídhe like a freight train. I heard a yelp, then a lot of snarling and ripping noises, then I was past the tussle and moving on.

"Shit," I yelled to Crowley. "We have to go back and help him."

"If we're to make a stand, it has to be out in the open where Herne cannot sneak up on us," he wheezed, pointing off ahead of us. "And it seems we'll have little choice."

Maybe one-hundred yards to the north, the forest thinned out completely, revealing a broad, flat, grassy plain that seemed to stretch on for miles. We'd be hard-pressed to outrun Herne and the Hunt on that terrain, but there'd be no place for them to hide, either. I weighed the risks and made a split decision.

"Keep going," I yelled as I skidded to a stop, reaching for Dyrnwyn as I did so. "I'll catch up after I thin the pack!"

"You'll die!" Crowley yelled as he swung around the trunk of an alder tree, slowing his momentum to address me.

"Maybe—but at least I'll die facing my enemies."

As I pulled Dyrnwyn from its sheath, the sword lit up in white hot flames along its length. I jogged back to the spot where Failinis had saved my bacon, just in time to see him rip the foreleg off a downed cú sídhe with a single snap of his jaws. As the great gray hound spat out his pound of flesh, seven more pony-sized black dogs emerged from the forest, teeth bared and snarling as they formed a half-circle before us.

I took up a position to the right of Failinis, squaring my stance and rolling my shoulders out as I readied to face Herne's Hunt.

"Alright you smelly, overgrown pack of jackals," I said, locking eyes with the biggest of the bunch. "Let's fucking do this."

Granted, I had no desire to face Herne, if what Crowley had said about him was true. However, I wasn't about to leave Failinis to face the Hunt alone. If I could thin out the pack before we fled to the plain—while saving Lugh's hound—so much the better.

Failinis stood to my left, hackles raised and teeth bared, his growl vibrating in my chest like a rumble of thunder. Before us stood seven of the largest, meanest looking cú sídhe and cŵn annwn I'd ever seen. The one Failinis had killed looked to be the runt of the bunch, because the rest were sized more like horses than ponies.

If I had a large-caliber firearm I might've shot a couple right then and there. However, all I had on my hip was a nine-millimeter pistol. Although it fired a round that was perfectly suitable for shooting man-sized creatures, Mr. Luger didn't design the cartridge to take down large prey.

Even if I still had my rifle, it was chambered in 5.56, another undersized round—a small, high-velocity cartridge the folks at Fabrique Nationale designed specifically so soldiers could carry more ammunition in the field. There was a good reason why folks didn't carry military rifles in bear country.

Guess we're doing this the hard way. But that doesn't mean I can't even the odds with a little magic.

One of Herne's hounds of the far left lunged at us, and Failinis turned to meet the attack. Now that Lugh's hound was looking away, that left an opening to fire off my flash-bang spell at the hounds arrayed to my front and right. Covering my eyes with my sword arm, I loosed the spell in their general direction, blitzing forward while the after-image was still imprinted inside my eyelids.

When I met them, my half of the pack was backing away, shaking their heads and pawing at their eyes and ears in confusion. For a split-second I felt a pang of guilt regarding what I was about to do, then I remembered these animals were intelligent fae creatures. Dyrnwyn wouldn't have lit up like a roman candle if the damned things weren't evil to the core. Sometimes it was nice having my own personal "detect evil" spell worked into my sword.

I waded into the line as silently as possible, swinging my blade like a man possessed. Possessed by fear, that is, because I needed to get this done before Herne showed up. I lopped the first hound's foreleg off above the knee with my initial cut, then I turned to deliver an overhead attack at a second hound's neck, cleanly severing the canine's head from its shoulders.

Two down, five to go.

I spared a glance at Failinis, who was shaking one of the hounds like a rag doll while two more of them were attacking him from his flanks. There was no time to help him, as I still had two dogs to deal with on my side. With big, bounding strides, I rounded the tail end of the faery hound I'd crippled, coming up behind the next in line and running my sword straight up its ass.

Most people never thought about stabbing someone or something in the rectum—too distasteful. That said, Maureen had taught me early on there was no such thing as an honorable way to fight against the fae. I took her lessons to heart, learning every dirty trick in the book, and stabbing a motherfucker in the taint was one of them. The faery hound yelped and fell to the ground, whining and snapping at me blindly as I passed.

Only one left—where'd it go?

A huge black shape barreled into me from the side, latching its bear-sized maw on my left upper arm and biting down. I felt its teeth pierce my human skin and Fomorian flesh down to the bone. While I screamed in anger and pain, I reached around and stabbed the hound in the side once, twice, three times, twisting and slicing sideways as I pulled the blade out on the last stick.

Dyrnwyn must've been pissed, or as pissed as a semi-sentient sword can be, because it cut through that cú sídhe's rib cage like it was made of wax. The hound yelped, releasing my arm as it staggered away a few steps, then it fell over like a ton of bricks. My arm was bleeding rivers, but on flexing it a few times, I found it was still functional. I thanked everything holy and good that my Fomorian bones were tougher than steel, then I turned to help Failinis.

A cŵn annwn lay in a broken, bloody heap off to the side, but the final two had their teeth dug in to Failinis and they weren't letting go. One of them had hold of the bigger hound's right rear leg, while the other had latched onto his flank. Both were tugging and holding on for dear life, pulling Lugh's hound off balance so he couldn't turn on them to fight back.

Being the sort who always hated seeing someone get ganged up on, I burst forward with a mighty overhand cut that chopped the former hound in two, just forward of its rear legs. It took a moment for the thing to realize it was all but dead, and while it managed to hang on for a second, it had no leverage. That allowed Failinis to turn and bite it round the neck, ending its suffering immediately.

Unfortunately, the great gray hound couldn't reach the last cú sídhe, as it kept tugging and moving away, timing its footwork against Failinis' efforts to dislodge it. I decided to intervene, although there was no way I was going to get in front of the larger hound's massive, snapping jaws to attack. To avoid getting in the way, I took two bounding steps, then I leapt over the hound's back, flipping upside-down in mid-air so I could chop at the faery hound from above.

My blade caught the Huntsman's hound behind the ear. It was a shallow cut, but enough to make the hound loosen its grip. Once it lost its purchase on the larger animal's flesh, the cú sídhe went flying. Failinis turned and was on it in a heartbeat, snapping the dog's neck in his jaws with a vicious shake of his head.

The gray dog raised its head to the sky and let out a piercing, triumphant howl. Somewhere very close by, Herne's horn sounded in response, so loud it shook the leaves from the trees.

"Good boy, Failinis, good boy," I said. "Now, come— we gotta' go."

Failinis looked at me, then at the forest to the south.

"Come on, boy, let's go."

The hound looked at me again, then with a last low growl, he loped toward me.

"Oh, thank goodness," I said as I turned to run with the hound at my side.

We hadn't gone two steps when a spear-sized, black-feathered shaft whooshed past my head. Failinis yelped in pain and confusion behind me. When I turned to look, I saw the tail end of the shaft quivering where it struck the hound in the right side of his chest.

I swiveled my head around to determine where the huge arrow had come from. There was Herne, striding toward me with his bow in one hand and an unconscious Crowley dangling from the other.

14

Herne was a giant, easily twelve feet tall with coarse, primitive features reminiscent of the depictions of Cro-Magnon man I'd seen in school. He had a high, wide forehead over bloodshot eyes with dark brown irises, a broad, blunt nose, and a matted, untamed brown beard that covered the lower half of his face. The Celtic god of the hunt wore his hair long and wild as well, but his great shaggy mane was dwarfed by the massive rack of antlers that stuck out from either side of his skull.

At first, I thought it was a helmet, then I realized they were attached to his head. The rack was a cross between deer or elk antlers and moose, broad and spoon-shaped just past the base, then spiked and bifurcated at the front and ends. How he moved through the woods without catching them on anything was a mystery to me, until I saw the trees part their limbs and lean away from the god at his passing.

His clothes were what I'd have expected—all leather, fur, and bone. A long hunting knife with an antler handle sat on one side of his wide leather belt, a hip quiver on the other, and a short killing club hung from his belt next to it. His buckskin pants and shirt had strange markings on them that at first I couldn't identify. It took a moment, then I realized they were tattoos. He wasn't wearing buckskin, but human and fae skin instead.

Why am I not surprised?

I glanced over my shoulder at Failinis. The hound's breathing was labored and weak, but he was still alive. Turning my attention back to the Hunter, I glared at him with all the menace my boyish face could manage.

"I'm going to kill you for that," I growled. "Just like I killed your hounds."

He smiled a predator's smile at me, revealing an extra row of teeth like some species of giantkind had. I glanced at his left hand, the one that carried his bow, and sure enough he had an extra digit. His right hand held an unconscious Crowley by the neck, who he dropped unceremoniously to the ground.

"I can get more hounds," he said in an Andre the Giant-like voice.

Between his deep voice and trilling, romance language accent, I almost couldn't make out his meaning. It took me a second or two to suss it out, then I pointed Dyrnwyn at his chest.

"Can't get another you, though."

"Big words, whelp," he replied. "But you and I both know you can't back them up."

"I can try and force you to kill me. Then whoever's pulling your strings won't get what they want." I spat on the ground. "Tell me, did Badb hire you?"

"Nay, she only set me on your trail. My client waits on yonder plain, and if you have a grievance to bear, she's the one you should address. I am merely the messenger."

"And him?" I said, pointing Dyrnwyn at Crowley.

"He goes to my other client," Herne replied, inclining his great horned head in the direction from which we'd traveled.

"Over my dead body," I replied.

Herne gave a put-upon sigh. "My job is to fetch you, and failing that, to capture you. If she'd have wanted you dead, she'd have done it when you first stepped into this facet of the *Orbis Alius*. Let's not make this harder than it has to be, eh, druid?"

I laughed mirthlessly. "I thought every good hunter studied their prey. If you had, you'd know I'm not going to give up that easily."

"If I hadn't studied you, I wouldn't be here, and you wouldn't be in your current predicament. I know you by reputation, enough to know that you value the lives of others above your own."

With speed I didn't think a creature of his size could possess, he nocked one of those giant arrows and drew his bow in a single, smooth motion.

"Now, which one of your companions should I shoot, eh?" He pointed the arrow at Crowley's inert form. "The changeling? Or should I finish off the hound?"

Herne raised the bow, pulling the string back further as he pointed the arrow at Failinis. I did the math in my head, and while I could deflect the first arrow, I didn't think I was quick enough to stop him from putting a second in Crowley's back. While I doubted he'd give up his bounty, I also knew there were places you could skewer someone without killing them immediately.

If the giant hunter had been hired by Fuamnach, she'd simply heal her adopted son anyway. Then she'd likely torture him near to death, only to heal him again so she could continue the cycle. Despite the likelihood of that happening, I couldn't risk getting Failinis killed. The hound was dying, without a doubt, but there was still a remote chance that Lugh would find him and heal him.

Very remote. But still a chance.

I lowered Dyrnwyn. "Fine, you win. But I'm still going to kill you."

Herne laughed. "You have pluck, I'll give you that." He inclined his antlers at my sword hand. "Best put that away. Won't do you any good against her, and it'd be a shame to lose that sword. I suggest you place it in the

Bag; that way, another MacCumhaill can wield it someday."

"There are no other MacCumhaills," I replied.

Herne frowned. "Damned shame then. But tuck the sword away all the same."

I did as Herne asked, sheathing Dyrnwyn and stowing it inside the Bag. Herne relaxed his arm, releasing his draw while still keeping the arrow nocked. He stepped aside, watching me closely as I passed him on my way out of Lugh's forest. When I reached the edge of the woods, I turned and called out to him.

"How do I find this mysterious goddess?"

Herne chuckled ominously. "Just keep walking until you reach the river."

More water. Peachy. Just peachy.

I headed down a long, gradual slope that led from the marsh woods to the flat, grassy plain I'd seen earlier. Loping along through the fields, I snagged a stem of grass to chew, breathing in the relatively fresh air as I noted the mingled scents of grass, wildflowers, and summer. The springtime aromas overshadowed the pervasive, sickly-sweet smell that dominated most areas of Underhill, and while that odor had abated considerably since I'd closed off the gates, it was still there.

This place is a cancer, or at least, cancerous. Funny how

Mag Mell didn't smell like that back home, after I wrested control of it from Tethra.

On our last trip, we'd learned that Underhill was slowly dying due to all the magic being drained off it by the Earthbound fae. As the story went, back in the day when the new religions were replacing the old, and belief in the gods and fair folk had waned, the Tuath Dé pooled their magic to create Underhill. It was meant to be their new home, and a sanctuary for gods and fae alike.

What humans in the know didn't realize back then was that some of the gods only saw it as a temporary measure. And at the time the fae who stayed on Earth didn't realize they'd have to siphon Underhill's magic through the gateways between the two realms to use it. I don't think they could've stopped the gods from creating Underhill, even if they had known. But certainly more fae would've chosen this realm over Earth if they had, maybe even all of them. Then we might have rid ourselves of them for good by closing the gates.

And if wishes were fishes, I'd have some to fry.

After the last trip I closed the gates, mostly to piss off Maeve, née Niamh, because I'd grown sick of her yanking my chain. But to the Earthbound fae, that act made me the most hated human on Earth. In hindsight, I probably should have thought my plan through before acting so rashly. Cutting off magic from the Earthbound fae had likely contributed to the chain of events that started this whole Faery War. No way would the vamps have gotten their help if the Earthly fae weren't so desperate to regain the magic I'd taken from them.

Hindsight is always twenty-twenty, but fuck the fae. And fuck this mysterious goddess with an axe to grind, too.

I had reason to be bitter. All the gods and fae behaved the same—they treated humans like they were pawns to be moved around on a game board. Or worse, they saw us as an expendable commodity, slaves and serfs to be used and used up at will, then discarded. No wonder the fae and the Vampyri had allied together—they were two of a kind.

And me? I'd been on the losing end of that dynamic too many times. That was why I'd started fighting back. Others might say it was a futile gesture, but someone had to stand up to these pricks—no matter the cost.

As I walked for miles along the plain, toward the winding, blue-gray river that snaked across the land in the distance, I considered how I'd gotten to this point and all the actions that had preceded it. I thought about my frenemy, Crowley, one version of whom now likely suffered at the hands of Herne or Fuamnach. I thought about how Finnegas, Maureen, and Belladonna had perished in the apocalypse in this timeline, and how Finnegas had died in mine.

I remembered Elmo, Ed, and Sabine, friends and family I'd lost to my war with the fae and the gods. I thought back to my own dad, how I thought I'd lost him to one war, but instead he fell to another, taking his own life rather than allowing the Fear Doirich to steal and inhabit his body. I thought about the kids, and Mickey and Anna. I considered Guerra, and how much he'd sacrificed to keep them safe. And I remembered Brian, who was just a sweet, snot-nosed kid who happened to be born in the wrong timeline.

Finally, I thought about Jesse, the very first casualty of the conflict I was born into, and how her initial passing sent me down a path of retribution, destruction, and death.

Never enough. It's never enough to pay them back for what they've done.

As I considered those events, I reminded myself that none of them deserved it. Nobody ever asked to be victimized by the fae or the gods.

The Tuath Dé and aes sídhe just took, and took, and took. When you fought back, even if you won a small battle or two, they'd come back at you twice as hard. Whether out of spite, or hubris, or simple capriciousness, they'd punish you worse every round after the first, grinding you down over time.

And they have time in spades.

That's why I hated them, and it was why they'd become the cause for my continued existence. Because someone had to stand up to them, someone had to fight them, somebody had to take the weight. Yes, there were unintended casualties, and I wasn't about to shift the blame to make myself feel better. I could've lain down from the beginning and given up, let them kill me or use me or punish me as they saw fit.

But that wouldn't have ended the cycle. Giving up would only encourage them to continue the same way they had for millennia. They would've continued preying on the frailty of humans, who had little magic of their own. That was why the Dagda gave druidry to humanity, to balance the scales, right those wrongs, and give us a way to fight back against the fae and dark gods.

I was the last druid, the last true protector of humanity, whether I liked it or not. That meant this wasn't just a personal beef between me and the supernatural realm —this was a war for the survival of humankind. I had a moral responsibility to win it or die trying.

May the innocent dead forgive me, but I'm seeing this through to the end.

After covering miles of grassland and years of memories, I finally reached the low, sloping valley where the river resided. As for the waterway itself, it was as picturesque as any river could be, here or on Earth. It was a crystal-clear, shimmering, dancing serpent that split the terrain without defiling it, adorning the lush green fields like a strand of sapphires against the gentle slope of a woman's neck.

The way it ran and flowed across the plain, snaking a slow course as it gradually wore a path through this peaceful, verdant plain, well—it was poetry in motion, a scene worthy of capturing and preserving on canvas for time and times to come. But like everything the fae and dark gods created, it was a glamour designed to conceal a much harsher and deadlier truth.

I saw her from afar, next to the river—the woman in white, the very same one I'd seen in the swamp. Flowing dark hair, ivory skin, bright green eyes, and features that Michelangelo would've given his left nut to etch in marble. She was graceful and slender, even as she sat in repose next to the river, reclining on her side across several large, black stones that lined the water's edge.

Around her neck she wore a gold pendant or charm of some sort, which hung from a thick leather thong. The gods didn't have the same aversion to metal as the fae, but I found that curious, as she wore no other jewelry or adornment of any kind. The charm had been fashioned in the shape of a lowered-cased "h" with a line through the upper stem—a simple design. It might've been a magical rune, but if so, it was one I was not familiar with, as the warding runes I used came from Ogham script.

As I approached, she dipped her hand in the water, lifting it to watch droplets trail away through her fingertips. She paid me no heed, which I expected, a subtle flex that typified the attitude of the pissiest gods toward humankind. Dismissiveness was the first resort of petty people, an insult they could toss about with abandon, one that required zero wit and little effort. Personally, I couldn't give a fuck. I just wanted to see what this was all about so I could deal with it and move on.

I stopped a few feet away from where she sat, and she continued to ignore me. Figuring I was already on her shit list, I picked up a large rock and winged it into the water next to her. The stone hit hard enough to create a splash, but none seemed to land on her, even though the resulting spatter drenched the rocks all around.

Let's see... river, water powers, goddess. Add in the continual harassment, the curse, and the Hunt, and suddenly this makes perfect sense.

"Boann, I presume."

"It certainly took you long enough to reach that conclusion." Her voice and tone reminded me of the river—gentle, elegant, and peaceful, but with a dangerous undercurrent residing just below the surface. She gave a tinkling laugh before continuing, and she continued to play with the water as she spoke. "For someone so slow, you certainly do cause the gods much strife."

"From my perspective it's the other way around, on both counts. How'd you follow me here?"

"Come now, the trickster isn't the only immortal who dabbles in time magic." A delicate smile played across her lips, there and gone in an instant. "Once I made my purpose known, help wasn't hard to find. Although, this would've been easier if you'd stayed in your own timeline."

"I take it you're the one who cast the curse on me?"

"As I said, when I made it known that I meant to

hurt you, assistance followed soon after." She turned her gaze on me, and I saw she had heterochromic eyes like Sophia Doroshenko, a vampire I knew from my own timeline. Boann's left eye had a bluish tinge I hadn't noticed earlier, a subtler difference than Sophia's blue and hazel eyes, but no less striking. "You aren't the most popular individual, you know, amongst the gods of any pantheon."

I shrugged, moving the grass stalk I chewed from one side of my mouth to the other. "Meh. Some people collect stamps, others baseball cards—I collect divine enemies. Generally speaking, I kill the ones I don't want to keep."

Her eyes narrowed slightly, but if the verbal jab bothered her the rest of her face didn't show it. Instead, she smiled in devil may care fashion, tossing her hair with one elegant hand, while gesturing discursively with the other.

"That's what makes your struggles so amusing, wouldn't you agree? While humans pass away, the gods never *really* perish. Slay us, and then what? We cross the Veil and back again, returning to life long after you've rotted away to dust." She tsked, looking across the water. "This war you wage is futile, and even if it were only against the fae and *neamh mhairbh,* it would make little difference in the grand scheme. Humans rebel, yet we persist. Your struggles are for *naught.*"

"Then why nurture this grudge? I'm just going to die

anyway, right? And come to think of it, I didn't even kill Aengus."

Although I would've if given the chance.

Her tone grew venomous, her expression taut. "I choose to punish you because you presumed to pass judgement on Maccan Óc, the fairest and most blessed of all the Tuatha Dé Danann. He among all our kind shed light on your accursed world. His laughter brought summer after winter, his smile was sunshine at dawn, his touch warmth after frost."

Wow, Oedipal, much?

I pointed in her general direction, spinning my finger in a small circle. "You, uh, skipped a season there. And he came after me first, in case you didn't know."

"You had no right to lay hands on my son, you insolent newt!" She leapt to her feet, face drawn in pale fury, and geysers of water shot high into the sky behind her as she spoke. "His loss pains me greatly, even if it is only for a brief passage of time, and the knowledge that he suffered stings all the more. As his mother, it is my duty to bring those responsible to justice, and I will not be denied."

Despite myself, I took a step back. This woman was pissed, and that was a fact. But it was like Herne said—if she'd wanted to kill me outright, she could have done it long ago. No, she wanted me to suffer, and I needed to glean all the information I could if I was to get out of this and get Crowley back.

"I hate to tell you this, lady, but your son was a right

prick. I never did a damned thing to him, yet he decided to ally himself with Badb and Fuamnach and come after me. The fuck did I do to deserve that?"

"Deserve," she spat. "You think you deserve anything? All you pale monkeys believe you're worth something, as if you mean anything in the grand scope of creation, as if you hadn't just crawled out of the mud and shed your vestigial tails."

"That's a bit racist, don't you think? I mean c'mon, who insults someone by comparing them to monkeys in this day and age? Speaking of which, I'm about to go apeshit on you unless you give this crazy vendetta up. Because honestly, I've got stuff to do and vampires to kill. You feel me, momma?"

"We both know you lack the power to do much more than annoy me in your current form. But please," she said as she crossed her arms over her chest. "Do your worst."

"'Kay then. Let's dance."

15

In my current, age-reverted state, I knew I wasn't
going to beat Boann. While she might have played a
minor role in Celtic legend, she was a river goddess, and
thus held all the force of the Boyne at her command.
That said, I was pretty sure she wasn't going to kill me—
not until she'd made me suffer. I might get banged up
fighting her, but the best way to learn your opponent's
strengths and weaknesses was by observing them in
battle.

Since I hadn't had the opportunity to face Boann
before, the best I could do was goad her into a fight and
try to avoid dying while I learned what I could of her
magic. I took Herne's advice, leaving Dyrnwyn and most
of my other metal weapons in the Bag. I'd considered
pulling out the Red Spear, but kept it safely hidden
along with the rest of my kit, based on a hunch I had
about this goddess's tactics.

Time to test my hypothesis and see if Herne really was doing me a solid. Here goes.

Quick as a wink, I drew my Bowie knife from my belt and burst forward, stabbing at Boann's chest with a straight thrust that relied more on speed and surprise than skill. As the knife's tip touched her flowing, toga-like dress, three things happened.

First, she pivoted expertly to let the blade pass. I'd seen one of my Filipino weapons instructors do something similar, pivoting right and left, clockwise and counter, all while someone stabbed at her with a live blade. Never once did the blade touch her, and even I was impressed by that feat when I saw it.

Boann wasn't exactly flat-chested, but she wasn't Dolly Parton, either. Thus, I didn't even snag a nipple on the follow-through, which elicited an internal sigh of relief on my part. I mean, what dude wants to say they stabbed a woman's breast in a fight? Not me, that's for sure. Considering how Boann moved, there was no danger of my turning her into an Amazon, even if I'd wanted to do so.

Yet, that wasn't even close to the wildest thing that happened. Next, that crazy left eye of hers flashed like a sapphire in the sun, then it swirled in whirlpool-like fashion. I realized then that her eye had turned to water, or maybe it had always been in the first place, and I didn't realize it. Regardless, I was still following through on the stab because I hadn't recovered my balance yet, and my knife was heading right for her left upper arm.

Huh. Might score a lucky cut, yet.

Here's when the third and weirdest thing went down. As my blade stabbed Boann's left bicep, her skin lost its opacity, going from alabaster white to clear translucence in an instant. The knife went right through with zero resistance, and that's when I understood that her arm had gone liquid as well.

Neat trick, that.

Recovering at the end of the thrust, I pulled the Bowie knife out and pivoted left to make another cut. But while I hadn't felt resistance when the blade went into her arm, I certainly did on the way out. Indeed, a thick pseudopod of pale blue-green water clung to the blade, preventing me from cutting her again or even turning to attempt an attack.

We became stuck for a moment like that, she and I. For my part I continued tugging at the knife, willing it to be freed so I could stab this shrew in her crazy, tidy bowl eye. Meanwhile, Boann wore a wicked, knowing smile as her arm *made of fucking water* clung to the blade like road tar on a tire in July.

A fraction of a second later, the liquid pseudopod expanded to envelope the Bowie knife to the hilt. The water that constituted that flexible appendage turned from blue green to rust brown, then the knife pulled free. Or rather, what was left of it—a jagged two inches or so of crumbling, rust-riddled steel.

Guess my hunch was right. Damn, I liked that knife.

Seeing as how I didn't have a blade anymore, I

decided to make do with what I had. When life hands you lemons, you don't make lemonade—you drink iced tea. I still had something in my hand, and it made a pretty good fist load, so I punched the bitch in the face.

Being that I was in my half-Fomorian form, I hit her pretty damned hard. Her nose shattered beneath my fist on contact, the cartilage exploding into fragments with the impact. She staggered back, blinking rapidly as pink, watery fluid flowed in thick rivulets from her nostrils. Unfortunately, she'd stepped backwards onto the water, as in *on top* of the water. No way was I following her there to follow up the attack.

"That's the thing with you gods and goddesses. You aren't used to pain," I spat as I flashed her a big, shit-eating grin. "Hurts, don't it?"

Considering what she did next, I had to give her credit—Boann wasn't the powder puff I thought she was. She reached up with both hands, one flesh and blood, the other water given form, and she straightened and set her nose. Having your nose broken was painful, let me tell you, but setting it straight again was far, far worse.

Color me impressed.

"Oh, I know pain, druid," Boann said, speaking now as if she had a cold. "When I wanted the knowledge held in Nechtan's Well, I taunted him by walking *tuathal* 'round the water's edge three times. The legends call me a fool, but I knew what I was about. When the waters rushed up to drown me, I snatched wisdom from his grasp, swallowing it even as my husband dashed me against the rocks."

"Unearned knowledge is a curse," I said, meaning it.

I'd inherited some of the same magic from Fionn, who absorbed it from the salmon that fed at the well. Back in the day, Finnegas caught the salmon and asked Fionn to prepare it. My idiot forebear burned his thumb in the process, and when he sucked it, he absorbed most of the wisdom that fish held. As the story went, Finnegas made him eat the rest and didn't speak to the bumbling moron for months after.

To this day, sucking on my thumb would trigger the fae magic, opening my consciousness to facts, events, and connections I could never piece together on my own. But that magic came at a price, like everything else the fae and the gods gave. Whenever I used that gift, I got all puffed up with confidence, barreling into whatever disastrous situation had caused me to use the gift in the first place. Inevitably, the knowledge it gave wasn't enough to avert disaster, and usually someone got hurt or died as a consequence.

Boann hissed, reminding me I had a pissed off goddess to deal with.

"Short-sighted fool. You inherited only a tiny sliver of it, while I took it from the source. What you see as a curse, I saw as my salvation. With the knowledge I stole, I took power from Nechtan, directing his well to further overflow and create the River Boyne. I lost an eye, an arm, and a leg, but forever after, the river has been mine alone to command."

"No one was meant to have that knowledge, Boann," I said, thinking back to when I chanted the *teinm laida* to learn time magic and master druidry. I'd only been able to retain a tiny fraction of the vast knowledge the spell revealed. Honestly it had scared the shit out of me, and I was glad I couldn't retain it, because no one should have that much power. I shook my head ruefully as I continued. "Not men, and certainly not the gods."

"As if such things were yours to decide." She wiped a thin trickle of blood from her nose with the back of her hand, a decidedly un-ladylike gesture. "You helped slay my son, and you deigned to lay hands on me. As punishment, you'll see firsthand what power I gained in sacrifice."

It was one thing to know that a god or goddess had powers, but it was quite another to see those powers unleashed. As a druid I could exercise power over water —at least I could until this vengeful woman cursed me with a second chance at prom. And fuck if I didn't regret getting her angry, because her skill with water magic made mine seem like a squirt gun next to a fire hydrant.

The river's waters began churning and boiling up behind Boann, first ten, then twenty, then fifty feet high in an amphitheater-like wall that circled around behind her. Along the surface of that great half-cylinder of liquid, figures bubbled up in the foam and froth, large and vaguely man-like, with mouths twisted in rage and thick limbs that looked like they could smash me to bits. I didn't know if Boann had simply done this for effect, or if they were elementals of some kind, captured by her magic to do her bidding. What I did know was that I didn't want her to unleash them on me.

I began to backpedal, slowly, as I thought of ways to appease her. "You do realize that Aengus still lives, or at least a version of him in this timeline does, right?"

Her expression softened slightly, and she almost looked sad as she spoke. "That one is *not* my son. He belongs to another, and she is unwilling to share his company. Yet she understands what I seek and will not stand in my way as I avenge my own son's death."

"You *spoke* to your counterpart in this timeline? Are you fucking crazy?"

Click had warned me against that, once. While he didn't go into specifics, he did suggest that it could cause all kinds of trouble. I could think of a multitude of reasons why it would be a bad idea to meet my counterpart in another timeline, not the least of which was influencing events and causing a timeline to go completely off the rails.

Boann glowered at me, and a darkness fell across her features that hadn't been there previously. As she spoke, her voice echoed and boomed with all the fury of a river's rapids. "Indeed, I am mad—mad with grief. I swear, you'll suffer as I have, every minute of every day until Aengus crosses back across the Veil once more."

In an instant, the wall of water crashed down on me from either side of the goddess, barely giving me time to take a breath. One second I was on my feet, standing on dry land, and the next it felt like I'd been thrown in the spin cycle inside the world's largest washing machine. I was spun and tossed and smashed against the ground, rushed along in a giant, living whirlpool that possessed all the power and intensity of a raging river.

Even worse, things inside the water battered me all the while. First it was just boulders and logs, bouncing and bashing into me as I spun and spiraled in the whirling mass of water. Then I felt cold, watery hands grasping at me, pulling my arms and legs in opposite directions, preventing me from balling up and protecting myself. I must've been struck twenty times, forcing the air from my lungs each time, breaking ribs and crushing my internal organs. It was like the flood at the creek, but a hundred times worse.

Boann's magic swooshed me around, stretched me out, and beat me up, then it would relent for several seconds and start all over again. Somehow, I managed to hold my breath, or what was left of it, until my lungs ached and my heart beat so fast, I thought it would explode from my chest. Then, the water began to force its way into my nose and mouth, pushing and creeping down my throat until I choked on it.

When the water filled my lungs, I blacked out, only

to come back to reality coughing and gagging on the water's surface, high above the plains below. I drew a few ragged breaths, then the river sucked me down again, back into the depths of that watery maelstrom. This went on for an interminable length of time, until I finally reached a point where I stopped fighting, losing even the will to expel the water from my lungs and breathe.

At that point the waters receded, and I was dumped unceremoniously at Boann's feet, there on the rocky bank of the river where the whole magical water-boarding session had started. I lay there, gurgling and panting, spent of all energy, badly battered and with bones grinding in my chest at every intake of breath. And that wasn't the full extent of my injuries, either.

Something was wrong with my left arm and right leg, although I wasn't certain if they were fractured or dislocated. Additionally, one eye had swollen shut, the other I could barely open, and I had gashes and bruises all over my body. I was pretty sure I could only hear out of one ear, and based on the piercing pain in the other, I was certain I'd ruptured an eardrum. On top of all that, my head was pounding, and I was nauseous due to the effects of multiple, repeated concussions.

If Boann wanted to break me, she had done a thorough job of it.

I heard rather than saw the goddess walk over to me, and I turned my head toward the sound with great effort. Cracking one eye open a fraction, I watched as she squatted beside me on a leg of flesh and one of sculpted, ensorcelled water. With all the energy I could muster, I spat water, blood and mucous at her, but unfortunately it ran off her seemingly hydrophobic robes like water off a duck's back.

Boann smiled cruelly at the tiny, vain act of defiance. "Brazen as ever, I see. No matter. A few decades of treatment like this should cure you of whatever spark of rebellion remains. Now, let's get you somewhere safe, so you can heal up in time to do this all over again."

She reached out with a translucent hand made from ensorcelled water, covering my mouth and nose. I could barely lift my head, much less struggle against her grip, and when water began forcing its way up my nostrils and into my mouth, I knew it was futile to resist. Giving in to the inevitable, I allowed myself to slip into dark, blessed unconsciousness.

16

When I woke up, I was supine on a hard, damp stone floor. I cracked open one eye, wincing at the pain even that small amount of movement caused me. Although I still wore my tattered clothing, all my weapons and gear were gone, even my Bag. High above, I could see the dark, starry night through a small grated opening in what must've been the ceiling high above me.

So, I'm at the bottom of a pit, badly injured with no weapons, armor, or resources to speak of. Eh, could be worse.

The Bag would show up, eventually, unless Boann was smart enough to ward it. It was a semi-sentient artifact, having a mind of its own. Whenever I'd lost or misplaced it in the past, the Bag always seemed to show up again, usually when I least expected it and sometimes long after I had need of its contents. For the moment I'd have to make do without it, doing the best I could with what I had.

I lay there for several long minutes, taking shallow, painful breaths while I assessed my remaining injuries. I could see, just not in the dark, which meant my eyes hadn't healed enough yet to fully regain my Fomorian eyesight. That was the way my healing factor worked, first by fixing muscles and bones and taking longer to repair complex organs and nerves.

Breathing was difficult, as I had a rib sticking out of my chest that needed to be put back before it could heal properly. With a grunt of effort, I used my thumb and forefinger to force the bone back into place under the skin. That grunt turned into a scream of agony, but despite the pain I continued on, forcing the jagged ends of the fractured bone to meet by sticking my fingers into the wound itself.

After that, I spent several minutes breathing as shallowly as possible as I allowed the bone to knit together again. Once my chest wasn't grinding every time I took a breath, I was able to move more easily. Obviously, that meant it was time to see how the rest of my body had fared.

For the next half-hour I busied myself with popping dislocated joints back into socket, straightening other displaced fractures, and re-breaking bones that had managed to heal improperly while I was unconscious. It was a long, agonizing process, to say the least. Once I finished, I rested again, letting my Fomorian healing factor take over to get me back to some semblance of health and functionality.

After a short bout of fitful, exhaustion-induced sleep, I awoke to find that the position of the stars above had moved. I wasn't sure if I was still in Underhill or if Boann had transported me to Earth, because I couldn't remember if there were stars in the night sky on my last trip to Tír na nÓg.

The fact that I didn't recognize any of the constellations told me I was probably still in the fae realm. A brief effort to extend my druid senses out from my makeshift prison confirmed it. While I couldn't reach beyond the walls of my prison—it had been warded against such attempts—Underhill's magic was present in the very stones and mortar that made up my cell.

That settles that. Let's see if we can find a way out of here.

I groaned and pushed myself to my feet, stumbling and staggering due to injury-induced stiffness and general weakness after expending so much energy healing. On reaching out to steady myself, I found that I could nearly touch both sides of my cell at once. I felt around to explore the space more fully, which gave me something to do while I waited for my eyes to fully heal so they could adjust to the gloom.

After another hour or so, my eyes had healed enough to allow me some night sight, and I was able to make out the space around me. The floor of the cell was roughly seven feet across, which allowed me to stretch out almost to my full height when lying down. Just above head height, the walls began to close in, narrowing and taking the shape of a long upside-down funnel.

On closer inspection, I noted that the walls stretched high above, perhaps thirty feet or so to the narrow opening that allowed me to see the sky overhead. Water seeped out of the moss and slime-covered walls above, forming tiny rivulets that ran into small, slotted drains that had been cut at intervals around the circumference of the floor. Over time, the steady trickle of water had worn the walls slick, because it was nearly impossible to find a crack or foothold anywhere.

The water did appear to be clean, however, having been filtered through the earth and stone walls on its way into the cell. It occurred to me that I was very thirsty, and I groped around until I found a relatively robust trickle of water on which to slake my thirst. After a few minutes of lapping at the wall, I had filled my belly with enough water to re-energize myself and attempt to climb out of my prison.

After exploring the walls further, I attempted to stretch out and gain purchase on either side with my feet and hands. Soon I realized that the design of the cell had been intended to prevent this very thing. Although at first I thought I had been imprisoned in a dry well, I soon realized that I had been dropped into an oubliette.

Oubliettes were one of the cruelest forms of torture

from the medieval ages. A unique type of prison cell designed for discomfort, the oubliette was also intended to engender a complete sense of hopelessness in a prisoner. Back in the day, the authorities would drop a prisoner into an oubliette to be forgotten. Oh, they might toss a scrap of food down to them every now and again, but mostly they'd just piss on them and leave them to rot—a lonely and terrible way to go.

For a moment I imagined what it would be like to be caught in a cell that was impossible to escape, slowly dying of thirst, hunger, and emaciation over the course of many long years. It would've been horribly, maddeningly lonely to only see a human face every now and again when some guard would peer down into the darkness to discover if you were still alive. Then I realized that was the exact fate Boann intended for me to suffer in this cell.

Certainly, if I were left alone long enough, I might eventually gain enough strength to leap out of this prison. However, the river goddess would never allow that to happen. Instead, it was likely she would fetch me just before I grew strong enough to escape, only to subject me to the same watery torture I was recovering from now.

That was what she'd promised—that I would suffer in the same manner, over and over again, until such time as her son returned back from across the Veil. Knowing what I knew about primaries, those gods and supernatural creatures who were so powerful that they could not truly die, I realized it could take decades or even centuries for that to happen. Combined with the recent genealogical revelation that I was a demi-human with a highly extended lifespan, it made for a fairly hopeless situation.

Well, shit.

I sat down on the damp floor of the cell, hugging my legs and resting my chin on my knees as I assessed the situation. Crowley had been captured. Poor Failinis was probably dead. Lugh was busy protecting his castle from a siege and completely oblivious to our plight. Finally, not only was I stuck here, but I also had no way of finding or summoning my Oak, much less bonding with it to get my powers back.

Dire? That wasn't the half of it. To put it bluntly, I was fucked.

With nothing better to do, I spent the next few hours staring up at the nighttime sky, wondering how the Tuath Dé had managed to fake those stars. As far as I knew, there was nothing out there beyond the sky but void and darkness, so it had to be a glamour, and a big one at that. Trying to come up with various ways they might have done it kept me from wallowing in self-pity and wondering why I had ever decided to get mixed up with the Celtic gods in the first place.

Oh yeah, I didn't decide that. It was decided for me when I was born a McCool.

I'd been over my "poor me" stage for some time, so I wasn't about to get all melancholy because I'd been dealt a raw hand. However, I didn't have a plan for getting out of this prison yet, and I wasn't strong enough to do so, anyway. The best I could hope for was to heal faster than Boann expected. Then maybe I could jump up and lodge myself against the walls and climb my way out of here.

Knowing I needed sleep to further heal, I allowed myself to doze off. I dreamt I was back in my bedroom in Farmersville, snugly tucked under a thick quilt, sleeping in on Saturday morning. Mom always cooked me pancakes on Saturdays—or did she? I was still sorting my real memories from the ones the old man's geas had created, but it was a good dream, so I let it ride.

The next thing I knew someone was calling my name. Probably Mom calling from downstairs, telling me that breakfast was getting cold.

"Just five more minutes, Mom," I mumbled.

"Colin, wake up, lad."

Hang on—even when she's pissed, Mom's voice isn't that deep.

"What?" I said as I sat up and remembered where I was.

Oh yeah, I'm in an oubliette in Underhill. Fuck, what a waste of a good dream.

I rubbed my eyes and swung my gaze to the opening

overhead. There, a shadowy figure looked down on me, although I couldn't make out any features because he was backlit by the sky above. His smooth, baritone voice was unfamiliar, although his accent reminded me a bit of Lugh's. Yet the lilt was much less pronounced.

"Who are you? And what do you want?"

"Who I am is not important. Why I came, is." He paused and clucked his tongue. "You're stuck here, you know. No one has ever escaped these pits, not unless they were pulled out for torture."

"Not that it's relevant to the discussion of escape, but where exactly am I?"

"You're somewhere on the grounds of Fuamnach's fortress, a place that few humans ever return from. Although I did hear that you snuck in and got out again some time back. Quite the achievement, that."

"I had help," I said, stroking the wispy hairs on my chin as I looked up at the stranger above me. "And to be honest, we got lucky."

"If you say so," the stranger replied, unconvinced. "Although it appears luck is not on your side this time."

"And?"

"And I might be persuaded to shift it in your direction. But only on certain conditions, of course."

"Uh-huh. Before you tell me what you want, prove you're not one of Boann's henchmen. For all I know, this might be a ruse meant to give me false hope of escape."

"That could be true. And we could sit here wasting precious time going back and forth over whether or not you have the right of the situation. Or you could listen to me and potentially find a way out of your current predicament. Which do you choose?"

It only took a second for me to consider the options, because his logic was spot on. If he was pulling my leg, then I was going to be tortured no matter what I said or did. But if he was actually here to help me, I certainly couldn't afford to refuse his assistance.

"Okay, fine. But at least tell me why you're helping me."

"An excellent question. Let's just say I have a score to settle with your captor. And, I was sent here by a mutual friend."

Although I was severely weakened after recovering from my injuries, by this time my eyes had fully healed and completely adjusted to the dark. My Fomorian vision wasn't as sharp as that of a werewolf, but it was better than a human's, and I began to make out certain features in the stranger's silhouette. Of particular note, something was weird about his right arm, as it didn't seem to have the same shape as his left.

Additionally, I heard strange noises in the background—little whirs and clicks, like clockwork gears turning in some odd, steampunk mechanism. Every once in a while, I'd hear a *whoosh*, and a burst of air or steam would blow his cloak away from his arm. That's when I figured out who he was and said as much.

"You're Nuada," I stated with certainty.

"Despite my desire to maintain anonymity, it

appears I've been found out." He chuckled and lowered his hood. "That is what I'm known by, yes—among other names. I also go by Nechtan of the Well, and some have known me as Elcmar, Lord of Horses. When you live as long as I have, you tend to take on many identities over the centuries."

"They also once called you *Airgetlám*, 'silver arm.' But I thought Dian Cécht had since replaced it with one made of flesh."

"Oh, he did at that," Nuada said with a nod. "However, recent events have forced me to bring my old one out of retirement—with some improvements."

He extended his right arm to the side, slipping it from beneath his cloak. The light wasn't the best, but I saw enough to know I'd identified those weird noises accurately. The limb looked to have been mostly made of gleaming silver metal, with brass tubes and copper fittings here and there in odd places, directing the steam and magic that powered the hydraulic pistons and clockwork mechanisms that made his arm function.

Obviously, he was showing off, because his robotic hand spun clockwise and counterclockwise in a manner no human hand could duplicate. For several seconds he produced various knives and tools from his fingers and forearm, causing them to spring out and back, switch-blade-style. Then his hand folded away, and a large gun barrel slid out from his wrist, ratcheting mechanically until it protruded a good six inches beyond his hand.

While I was still geeking out at what his arm could

do, gears whirred, and steam belched forth from his prosthetic. In an instant, he retracted all the accessories Inspector Gadget-style, then he folded the wondrous limb back beneath his cloak.

"Quite a marvel of engineering and magic, if I do say so myself," the former leader of the Tuath Dé said with apparent self-satisfaction. "Dian Cécht out did himself with this one, albeit with Goibniu's help. It amazes me that, all these thousands of years later, it still works better than anything your modern technology has produced."

"Okay, color me convinced," I replied, trying hard not to sound too impressed. "You're one of the good guys, and you're here to help. So, why don't you open that grate, drop a rope, and get me the hell out of here?"

Nuada seemed to rock back on his heels, although it was hard to tell from my perspective. "Hmm, yes. I'll be right up front with you, lad. I can't offer you any direct assistance in getting out of there."

Then, it clicked. "Damn, your Boann's husband."

"Estranged, but yes. Love is a funny thing, you know, and it can make you act against your better nature to protect the ones you love." He gave a weary shake of his head. "Although, in this case I'm stumped as to why she went on the war path against you."

Ah, he's the Nuada from this timeline. Better watch what I say.

"Who knows? Maybe she sees me as a threat to the gods. Wouldn't be the first time one of your fellow deities used that excuse to come after me. Regardless, I really don't want to be around here when she comes back for a second round."

"Doesn't make sense, though. She may be many things—an adulterer, a thief, and power-hungry, to name a few—but she's not prone to committing violence without reason." On hearing that, I laughed bitterly. "Oh, you've something to say on that matter?"

"It's just that, from my perspective, your kind never need a rationale for visiting injury on humans."

"Not all of us are like that, druid. Give credit where credit is due."

"My apologies, Nuada. I don't mean to look a gift horse in the mouth."

He inclined his head slightly, ignoring my blatant reference to Greek mythology. "Apology accepted."

"Great. Back to our discussion of how exactly you can help me...?"

"Of course. Since I'm disinclined to act directly against my spouse, the only thing I can offer you is my counsel."

"Advice? That's it?"

Nuada's voice was taut, dangerous even as he replied. "Do not discount the value of a god's counsel, boy."

"Ahem," I stammered as I prepared for some verbal

backpedaling. "You are absolutely right. My mistake. Please, go on."

"As I was saying, I am perfectly willing to advise you regarding your current situation. On one condition."

"That is?"

"You can't kill her. You can stymy her, foil her plans, restrain her, and otherwise prevent Boann from doing you harm. But if you kill her, you'll have made a much more powerful enemy than you have now. Do I make myself clear?"

"Crystal."

"Good, then let us discuss how you might extricate yourself from your current, unfortunate circumstance."

"I don't mean to contradict you, nor do I intend to reject your input, but I really don't see how I'm getting out of here of my own volition. I lost most of my magical abilities when Boann cursed me, so I can't spell myself out of here. I can't shift into my more powerful form, and even if I could, I wouldn't fit through that hole. And, in my current state, I'm too weak to climb out of here before Boann comes back to kick my ass all over again."

Nuada must've been tired of leaning over the oubliette's opening because he sat cross-legged, half on and half off the grate. Then, he produced a pipe from his cloak, taking his time as he packed it with tobacco. Before Finnegas took up smoking cigarettes, I'd seen him perform the same ritual many times. I always knew not to interrupt him in those moments, because it was his way of filling time while he pondered a problem.

Figuring Nuada was doing the same, I shut up and let him think.

"You know, I was known for being a bit of a magician in my day," he said after lighting up and taking a puff. "Comes from being master of the well, you see. As you know, your teacher wanted some of that knowledge for himself, but Fionn botched that up for him. Not the sharpest blade, that one."

"I only know him by reputation, but I have to say, I'm not his biggest fan either."

"Not many of the gods cared for him, and that's a fact. He had a tendency to make enemies wherever he went, and powerful ones at that." Nuada punctuated that last comment by poking the stem of the pipe at me. "A familiar story, yes?"

"Point taken. But how does reminiscing about my ancestor's screw-ups help me get out of this pit?"

"Patience, I'm getting to that." He puffed on his pipe, blowing smoke circles into the rapidly fading darkness. "Did you ever wonder why Finnegas gave up on catching that salmon?"

I shrugged. "No idea. I just figured it was the only one."

"Really? Just one salmon, in the entire spring that eventually comprised the headwaters of the River Boyne?" He tsked. "Come now, lad. I thought you were smarter than that."

"Okay, so there were other fish. Maybe Finnegas

thought it wasn't worth the effort after all. Or he got so frustrated after Fionn screwed things up, he gave up."

"Honestly, lad—did you ever know Finn the Seer to be one who gave up easily?"

"No, he wasn't a quitter. So, what's your point?"

"Maybe he realized he didn't need what the salmon could give him. Perhaps he determined that he possessed a gift far greater in its value—one that could never be taken away."

"You mean druidry—is that what you're getting at?"

"Got it in one."

"But that's where you're wrong. Druidry can be taken away. That's what Boann did when she cursed me with this weird de-aging spell. I lost great swathes of my memory, along with all the things I learned when I mastered druidry." I sighed and slammed my fist against the floor of the oubliette. "Now I'm just an amateur, an apprentice-level druid. I could barely cast a cantrip right now, much less create a spell to get me out of here."

"*Cast* a spell? Since when is druidry reliant on symbols and incantations, hmm? Did your master teach you to create circles and runes, to follow recipes, or to keep a grimoire with records of all the magic you've learned?"

"Well, no, not really. I mean, I learned some of that stuff over the years, but Finnegas always said it was a crutch, something to help me until I mastered druidry."

"He was right. Druidry isn't something you learn, boy, it's something you possess. The Dagda—conniving, wife-stealing bastard that he was—*gifted* it to humankind. That's why you didn't learn it in some academy, earning its usage through knowledge gained from books and tomes. No, you inherited it as your birthright, a legacy passed down to you by blood and from master to student." He hissed, blowing pipe smoke through his teeth. "My wife could no more take that from you than she could paint the ocean pink."

I wisely decided to avoid telling him I thought his wife *could* paint the seas pink if she chose, merely by tainting them with a sufficient amount of human blood. Instead, I steered the conversation closer to a definitive solution for my predicament.

"What you're saying is—"

"What I'm saying is that you possess everything you need to get yourself out of this mess." He puffed at his pipe again, exhaling smoke that combined with a gout of steam blowing from his arm. "Tell you what, here's a bonus for you. How does a river goddess acquire mastery over advanced time magic? Considering that her purview consists of water and currents, rapids, and floods? Seems a bit out of character, don't you think?"

I didn't have anything to say to that, because Nuada's statements had already started the wheels turning in my head. While I chewed on what he'd said, he stood, brushing himself off.

"It seems you've a lot to consider, and I have needs to abscond from these premises before my spouse gets wind of my presence." He tapped his pipe out on his shoe sole, shaking the stem at me as he offered a final bit of counsel. "If you ever get married, druid, do yourself a favor—don't ignore your wife. Leave her pining too long, and you'll be paying for it the rest of your life."

He turned away from the pit, and I called out to him. "Nuada?"

"Yes, boy?"

"Your, um, counsel is wise, indeed."

He chuckled. "That's a good lad. Now, do your teacher proud."

17

After mulling over my conversation with Nuada, it boiled down to the following: I had to devise a way to defeat Boann, using druid magic that I couldn't remember how to use, all while avoiding lethal measures. This was going to be a challenge.

First things first—let's see if Nuada was right about my ability to access the loftier and more potent mysteries of druid magic.

I sat cross-legged on the floor of the oubliette, eyes closed as I prepared to enter a druid trance. After going through several long cycles of deep, metered breathing, I sank into the depths of my own consciousness, leaving the aches and pains of my rapidly healing body behind. Extending my senses out as far as I could, I began by extending my awareness to the boundaries of the oubliette's magical constraints.

Yep, wards are still there. Let's see what I can recall of Finn's lessons.

The immediate challenge was obvious—I'd forgotten virtually everything I had learned about druidry and time magic over the course of the last several years. As far as my memory was concerned, I was exactly as I'd described myself to Nuada—a druid apprentice and nothing more.

Yet, Nuada seem to think that I had greater power at my disposal. Based on what I remembered of my earliest lessons, Finnegas had never taught me druidry by rote. Whether Airgetlám was right about druid magic being something you possessed as a matter of course, due to inheritance or by right of ancestry, well... that remained to be seen.

If that were the case, it meant that using druid magic was something you did more by feel than by procedure. I thought back to the times when I used druid magic after I had bonded with the Oak and chanted the teinm laida. Clearly, Finnegas had intended that I use the chant to cheat my way into druid mastery. By retaining a tiny sliver of the vast knowledge and understanding the chant revealed to me, that was exactly what I had done.

That said, when I used druid magic after the chant, it seemed as though it was something that came to me naturally and without much effort. Although I couldn't remember exactly how I had done it, I did recall there weren't any spells to chant, or runes to draw, or ingredients to mix before I made the magic happen. Instead, I simply connected with nature's energies, forging whatever magical effect I needed using nothing more than thought, will, and potential.

Question is, can I do that now?

To quote the wise and powerful Morpheus, "there's a difference between knowing the path, and walking the path." Nuada had presented me with an idea that provided a ray of hope, but it fell to me to make something of it. I only hoped I was up to the task.

Knowing I had scant time before Boann returned, I descended deeper into my druid trance, familiarizing myself with the ebb and flow of Underhill's energies. I met with some difficulty at first, because the wards around the cell blocked my efforts. After quite a bit of trial and error, I extended my senses up and out through the entrance to the oubliette above, at which point I began to probe the grounds of Fuamnach's fortress.

What I couldn't see with my own eyes, I could feel through my senses. As I gave myself over to the trance, I detected spaces, walls, and even Fuamnach's remaining garrison through every blade of grass, every tiny insect, and every pebble strewn across the courtyard. In retrospect, it was quite similar to what I had done in the swamp during the grindylow attack when I sensed their positions around me. On a whim, I searched the grounds for Crowley, but he was nowhere to be found.

Damn. Time to go deeper.

Fuamnach's fortress wasn't exactly bustling with activity, and I could only assume she'd taken the bulk of her forces on campaign elsewhere in Underhill. I made note of how many of her soldiers remained, then I moved on to explore beyond the castle walls. There I felt the remnants of the sorceress' presence, a warp of corruption left over many centuries of her evil influence. Beneath that, however, I sensed something greater, a thing so vast and timeless, it dwarfed the life signs I'd sensed in my immediate surroundings.

Moving at the speed of thought, I dove into the deeper currents of Underhill's magic, riding the ebb and flow of her energies until I'd tuned into the source. There I discovered a presence that pervaded all of Underhill, much in the same way the demesne's consciousness permeated every square inch of Maeve's realm. This was the entity that kept Underhill going, a sort of magical AI that powered the land, sky, and sea of this realm, nurturing life by maintaining checks and balances that kept the ecosystem stable.

It would be an understatement to call it incredible. Its presence was so overwhelming, I nearly lost my sense of individuality in the shadow of Underhill's colossal magnitude. Yet to say it was aware would be a mischaracterization of its nature. It was vast, and it contained power beyond imagination, but it was not a singular awareness in the manner that I was, a person with my own beliefs, quirks, and experiences. Underhill —the arcane, algorithmic intelligence that kept it alive and functioning—simply *was*.

As I examined the warp and weave of the energies

that had been used to create Underhill by the Tuath Dé millennia ago, I realized something—*Underhill had been fashioned after Earth*. It was a poor facsimile, despite all its splendor and strange wonder, but the energy patterns here definitely reflected those I felt through my connection with nature back home. If that were the case, I should be able to tap into and direct Underhill's magic, just as I had Earthside, before I was cursed by Boann.

However, I was well aware that these were Fuamnach's lands, and ultimately under her control. Yet I didn't sense her presence anywhere near, so I had to assume that she was off somewhere fighting the Fae war. In her absence, perhaps I could subvert her magical hold on this demesne for a time and use it to escape and defeat Boann.

Mag Mell accepted me as its master, back in my own timeline. Let's hope this small part of Underhill will accept me as well. Only one way to find out.

Acting with a sense of desperation born out of fear I'd never escape Boann's grasp, I poured myself into Fuamnach's demesne. It was delicate work, because I needed to introduce my presence and establish myself as a non-threat, while familiarizing myself with the strange patterns and magics that made up the sorceress' lands. At first my overtures were rejected, then I remembered what I had done to get Tethra's demesne on my side.

I need to do something to heal this land.

Without hesitation, I extended my senses beyond

the immediate grounds of the castle, searching the area for abuses that had been inflicted on it by Fuamnach. Thankfully, such atrocities were not hard to find. Over the centuries, the sorceress had warped and corrupted the land, turning a paradise into a living hell. She'd converted clear, freshwater springs into acidic pools and swamps, changed fruit-bearing plants and trees into predatory carnivores, and altered the local fauna's DNA with magic, transforming them into monstrous creatures that were never intended to exist within the algorithms of Underhill's core functions.

I couldn't undo two millennia's worth of damage in a few hours. However, I could plant the seeds of change with druidic magic by encouraging Underhill to reject Fuamnach's evil influence. Hopefully, the land would correct and heal itself over time, shirking her domination and reverting back to its original core directives.

It was a slow, arduous process, and with every passing moment I worried Boann would return before I finished. Having no other choice, I continued working diligently at my task until I felt I'd made enough headway to gain a modicum of acceptance from the land. If Fuamnach's demesne did not see me as a close ally, then at least I'd not be perceived as an enemy, should I attempt to tap into its vast reserves of energy when I faced Boann.

After that was done, I slowly began to come out of my trance, wondering if it would be enough to help me defeat the river goddess. Moreover, even if the demesne did not reject my presence outright, I worried that I would not be able to control its magic. After all, I wasn't a druid master anymore—the curse had seen to that.

Regardless of my reservations, the time for worry was over. Through the connections I'd established in the trance, I sensed Boann as she portalled in above. As I returned to the present, I opened my eyes just in time to see water begin to burst out of the walls of the oubliette, flooding my cell.

Considering how quickly the stone-lined pit filled with water, any doubts I might have had regarding Boann's absolute control of that element were extinguished. I barely had time to take a breath before the water was over my head, swirling round and round in a never-ending whirlpool that sent me careening against the floors and walls. Yet this time I was ready for her, and I was able to use my connection with the demesne to my advantage.

Fortunately for me, Boann didn't seem to have the ability to create water from nothing. Meaning, all the water she controlled had to be drawn from the local ecosystem, here in Fuamnach's demesne. Since I had established a rapport with the magic that sustained and maintained the area, I was able to influence it to reduce the damage I took from this second thrashing.

The trick was in keeping Boann from noticing what

I was doing. Any significant display of magic would cause her to redouble her efforts, or to bolster the wards on the cell with negation spells—or both. I had to play this close to the wire to make it work, and that's what I did, using druidry to give myself a tiny nudge here, a softer landing there, just enough to avoid the broken bones and concussions I'd suffered the day prior.

Yet I couldn't protect myself too much, as Boann would just kick my ass all over again if I wasn't sufficiently subdued when she pulled me out of the oubliette. For that reason, I took some scrapes, cuts, and bruises, enough to make it seem as though all the fight had been drowned and beaten out of me. By the time the current inside the oubliette brought me to the surface, I must've looked like a bloody, drowned rat—but I was still functional.

Boann's makeshift washing machine spun me around several more times, then the entire body of water surged up underneath me, pushing the grate open and blowing me out the top. I flew roughly twenty feet in a short, high arc above the opening before landing in a heap at the river goddess' feet. Coughing and spitting up water from my lungs, I hugged my arms to my chest and curled into a ball, doing my best to look like an injured, helpless human.

Not a difficult role to play, after all that.

"My, but what a mess you are," Boann chided with mock sympathy. "I must say, you've disappointed me,

Colin. Based on your reputation, I expected a lot more fight from you."

"Lift this curse," I muttered as I cracked one swollen eye open, "and I'll show you what I can do."

"Oh, I think not," she replied. "I have plans for you, plans to make you suffer. Lifting the curse would only give you opportunity to escape, then I'd be forced to have Herne hunt you down all over again. While I might enjoy that, I'm rather eager to explore what Fuamnach's dungeons have to offer."

"Speaking of that witch, where is she?"

"Off somewhere fighting this silly war. Herne has already delivered the Changeling Prince to her, in case you're wondering. That was our deal, that I capture her adoptive son, and in return she'd provide me use of her dungeons for as long as I needed them."

"So Fuamnach loaned you her pad." I rubbed my jaw, covering my mouth so I could purposely bite my lip. The coppery taste of blood flooded my mouth, and I spat some in the dirt. "What are friends for, right?"

She chuckled at that. "I see a small sliver of that acerbic wit has returned. No matter, the sorceress' head torturer will eliminate it shortly. I wonder, how long will it take you to grow your tongue back after he cuts it out?"

Boann clapped her hands, and two bugganes marched into view on either side of her.

"Mistress?" one of them grumbled.

"Bind him, then take him to the torturer to be put on

the rack. Instruct that he should not kill him, but he should spare him no pain, either. After he's screamed himself hoarse, come find me in the baths." She waved her hand at me in a sort of shooing motion as a portal appeared behind her. "Go now, remove this creature and see that he is properly broken."

"Yes, mistress," the buggane replied as he bowed fully at the waist.

Boann stepped through the portal, disappearing as it closed behind her. Immediately the two bugganes laid hands on me, hog-tying me with magically strengthened leather straps that tightened automatically after they had been knotted. Figuring I needed to make it look good, I struggled a bit, earning a cuff across the jaw from one of the creatures, and causing the straps to tighten further in response.

"That'll be enough o' that, now," the other buggane said. "Me 'n Hamish gots stuff to do, 'n we don't have time to be pissin' about with the likes o' you. Ain't that right, Hamish?"

"S'right, Inry," the first buggane said. I could hardly tell them apart, except that Inry had the thicker accent. "You just settle down there, mister drood, and take your licks. Once our lady's tormentor is done with you, we'll have you back in this here hole, as snug as a mouse at the border."

"Nuthin' fer' it, no how," Inry added. "So be a good lad, 'n don't be causin' a fuss, 'n make it worse on yerself 'n it has ta' be."

In response, I did my best to look properly defeated, lowering my eyes and nodding in silence. Behind my back, however, I began working on freeing myself by unraveling the magical weaves powering the enchantments in the restraints. Doing so required zero movement or struggle on my part, and since bugganes weren't very good at magic, it was doubtful that either of them would know what I was doing.

"That's a good lad," Hamish said. "Grab him, Inry. My back's all kinked up from fightin' the lady's whelp."

"Oh, woe is you," Inry replied in a mocking tone. "I told ya' it'd be a good idea ta' wallop 'im afore ya' laid hands on 'im."

"Well, he looked half-dead, didn't he? Weren't like Herne was no gentle caretaker to him."

Inry grabbed me by the ankle with one huge, hairy hand, then he swung me up and over his shoulder with no more effort than it might take to lift a sack of groceries. "Told ya', that Hound's a tough'n, he is. Ya' weren't here when 'e was doin' the lady's biddin', 'an ya' didn't see 'is handiwork."

"Well, I know now," Hamish said as he knuckled his lower back. "S'let's get this one down to the dungeons right quick, so's we can tap that keg whilst everyone else is away."

"Now yer' talkin'," Inry replied, taking the lead and marching toward a large oaken door on the other side of the castle's courtyard.

I'd already gotten the lay of the land when I was in

my druid trance, but it wouldn't hurt to verify that info with my own eyes. While Inry carried me across the courtyard, I glanced this way and that, noting all doors, passages, buildings, and landmarks from my upside-down perspective. While I was conducting my visual scan of the area, something in the sky high above caught my eye.

I zeroed in on it, which was hard to do with my head bouncing off Inry's greasy, furred back with his every step. It was a large, winged reptile, that much I could tell, but it was too high in the sky to determine if it was a dragon or a wyvern. Before Inry could duck through the doorway that led to the bowels of the castle, I reached out to the creature with my druid senses, brushing up against its consciousness more out of awe and curiosity than anything else.

Wow, a real, live dragon. Amazing.

As with most animals I linked with, I was able to scan its surface thoughts and see what it saw. Correction, *her* thoughts, because "it" was definitely a she, and she was mostly concerned with establishing and securing her territory so she could raise a brood. From what I could tell, this involved eliminating threats like rival wyrms—wyverns, drakes, oilliphéists, and the like—and hunting down manticores, gryphons, and other creatures that liked to eat young, defenseless dragonlings.

Badass.

At first, I didn't think she sensed my presence, then I

realized she had. She was barely an adult, that much I could tell, and she seemed to be as intrigued by me as I was of her. Before I could communicate further, Inry took me inside the castle where Fuamnach's wards blocked my druid senses. Instantly, the connection was gone.

Damn. Well, if I die, at least I can say I touched a dragon's mind. Cool.

By the time I opened my eyes again, Inry was carrying me down a torch-lit stone stairway that led beneath the castle proper. A macabre symphony of noises echoed up the stairwell—screams of agony, the softer sound of someone weeping, and the meaty, brutal smack of fists on flesh. As we descended first one flight of steps, then another, I was assaulted by mixed odors of fresh and old blood, burning skin and hair, human filth, rotting flesh, and troll stench.

As for the prior scents, they were exactly what I'd expected to smell in a torturer's dungeon. However, the troll musk was entirely unexpected, as the majority of their number lived Earthside, shunning Underhill despite the favorable conditions that a lack of real sunlight provided. The sun's rays were anathema to trollkin. Any of their kind that was unfortunate enough to be caught in full sunlight would be turned to stone and perish almost instantly.

At first, I thought that the troll scent might be coming from Fuamnach's torturer, speculating that perhaps she'd managed to acquire the services of a rogue troll by means of threat, bribe, or coercion. Then we passed a line of cell doors, and I spotted a mottled, lumpy, gray-green face peering out between the iron bars of a small, head-height window. Although the troll was emaciated and scarred, his was a face I recognized.

Guts, I mouthed as his gaze met mine.

Guts, whose full name was "Eats-Guts-With-Bare-Hands-And-Salts-The-Earth-After-Battle," was a warrior of the Toothshank Clan back on Earth. I'd become an ally of the clan after narrowly defeating Guts in a sort of trial by combat while acting as Maeve's representative. Despite losing the match, the fight allowed Guts' clan to save face, and by helping them do so I gained their favor along the way.

Guts and I had been through a lot together, fighting off an undead army and traveling to Underhill with Crowley and Sabine to rescue a bunch of fae-trafficked kids. Although trolls from bloodlines originating in the United Kingdom looked quite a bit different from the mountain trolls of Scandinavia, Guts was just as loyal as my friend Ásgeir ever had been, and nearly as fierce in battle. In short, I'd trust him with my life.

The troll gave no indication he recognized me. However, Inry noted his interest as we passed. "Don'cha be gettin' any bright idears, troll. This'uns goin' right back in the pit when ol' Urman's done wit' 'im. The lady's guest 'as plans 'fer 'im, so 'ere won't be no scraps nor bones 'fer ya' ta' chew on after."

Guts grunted, stone-faced as he replied through the

bars of his cell. "A rat makes an easy meal, but wolverines are hard to kill."

"What'd 'e say?" Inry asked his companion.

"Who knows, the way all them trolls are always rhyming? Ignore him. We can come back and beat the shit outta' the troll later."

"Sounds good ta' me," Inry replied as he dropped me in a heap before a large, brass-bound oaken door. "Welp, 'ere we are, drood."

Hamish knocked on the door, causing it to shake in the frame. "Oy, Urman! We got a fresh one for you. River goddess wants you to give him the full monty, jest don't kill him." He glanced down at me, speaking as if to a child. "Take your licks and do what Urman says, drood. Inry and me will be back for what's left of you at the end o' the day."

The two bugganes sauntered off down the hall, laughing and roughhousing like a couple of high school bullies. Shadows shifted in the torchlight that filtered through the crack beneath the door, and I heard the approach of heavy shuffling footsteps on the other side. I tried to rip the bindings around my wrists and ankles apart, but it seemed I'd only weakened the enchantment on the straps enough to loosen them. Knowing I only had seconds to act, I began working furiously at the knots in hopes of getting free before Urman the Torturer had me at his mercy.

18

There goes one knot. Now, for the second—there!

The bonds around my wrists slipped free, and I gripped them tightly to hold them in place as the door opened. As the heavy oak and brass monstrosity swung wide, I stared up in shock and horror at the huge thing that stood over me. He—it?—was easily seven feet tall, with broad but stooped workman's shoulders, long arms, meaty, almost oversized hands, and feet that must have been size twenty in human shoes.

Urman wore a thick leather apron over his bare chest and torso, and beneath that he wore simple cotton leggings tucked into sturdy but worn leather boots. Both the apron and the boots were splattered with blood and other organic material, most of it old and blackened, some of it glistening and fairly recent from the looks of it. Plain pockets of sewn leather had been worked into the apron, in which sat a variety of tools, blades, corkscrews, pliers, tongs, and other instruments.

All of these details added together would make for a very intimidating torturer indeed. However, it was Urman's other physical traits that had me most concerned. His skin was a pale, uniformly grayish-white, unblemished except for the road map of cyanotic veins that ran beneath the surface and the stitches and staples where his flesh had been sewn together at various joints and junctures. On closer inspection, I realized that his arms and hands were mismatched, with one being shorter and more muscular, the other being longer and thinner, but no less massive.

His skull was ogrish and overly large, with a high, bulbous forehead and a shock of short, dark hair that stood at attention on top like a bundle of soot-blackened broom bristles. He had small, cauliflower ears that stood out like car doors, surrounded as they were by nothing but stubble and skin, as his hair had been shaved short around the sides and back of his head. His face was dominated by a pronounced brow that jutted out an inch or more over a squat, crooked nose that looked to have been broken and never reset. Beneath that sat a flat, nearly lipless mouth punctuated by two lower canines that stuck out above his upper lip, giving him the look of a demented, very mean bulldog.

Urman pulled those thin frog lips into a tight sneer as he looked down at me. "A human," he observed in a deep, rumbling voice marked by a thick cockney accent. "'Aven't seen one o' your kind down 'ere in ages. Fragile fings, humans. Doubt this'll take any time t'all."

My hand and fingers were still tingling from being restrained so tightly, and I didn't trust myself to take Urman out just yet. Besides, my ankles were still tied together, as I hadn't had the opportunity to unfasten those knots as well. I decided to bide my time, to wait until the moment to strike was right before making my move.

Unfortunately, when Urman grabbed me, he tried picking me up by my right upper arm, suitcase style, causing my semi-numb fingers to lose their grip on my restraints. My arm slipped free, and instead of lifting me off the ground I ended up dangling by that arm, halfway off the ground while balancing on my bound feet with my left arm free.

"Whazzis now?" Urman said in a tone that registered as inconvenience rather than surprise. He held onto my arm, lifting me in the air and turning me so he could examine my bindings more closely. As the leather strap fell to the floor, he tsked loudly. "Damned Inry, can't even tie a simple knot wi'vout sommun holdin' 'is hands."

"Sucks for you," I said as I grabbed a long, wood-handled chisel from Urman's apron, stabbing it to the hilt in his right eye.

Shockingly, he didn't even flinch when I did it. Nor

did he lock up in a trauma-induced seizure and fall to the floor, like I'd seen dozens of monsters and humans do before after suffering such an injury. Instead, he frowned and scratched his scalp absently with his free hand, as if he were figuring numbers in his head.

"Oy, whadja do that for?" he said as he plucked the chisel from his eye, replacing it in the pocket from which I had taken it. "Now I'll have ta' ask our lady ta' replace it when she returns from battle. Damned inconvenient ta' only 'ave one eye, ya' know. Make my work a right pain in the arse, fer' sure."

"What the fuck are you?" I asked in all seriousness. "Some sort of Franken-ogre or something?"

"I'm the proper naughty bloke Frankenstein's mum fucking warned him of," Urman replied, right before he casually backhanded me with one of his massive hands.

Momentarily stunned, it took me a second or two to recover. Meanwhile, Urman had decided to drag me over to the rack. When I realized what he was doing, I reached up to snag another tool from his apron. In response, the torturer lifted and shook me like a rag doll until my skull rattled.

"Are you 'avin a Turkish? Won't do you any good, mate. See, you can't kill me, cuz' I'm already dead. So, stop it, eh?" When I tried yet again to grab a weapon, Urman tossed me across the room, causing me to collide at speed with the stonework wall on the other side. I fell into a heap at the base of the wall, temporarily dazed as he rattled on. "See? It's hopeless ta' fight. Now, lie still an' mind yerself, whilst I get the rack ready."

I sat up and shook my head, shrugging off the dizziness I felt while the Franken-ogre fussed over a rather nasty-looking piece of torture equipment. While he was preoccupied with that, I cast my gaze about the room, searching for a weapon I could use to even the odds. Finally, I spotted a large cleaver with an eighteen-inch clip-point blade and a full-tang handle, sitting on a butcher block table next to an open, massive, gore-stained iron maiden.

Still a bit groggy from my collision with the wall, I pushed myself upright, only to trip and fall right back to the ground. This earned me an annoyed over-the-shoulder glance from Urman, who simply hissed before turning his attention back to preparing the rack. After being painfully reminded that my ankles were still tied, I inch-wormed myself across the floor toward the table that held the cleaver, pulling myself with my arms while scoot-pushing myself along with my legs.

When I reached the table, I grabbed the edge to pull myself upright. Leaning against the edge to steady myself, I grabbed the cleaver. Testing the edge first—it was wickedly sharp—I leaned over to cut the bindings from my legs, looking up at intervals to make certain Urman wasn't coming. The bindings were much tougher than leather straps should be, and it took a lot of sawing to finally slice through the top layer.

Once I worked myself free, I stood on shaky legs,

assuming a fighting stance just as the huge Franken-ogre finished setting up the rack. He turned around, moving slowly like he had all the time in the world. When he saw the blade in my hand, he clucked his tongue.

"Oy, fink I'm gonna let ya' stick me wif 'at? Have I got 'mug' tattooed across my forehead? Drop the cleaver an' let's get on wif' yer' torture, yeah?"

"Uh, nope. You're going down, and I'm walking out of here."

"Your funeral," he said as he marched across the room toward me.

I got the feeling that Urman thought he was nigh invincible, and I decided it was time to disabuse him of that notion. As such, it was fortunate that I'd had all night to heal and meditate before Boann and her goons brought me here. My Fomorian healing factor was working at top speed, so I was already shaking off the effects of Urman's not-so-gentle treatment. By the time he got within range, I wasn't one hundred percent, but I had enough juice to rumble.

Like most large brutes, the Franken-ogre relied on his size and strength to give him the edge in a fight, and he came at me just like I expected. He lunged to grab me, arms extended. I side-stepped, cutting his right biceps with a forehand cut as I parried his arm under mine with my left hand. I followed up with another slice to his triceps muscle on the same arm, then I stepped past him as I cut his quadriceps to the bone on his right leg, just above the knee.

Once I'd flanked him, I pivoted clockwise, turning to face him as I aimed a backhand horizontal slash at his neck. Urman turned out to be cannier than I'd expected, and he dropped and rolled onto his back before I could chop his head off. I was tempted to leap on top of him and go all Psycho with the cleaver, but it wasn't really made for stabbing, and the torturer still had one good hand with which to fend me off.

Instead, I backed away and circled, looking to come at him on his injured side. Urman lay face-up on the floor, his right arm hanging useless at his side. His right leg had curled up under him at an impossible angle, opening the cut I'd made so far that it looked like a gaping mouth above his knee. Considering that he was crippled, I was tempted to leave him so I could go find Boann. However, I worried that someone would find him and alert the rest of the garrison.

Better finish this.

I was about to move in on his right side and start slicing and hacking away when a strange thing happened. I sensed what I can only describe as a *shiver* of magic, a swell of mystical energy that released all at once in a single burst. As soon as I felt it, a translucent wave of magic swept over Urman from head to toe. When it passed his injuries disappeared, as if he'd never been hurt in the first place. As soon as he was whole again, he pushed himself up to a seated position and crab-walked backward away from me to give himself more room.

"Ya' heal pretty fast, for a human," he said. "But the Lady I serve didn't leave me wantin' in that department, neither."

Fuck.

I wasn't about to let him get back on his feet, so I rushed in, cutting and slashing with near-vampire speed, like a sushi chef on meth. He covered his face and head while I sliced and hacked at him until his arms were nothing more than ribbons of meat hanging off the bone. When I'd done enough damage to prevent him from raising his arms, I slashed one more time, right across his throat, so deep I felt the tip of the cleaver hit bone.

Then I stepped back, breathing heavily as Urman slumped forward, his head dangling on a partially severed spine and a thin piece of skin and muscle. I waited for him to recover—nothing. When I was satisfied he wasn't getting up, I turned and headed for the door.

That's when I felt it, that shiver of energy I'd sensed earlier when Urman healed the first time.

"Hang on there, mate," I heard him say behind me. "We ain't finished, yet."

Quick as a mongoose fighting a cobra, I spun around in a crouch, blade in a high guard and ready to fight.

"For the love of all that's holy, just die already!" I growled.

"Not so easy to kill me. The Lady of the castle made sure o' that."

Obviously, my current strategy wasn't working. For all I knew, I could slice him into confetti a thousand times, and he'd just heal again. Even my Fomorian stamina had limits, and I wasn't about to fight myself ragged just to beat the first-level boss in the castle. I thought about using druidry, but I resisted the temptation, knowing that it would alert Boann if I performed any significant feat of magic.

Urman was almost on his feet, and I was running out of options. I swept my gaze across the room, searching for something, anything I could use against him to finish this fight.

There.

A few feet behind the Franken-ogre, the iron maiden stood open on its hinges, just begging to be used. I judged the distance, deciding I'd best hit Urman before he got his legs underneath him.

Time to finally put all those tae kwon do lessons to good use.

Faking a slash as if I was about to slice him up again, I waited until Urman raised his arms, then I leapt into the mother of all jump spinning back kicks. Turning one-hundred-eighty degrees in the air, I kicked out like a donkey with my right leg, pulling my toes up to expose the heel completely. My kick landed dead center on the brute's sternum, forcing an *oof* from him as I felt his ribs crack.

Urman stumbled backwards, landing squarely in the iron maiden and skewering himself on a hundred long, sharp spikes all at once. However, I wasn't finished. I knew from experience that the only way to overcome a magically enhanced healing factor was to overwhelm it completely. If I wanted to finish the torturer, I needed to make sure the damage was more than Fuamnach's healing spell could handle.

As soon as I landed, I danced forward and round-house kicked the iron maiden's lid closed. Despite his injuries, Urman had the wherewithal to thrust his arms out, preventing it from shutting completely. Not to be deterred, I spin-kicked the door, forcing it shut. Thick, black blood oozed out from the bottom of the torture device as I stepped forward to latch and lock it shut.

"Heal from that, motherfucker," I hissed as I turned and headed for the exit. "Oh, and I'm keeping this cleaver," I added, just before I marched out the door.

Other than Urman and the prisoners, the dungeon was a ghost town. I'd sensed as much during my druid trance, but it was comforting to have that information verified by my own eyes. As soon as I decided the coast was clear, I headed for Guts' cell with a ring full of heavy iron keys that I'd snagged from the torture chamber. On approaching the door, I found the troll in the same position as before, staring out the bars and down the hall as if he'd been waiting for me to return the entire time.

"Knew it wouldn't take long, your escape was a conclusion foregone," he rhymed as I worked at unlocking his cell door.

"Man, your English has really improved since the last time I saw you," I replied as I continued to try the keys on the ring, one by one.

"Nothing to do in here," he said with a shrug. "Imminent death was a constant fear. Had to keep my mind occupied, otherwise I'd surely die."

Finally, I found the key that turned the lock. "Got it." The door swung open, and I stepped back to allow Guts to step into the corridor.

Now that I could see more than his face, I realized he'd been here for some time. For starters, he was emaciated to the point of starvation, and his tough, gray-green skin had taken on a pallid cast. Trolls healed very quickly, but they weren't immune to injury. The fact that he had scars all over his lanky frame told me that Fuamnach had been actively torturing him for some time.

One of these days, she's going to get what she deserves.

"Are there any more Toothshank Clan imprisoned here?" I asked, not bothering to insult him by mentioning his poor condition. Troll warriors were serious about their honor, and they rarely showed weakness no matter how dire their wounds.

"Seven still remain alive," he replied. "Along with more from other tribes."

"How'd you guys end up here, anyway?"

Guts scanned up and down the hall as he answered. "We fought for Queen Maeve. When we lost, we were enslaved."

"Damned sorry to hear that." I tossed him the keyring. "Guts, I need a diversion. I know I'm asking for a lot, but could your troll warriors help me out?"

"Not a question of if we could. Better to ask, 'Does a buggane shit in the woods?'"

I laughed and clapped him on the shoulder. "I never doubted it for a moment, but you know I had to ask. I'm about to go take care of the bitch who locked me up here—not Fuamnach, another goddess—and it'd be nice to have my gear. Any idea where they store that stuff?"

Guts shook his head. "No idea where she locked your magic bag up. Might have to defeat her to get your stuff."

"Eh, it's not as if my gear helped me the last time we tangled. I'll just have to make do."

The troll raised a rubbery, hairless, gray-green eyebrow at me. "Does the druid have a plan? Or will this be his final stand?"

"I have an inkling of one, yes. Like most of the Tuath Dé, she's powerful but overconfident. If I can get her out in the open, I think I may have a chance." I tossed him the cleaver, and he snatched it out of the air by the handle. "There's more knives and shit in the torture room, at least enough to get you to some real weapons. Give me twenty minutes, then I want you to tear through this place like a week-old bean burrito through a goose's ass. Just don't get yourself killed on my count, alright?"

Guts locked eyes with me, his expression one of fierce resolve as he answered. "The Toothshank Clan owes you the debt of our freedom. Our lives are yours if you should need them."

"Let's not see it come to that. I'd much rather have you around when I'm done here. I still have a lot of killing to do Earthside, and it'd be nice to have some Toothshank warriors at my back."

"Then we will survive to fight another day. Now, don't you have a goddess to slay?"

"Actually, the plan is to subdue her and turn her over to her husband. Then I need to find Lugh so he can help me get my Oak back." The troll looked at me askance. "Yeah, long story. Just remember, I need you guys alive. After you've stacked a few bodies, find an entrance to the sewers—if you follow them down, they should take you to Peg Powler's swamp. I'll catch up with you there."

Guts gave a formal bow. "Consider it done. Join us when the battle is won."

If I'm still alive, that is.

Smiling with a confidence I didn't feel, I clasped forearms with Guts, then I headed for the exit. It was time to find Boann and draw her out so I could end this once and for all. I only hoped that Nuada was right, because a lot was riding on me being able to cast magic that I had no idea how to use.

Fuck it. I've killed gods before with less.

Or so I told myself as I headed toward an almost certain doom.

19

Much like the dungeons, the rest of the castle was almost deserted. Sure, there were a few guards here and there, but they were lax and easy to avoid. After a few minutes of sneaking around, I found my way to the kitchens, mostly by following the smell of baking bread and roasted meat. The latter odor reminded me of barbecued pork ribs. Since I hadn't seen any pigs in the courtyard, I had no illusions as to what was actually on the menu.

When I snuck up to the entrance to the cooking area, I heard someone humming along with the occasional rattle of pans and crockery. Whoever it was, they were busy preparing meals for the day. I peeked around the corner and back again, only to spot a short, plump female figure working away with her back turned to me.

She wore simple clothing—flat-soled leather shoes, a rough, brown cotton dress, a white apron, and a white handkerchief tied round her head to pull her hair away from her face. The cook was mixing batter in a large bowl at a long table that faced one wall of the kitchen. Behind her, two large pots boiled over open fires, and to her left at the end of the room, bread baked in a brick oven. Over in the opposite corner from the oven, a suckling pig roasted on a spit atop an open pit.

Nope, not a pig. That's a child, a human child. Fuck.

Ducking back behind the wall, I resisted the urge to puke. Once I had my gorge under control, I tiptoed into the kitchen, sneaking up behind the cook until I was within striking range. While I wanted nothing more than to slit her throat, I was lost—and I had no idea how to find the baths.

Directions first, then I kill her.

Instead of executing her outright, I kicked at the back of her knees. In the same motion, I yanked her backward by her collar, pulling her toward me until she was leaning at an awkward angle with her head on my chest. Touching her throat with the tip of the butcher knife, I looked down at the creature as she cringed and covered her face with her hands.

Surprise and outrage struck me simultaneously as I realized she wasn't fae. "Shit, you're a fucking human."

"Aye, an' don't kill poor Nan for it, master," she pleaded in an archaic, low-born English accent, her fat jowls shaking beneath rosy, well-fed cheeks as she spoke. "Been working these kitchens since I was a young lass, I 'ave, e'er since the sorceress bought me an' made me her slave."

I pricked her throat with the knife, drawing blood as I inclined my head at the cooking pit. "You cook kids for her, Nan? You kill your own kind?"

"Not willingly, I don't. But what am I ta' do? She'll do worse'n kill me if I don't do as she says."

On a whim, I leaned in and smelled the cook closely, taking her scent deep into my nostrils. Back in the Hellpocalypse, I'd learned that cannibals gave off an unmistakable, sickly-sweet smell through their pores. Nan had it, sure as the day was long. On recognizing her for what she was, I gripped the knife so tightly my knuckles whitened. Somehow, I managed to stay my hand.

"I need directions, Nan. Where are the baths?"

"The baths, sir?" she whined.

"Yes, where Fuamnach bathes, you moron."

"Up the stairs 'at way, down the corridor past the great dining hall, and straight on through the throne room into the royal quarters. You'll find her private baths on the lower level o' the tower. Ya' can't miss 'em."

"Thank you, Nan. When you get there, tell them I'll be sending plenty more just like you."

Her expression became puzzled, and her eyes darted left and right with nervous confusion. "Where, sir? To the baths?"

"No, to hell," I said as I slit her throat from ear to ear.

Discarding the worthless piece of trash while she

was still choking on her own blood, I grabbed two large towels from the counter. Working quickly, I wrapped them around my hands, then I removed the child's corpse from the fire. Setting the poor thing down on the kitchen counter, I removed the spit and covered the body with the towels before saying a prayer over it.

"I'm sorry, kid," I whispered. "Wish I'd gotten here sooner."

After that was done, I grabbed two logs from the fire pit by their unburned ends, and I placed them on the shelf below the table. I repeated the process until there were no more logs, building the fire to a robust blaze until flames licked across the bottom of the tabletop. It might have been a futile gesture, but if I died fighting Boann, I wanted to make sure this kid had something of a decent burial. Failing that, at least they wouldn't be using the kitchen again anytime soon.

I swear, if I survive my fight with the river goddess, I'm tearing this place to the ground after.

———

With the kitchen ablaze behind me, I headed out the opposite door for the stairs. Just as I reached the top, I heard footsteps coming toward me from down the hallway. Ducking back into the shadows of the stairwell, I waited for the guards to pass, then I made a beeline for the royal wing of the castle, following Nan's directions to the letter.

Thank goodness they didn't smell the smoke. Let's hope Guts and his boys don't get antsy and start the party before I find Boann.

After passing the dining hall and the longest fucking table I'd ever seen, I followed the hallway where it ended in front of a set of massive double doors. I pulled the right one open just enough to slip through, taking a moment to peek inside before I entered the room. Once inside, I closed the door behind me and let out a low whistle at the absolutely ridiculous amount of wealth that had been wasted on the decor.

The room was longer than it was wide, roughly forty feet across and twice that in length, with a broad red carpet runner leading from the entrance up to the throne dais. Richly colored tapestries were hung on the walls beneath carved wood moulding and architectural accents covered in gold leaf and gemstones. Battle armor displays were arranged on the walls between the tapestries, each consisting of finely engraved breast-plates and swords, decorated in gold and silver filigree.

As for the throne itself, it was a massive, gaudy affair. Fashioned from some dark, exotic wood, it was carved all over with lions, dragons, and other appropriate symbols of regal power. Of course, the throne had over-sized armrests, a towering back, and thick velvet cushions upholstered into the seat and backrest with gem-studded gold tacks. If I hadn't been in such a rush, I'd have pissed on it just for spite.

I crossed the throne room at a quick jog, searching

for the exit to the royal chambers. Finally, I decided it had to be on the other side of a huge wall hanging behind the throne that depicted Fuamnach in all her bitchy sorceress glory. The artist had portrayed her flying high above a battlefield astride a dragon's back, tossing elemental magic around like a politician throwing candy from a parade float.

Below her, the Tuatha Dé Danann fought against the Fomorian host. In the scene, the Celtic gods appeared to be driving my people off a cliff into the sea. On the far right of the tapestry, the rearmost ranks of Fomorians tumbled from the ledge, only to drown in the ocean deep far below.

It was all bullshit, according to my mother. She claimed the Tuath Dé had tricked the Fomorians in order to steal their magic. If what she told me was true, that was how the Celtic gods were able to defeat their former masters. Logically, it followed that they would have used the same magic to create Underhill, which explained why a Fomorian like Tethra had been able to command such a large demesne.

Before I pulled back the tapestry, I hawked up phlegm and spat on it, landing a large, green wad of goop right on Fuamnach's face. Satisfied with my aim, I swept the wall hanging back with one arm. Behind the tapestry I found a short, low-ceilinged corridor that led to a regular-sized set of double doors no more than ten feet beyond the throne room.

Tiptoeing with care up to the doors, I placed my ear

against the right-side door and listened. The only sounds I heard were the faint echo of classical music in the distance—Chopin, if I wasn't mistaken—and the soft splash of water. I cracked the door open just a bit, ears pricked for the slightest indication that anyone awaited me on the other side, but the only thing that greeted me was the damp scent of lavender bathwater.

Carefully, ever so quietly, I slipped into the room, then I paused to get my bearings. I stood in what could only be described as a receiving room, just as ornately decorated as the throne room, but on a much smaller scale. Directly ahead sat an antique desk and chair, and behind that a matching bureau and console table abutted a semi-circular wall. Arched entryways book-ended the wall on either side, the left leading to a grand, spiraling staircase beyond. If I wasn't mistaken, the right-side entry led to Fuamnach's private baths.

Ignoring the door that led to the stairs, I chose instead to get a good look at what was behind archway number two. Leaning to my right, I saw water lapping at the edge of a huge in-ground pool on the other side of the opening. I found it strange that someone would have an indoor swimming pool right next to their entry foyer, but then again, Fuamnach *was* technically a goddess. Who could say what drove their whims and idiosyncrasies?

It occurred to me that, as I traveled the entire distance from the dungeons to these chambers, I hadn't seen a restroom or water closet of any kind. For all I knew, deities didn't need to shit or even bathe. If that were the case, it wouldn't surprise me in the least if she had installed a Roman bath in her castle solely for the sake of showing off her wealth.

Once I had Boann's attention, I was going to need a means of making a quick exit. Lucky for me, Fuamnach had tastes that ran on the far side of ostentatious. The floor-to-ceiling stained-glass window she'd installed on the right-hand wall of the bath chamber would do nicely.

Again the artwork depicted the Black Sorceress herself, this time nude and side-saddle on a large piece of granite jutting up from a body of water. A huge, winged serpent was wrapped around her exaggeratedly shapely figure—she had very few curves, in real life—in such a way that it strategically covered her breasts and pelvic region. Except for the fact that her enraptured expression made it look like she enjoyed having a giant snake between her legs, it might almost have qualified as a classy bit of art.

Just then, Boann's voice echoed from the other room. "Nan, I can hear you puttering around in there. If you're just now bringing my wine, expect to receive a caning when I'm finished with my bath."

Figuring a surprise entrance might throw Boann off her game, I stepped through the arched door with my back to the window. "Sorry, but Nan slipped and slit her throat. Looks like you're not getting that wine after all."

As soon as the goddess heard my voice, her head snapped around. She glowered as she stood, eyes narrowed, and lips pressed into a flat, angry line. Then she did that Lady of the Lake thing again, rising up from the water naked as the day she was born save for that weird, H-shaped pendant she wore. That is, if gods and goddesses were born naked—that was another mundane detail of deific existence regarding which I held incomplete information.

Regardless, she hadn't a stitch of clothing on her, obviously, because baths and stuff. But what was really weird was that it looked as though her left leg was missing from mid-thigh down. On closer inspection, I realized that leg was completely formed of the same crystal clear, lavender-scented water in which she bathed.

As her face contorted with rage, great gouts of water surged up from the pool all around her. She screamed wordlessly at me, releasing a primal, animalistic sound as she slung both her arms forward, causing the water to shoot at me like dual water cannons. Disappointingly for her, I had expected that move, and a split-second before the water hit me, I jumped up and backward at the window behind me.

When my back struck the panes of colored glass, they shattered outward along with all the bits of lead that had held them in place. The force of Boann's water geysers merely accelerated my flight through the window, pushing me much further than I would have flown otherwise. Fortunately for me, the baths were on the first floor of the castle, meaning the window was only fifteen feet or so above ground level—a very manageable distance to fall.

I hit the ground in a classic, three-point superhero stance, after which I immediately sprang to my feet. The same moment I landed, klaxons sounded throughout the castle grounds, signaling that the Toothshank Clan's escape and attack had not gone unnoticed by the remaining garrison. As proof, I noted several trolls engaged in combat with Fuamnach's troops at various locations across the courtyard.

Additionally, it appeared that one wing of her castle was completely in flames, as gouts of smoke and fire billowed from open windows near the kitchen area I'd set on fire earlier. Smiling at the chaos Guts and I had created, I glanced up at the broken stained-glass window some fifty feet away. There, a still naked Boann stood framed by shattered glass and swirling water, her face a mask of fury as she searched the courtyard for yours truly.

As soon as she spotted me, I shot her the bird with both barrels as I yelled across the courtyard. "This little pool party has been a blast, Boann, but it's time for me to yeet. Peace out, bitch!"

Then, I ran like an escaped ape for the front gates of the castle. Fate smiled on me again, as the Toothshank

Clan trolls had already opened it wide and lowered the drawbridge. I sprinted past a couple of skirmishes and straight through the arched opening, hotfooting it onto the gate-bridge like my life depended on it. Meanwhile, a pissed off river goddess chased behind me on a tidal wave of lavender-scented bath water, screaming her fool head off.

Fuamnach's castle sat on a mountaintop high above Peg's swamp. Immediately outside the walls, there was nothing but a long fucking drop until you got across the drawbridge to the opposite cliff and a road that led down the mountain. That was where I was headed, out where Boann would have little if any water to command.

However, at the very bottom of the chasm between the two ledges there was a moat of sorts—a long, boggy lake of swamp water and mud which I wanted no part of at all. Unfortunately, Boann had other plans. As I crossed the drawbridge, geysers of muddy bog water shot up at the gate, lifting it slightly and bursting through the planks.

"Run all you want, druid," Boann screeched. "You'll not escape the goddess of the River Boyne!"

"Fucking hell, woman," I yelled as I dodged the gouts of water that shot up through gaps in the bridge's timbers. "How many times do I have to tell you, the kid's not mine!"

Boann shrieked incomprehensibly, then something wet and heavy hit me like a battering ram right between my shoulder blades. The impact knocked me forward, and I sailed headfirst across the bridge, landing a good twenty feet on the other side. Somehow, I managed to roll with it, flipping forward and landing on my feet with enough balance to continue my mad dash to the dry, rocky cart path that led down the mountain.

The way my legs were moving, I felt like that cartoon roadrunner zooming through the desert with a wily coyote on his tail. I don't think I'd ever run that fast, not even when I was being chased through my junkyard by Thor's 'roided up, homicidal nephew. And hell if I didn't make it around the first bend of the road, and out of the goddess' immediate field of view.

However, I wasn't in the clear yet. Boann had a pool full of water and the power of a Celtic goddess to play with, while I only had a tenuous connection to the demesne's magic and my wits to protect me. Not the best odds, but I had an ace up my sleeve—if I could manage to slip it into play.

As soon as I was out of her sight, I leapt behind a large boulder that had been shorn away from the mountain above the path. It was only one of many such formations that lined the twisting road down, and I hoped like hell Boann wouldn't think to search it as she passed. Seconds after I got to my hiding place, I heard the roar of rushing waters coming down the path, and I scrunched down as far as I could in the cleft.

Tight fit. Good thing I lost a few pounds to that curse.

Instead of stopping and searching the rocks, Boann simply whooshed on by on her mobile tidal wave. I honestly could not believe my luck, but I also realized I had no time to question it, as she'd soon figure things out and loop back around. With only seconds to spare, I closed my eyes and slowed my breath, dropping into a druid trance as I initiated my connection to the demesne's magic.

I've always been a pragmatic sort, and I held no illusions that I would defeat Boann in a battle of magic. She was powerful in her own element, and even with my druid master abilities intact I doubted I could pull it off. I might be able to kick her ass with the Oak backing me, but it'd be close.

That's why I decided to take a different approach.

Underhill was a powerful source of magic, being formed from what was probably the largest pool of arcane energy in existence, aside from good old planet Earth itself. If I could tap directly into it and channel that energy—hell, I'd be golden. We're talking small-g, god-level power, but still.

The only problem was, I couldn't do that. When I was in my druid trance, I was definitely able to connect with the demesne, but it was ultimately Fuamnach's demesne, her primary source of power. As soon as I jacked in and started bleeding off magic, she'd portal in, cut me off, and help Boann kick my ass proper.

But that didn't mean I couldn't use Fuamnach's

resources to deal with the river goddess. Or rather, the land's resources, the flora and fauna that resided within this demesne. I doubted very seriously that Fuamnach cared much for what a dragon wanted, but I did—very much so, in fact.

Based on the tapestries and artwork inside Fuamnach's castle, I knew what she'd do to the dragon I'd seen earlier. She'd capture it, bind it, and subjugate it, then use it to do her bidding. Hell, she might even kill it and raise it again with necromancy, just to make it easier to control.

Well, fuck that. I wasn't about to let that happen, but to help the dragon find a better home, I had to survive Boann's wrath. Which meant that said dragon and I could help each other. All I had to do was convince her that I was a friend.

It took precious seconds for me to locate her in her aerie high up on a nearby mountain peak. Once I did, I reached out to her ever so cautiously, all while expressing my very friendly intentions. Surprisingly, as soon as I made contact, she spoke directly into my mind.

-Only the druids are able to commune to my kind thusly. Explain yourself.-

Her "voice," if you could call it that, was sonorous and smooth, yet very drake-like. It was like listening to Etta James, if Etta James drank whiskey and smoked three packs a day. If I had to describe it, I'd say it was silk over hot coals. I know that didn't make sense, but that's how it sounded in my head.

That's because I am a druid.

-How? Your kind were killed off, or so our oral history says. My mother's mother's mother was the last of my line to have known a druid.-

I'm actually the last of my kind. My master was Finnegas, have you heard of him?

-Finn Eces, Finnegas the Seer, Druid Master and friend of dragonkind. Yes, I have heard of him. I owe him a great debt indeed. When the little gods and their fey offspring began killing and enslaving us, it is said the Seer hid my mother's mother's mother in a druid grove, preserving our line.-

That's awesome! Anyway, I'm Colin.

-You could not pronounce my name if you tried, but you may call me Smokedancer.-

Gosh, I wish could chat more, but time is short. Listen, if you nest here, you're placing your offspring in danger.

-Go on.-

I could explain it, but maybe I should just show you. I sent her images, memories of the tapestry and the stained-glass window inside Fuamnach's castle. *She's evil, Smokedancer. I honestly think she'd try to enslave you and steal your young if you stuck around here.*

-Safe places to roost in Underhill are hard to find, young druid. What do you propose I do?-

I'm working on getting my druid oak back. What if I hid you inside my grove, after I bond with my Oak? Would that work?

-You would share your druid grove with me?-

Sure, but first, I have to defeat a river goddess who's trying to kill me—

"Ah, there you are," I heard Boann say from above me. "I tire of these games. Time to die, druid."

In a classic "oh, shit" moment, I cut off the connection with Smokedancer instantly. I opened my eyes and looked up just in time to see a torrent of water rush down the cleft at me. The force of the water pummeled me like a thousand fists, pounding me into the rock over and over again and driving me further into the space between the boulders.

This time, Boann wasn't fucking around. The water just cycled around and around inside the cleft, forcing me down and preventing me from taking a breath. Since she'd caught me by surprise, I didn't have time to take a deep breath to hold me over, and soon my lungs and muscles were begging for oxygen.

I struggled to push myself out of the cleft, but I was wedged in tight. Not only that, but Boann's magic was recycling a swimming pool's worth of water, hammering into me over and over like a thousand fire hoses. I was strong, but she was stronger. There was no way I was going to escape this one.

Oh well, at least I warned Smokedancer.

The Celtic water torture seemed to go on forever, and after a time, I was so weak I stopped struggling. I still hadn't tried to take a breath, but it was only a matter of time before I blacked out and my reflexes took over.

There were dark spots at the edge of my vision, and I could feel myself going under.

Whelp, this is it. I wonder, when you die in Tír na nÓg, do you die forever?

Then, I felt a warmth flood through the cold, lavender-scented water that had beaten me bloody for the last few minutes. As quickly as it had started, the water flowed away around me, and I felt sweet, sweet air hit my face. Gasping and sputtering, I took in a deep, full breath, then I coughed up half a lung's worth of Boann's bath water.

Belle Delphine weebs, eat your heart out.

Once I had some air in my lungs, I tried to crawl out of the cleft, but Boann had wedged me in tight. Suddenly, I heard a loud *crack*, then the boulder on my right fell away from me, revealing a two-story tall red dragon behind it. Smokedancer spread her wings wide, flapping them once, then she folded them against her back.

"Can I safely say 'thanks' to a dragon?" I croaked.

-Suffice it to say your thanks is welcomed.-

I looked around, only noticing now that the surrounding area was scorched black for fifty feet all around. Smaller stones had been turned to black, glassy slag, and larger stones and small boulders had been half-melted away. All around us, the ground smoked and gave off steam where Boann's ensorcelled water had touched the parts that were still lava hot.

"Aw heck—is she dead?"

-No, merely unconscious. Look.-

Smokedancer pointed with one huge, clawed fore-limb to where Boann lay on the ground a few dozen feet away. She looked unharmed, except her eye, arm, and leg were missing. And she was out like a light, just like Smokedancer said.

"What happened to her arm and leg—and her eye?"

-They evaporated when I breathed fire at her. It seems the river goddess has a weakness—fire and heat.-

"We'll have to restrain her before she wakes up again."

-No need, you merely need to keep her dry. It seems that much of her power resides in her missing body parts; the ones comprised of enchanted water. Without them, she will remain in her current state, alive but unaware of her surroundings.-

"Ah, that's good. I had a deal with her husband, you see—"

Before I finished my sentence, a portal opened up near Boann, and Nuada stepped through. He still wore his cloak and hood, but I was able to get a better look at him in the light.

"Never you mind, druid—I'll take it from here." He inclined his head at Smokedancer. "Dragoness."

The red dragon dipped her head slightly on her long, slender neck, acknowledging the god's greeting. Otherwise, she remained both telepathically silent and still as he swept his wife's body up in his arms. Nuada looked like he was about to step back through the portal, but I had questions yet, so I cleared my throat loudly.

"Um, Nuada?" I said, waving to get his attention.

He stopped and half-turned to face me while his weird, steampunk arm clicked and whirred. "Yes, druid?"

"When she wakes up, won't she just come after me again?"

"No, she will not. When she succumbs to dehydration, she loses much of her recent memory. I doubt she'll even remember that any of this happened."

"Ah." I frowned and nodded slowly. "So... are we good?"

Nuada smiled, and in the light, I realized he looked a lot like his brother, Dian Cécht. "Yes, we're on good terms. Lugh asked that I send you to his castle. He also said to tell you to ignore the army outside—a 'minor nuisance' is how he described them, I think."

"Will do." I held my arms up, taking myself in at a glance. "Maybe he can do something about this stupid curse when I get there."

A look of sudden recollection crossed Nuada's face. His mechanical arm made some funky noises, then it split into two thinner but equally long arms. He shifted Boann's weight from his real arm to the others, then he reached down and snatched the charm from her neck by snapping the thong.

"A good thing you reminded me. You will need to destroy this to break the curse. The dragoness can easily manage it if she'll agree to loan you her assistance again." He tossed me the necklace, and I snagged it out of the air. "Be well, druid."

Without another word, Nuada Airgetlám stepped into the portal, and it vanished behind him. I stared after him for a while, then I looked up at Smokedancer. "My offer is still one-hundred percent good, by the way, once I get my Oak back."

-I am glad to hear it- she replied, with just a hint of amusement in her telepathic voice.

"Cool." I glanced around again, wondering how far I could push it with a real, live dragon. After a moment's deliberation, I decided it was a DGAF sort of day, so screw it. "Say, Smokedancer—I don't guess I could impose on you to melt this thing and give me a ride to Lugh's place?"

20

Once Boann was gone, my Bag finally showed up. I turned around after Nuada split, and there it was, sitting on a small boulder next to the path. I snagged it immediately, digging around inside for a set of clean, dry clothes. When I put them on, I realized we still hadn't removed the curse, because I was swimming in the flannel shirt and jeans I'd donned.

"Guess we'd better melt this thing," I said, holding up the pendant for Smokedancer to see. When I looked at it closely, it seemed to blur and shift in the light, as if it wasn't fully corporeal. "Weird. You know anything about this?"

-It is a sigil of Saturn. It seems the goddess had friends amongst the other pantheons. Toss it on the ground and back away, young druid, and I will see to its destruction.-

I discarded the thing immediately, mostly because I was done being a sixteen-year-old kid, but also because the thing felt *wrong*, as if it had been made from warped magic. Not being an expert on dragon fire, I backed up a good thirty feet, only to have the dragon give me an "are you serious right now?" look. After I doubled the distance, she gently beat her red, leathery wings against her body, which I interpreted as the dragon version of a shrug.

Then Smokedancer pulled herself up to her full height, arching up on all four of her muscular, lacertian legs. She extended her neck to its full length, craning her head down so her muzzle and snout faced the pendant directly. The dragon inhaled and exhaled several times, expanding and contracting her chest until orange and yellow light glowed brightly from within. Despite the distance, I felt the heat coming off her in waves, and decided to back up another twenty feet or so, for good measure.

When Smokedancer spat flame over the pendant, it was as if liquid fire spewed forth from her gullet. The fire was white-hot as it exited her mouth, changing to pale yellow, gold, and orange flames as the fire spout reached the ground. There her breath formed a ten-foot-wide cone that completely enveloped the charm, obscuring it from sight for the span of thirty seconds or more.

I was glad I'd backed up more because the fire was so hot, I had to shield my eyes and face, even at that distance. When her breath was depleted, the flames died out, save for a few licks of flame around her lips and the lava-hot rock that smoked and burned on the spot where the sigil had been moments before. Of the necklace there remained no trace, but I felt no different, either.

"I hate to be a drag, but did you by chance blow that thing off the mountain?" I asked as I lowered my arms. "Because I don't feel a thing."

-Give it a moment. That pendant was made by a god, and it will take time for the magic to dissipate.-

Sure enough, I began to feel a tingling all over seconds later. As the curse lifted, I felt myself growing taller, a millimeter at a time. Likewise, my muscles swelled, filling out my frame until my t-shirt fit a bit more snugly than I remembered. Eventually I was forced to loosen and adjust my belt, although there wasn't an ounce of fat on my frame after weeks in the Hellpocalypse.

I pulled my phone from my Bag, powering it up so I could look at myself using the forward-facing camera. "Oh, it is so good to have me back. And look, ma—no acne!" I said as I touched and prodded my face. I glanced over at the dragon, who looked on with apparent amusement. "Thanks again, Smokedancer."

-Happy to have been of service. Perhaps we should be going? A god awaits you, after all.-

"Right. Um, how does the whole 'riding a dragon' thing work?"

-It is best if you straddle my neck where it meets my

shoulders. *Hang on tight, as I may not be quick enough to catch you should you fall.-*

"Er, roger that. Colin go splat, no bueno."

She crouched all the way to the ground, stretching her neck out so I could hop on. As I mounted, I noticed that her scales were shiny and iridescent up close, which explained how surprisingly slick they were as well. Once I was balanced on her back, I found that I could get my fingers under her scales, gaining purchase to hang on.

"That's not bothering you, is it?"

-Just don't pull one off. We dragons are rather particular about giving away our scales. Clamp your legs tightly as we take off, else you'll slide right off my back when I bank.-

I did exactly as instructed, somehow managing to hang on as Smokedancer ran and leapt off the side of the mountain. We plummeted for several hundred feet, then she snapped her wings out, extending them fully to catch the updraft. Before I knew it, she'd banked hard to the right, and of course I damned near slid off, despite her explicit warning.

Speaking telepathically, I asked her to do a quick flyover to see if Guts and his crew had made it out of Fuamnach's castle. Sadly, there were a few troll corpses amongst the fae and undead that had staffed the sorceress' fortress in her absence. However, Guts and the bulk of the trolls were nowhere to be found. The fire I'd set in the kitchens had also spread throughout the place, and much of the main structure was now a charred, smoking husk.

-I approve of your methods, druid. There is nothing like a good, hot blaze to cleanse the stench of evil from the land.-

I appreciate the sentiment. That said, I think it's best if we get far, far away from here before the owner shows up. I'd hate for her to see us together, because believe me—you do not want her as an enemy.

-I am a dragon of the cardinal line, and I do not fear these little gods. However, your concern is noted, and I will abide your wishes.-

She banked away from the smoldering ruins of Fuamnach's castle, gaining altitude and climbing higher as we flew well above the mountain range where my friend Hemi had lost his life. I spent a moment wondering where he was in this timeline, and if he'd escaped the Hellpocalypse. His mom was a full-on Maori death goddess, and his girlfriend was a minor goddess in her own right, so I was fairly certain he made it out.

As for Fallyn, this timeline's version was supposed to be safely ensconced at her mom's assassin academy in the Swiss Alps. The woman I loved was helping her mom run the Pack back home in Austin, in my own timeline. I didn't have to worry about either of them at the moment, and for that, I was thankful.

Crowley was another matter, however. Rescuing him from Fuamnach was going to be a Herculean task. But he'd been there for me when I needed him, so the least I could do was save his creepy, shadowy ass in return.

One thing at a time. First, I need to bond with that Oak.

Despite the altitude, Smokedancer's back was surprisingly warm, likely due to the fire glands that generated a constant, comfortable heat inside her. After a time, I managed to find a comfy position, wedging my fingers up under her scales as I hugged her massive neck. After that I must've have dozed off, because the next thing I knew the dragon was speaking into my mind to announce our arrival at Lugh's home.

-Look, druid—Lugh allows the fae and undead to spend their strength against his walls. The fools think they can stand against him, and they are wrong.-

Thousands of feet below us, an army of tiny specks milled about like ants, surrounding Lugh's castle on all sides. From this vantage point, I could easily see they hadn't made any progress at all. I couldn't spot a single breach, and every time the rebels catapulted a boulder over the walls, it landed harmlessly in his massive garden courtyard. After all this time, the worst the attackers had done was trample his roses a bit.

What about the opposing gods? You think they'll join the siege?

The dragon snorted smoke three times in quick succession.

Are you laughing?

-I am. They fear Lugh, druid, because he is not like the other gods. Lonnbéimnech is crafty, and not prone to come at his enemies from the front. If they had any among them who

were wise, the other gods would have left him alone.- She banked slowly, coming around over the top of Lugh's fortress. *-Speaking of, it seems we are being hailed.-*

Far down below us, a small green and red speck stood in the center of the courtyard. Smokedancer spiraled to descend, and soon the figure came into focus. It was Lugh, of course, wearing his customary green cloak over a red tunic stitched in gold, cinched at the waist with a wide, black leather belt. A silver brooch held his cloak in place, and he wore black leather breeches tucked into matching, calf-high boots. The god held a leaf-shaped spear in his right hand, and a late Bronze Age longsword was sheathed at his left hip.

As we made our final descent, a boulder the size of a motorcycle came flying over the wall. Lugh released his hand from the spear, and immediately it flew from his hand, the tip bursting into flame in mid-flight. Like a magic heat-seeking missile, the spear looped around the courtyard, homing in on the rock and striking it dead center, shattering it into a thousand smaller pieces.

We landed twenty yards away, just as the spear flew back into the god's hand. "Damned shame, that," he said as he approached. "The stone I kin' use for repairs on the walls, but I've little need fer' gravel."

Smokedancer lowered her herself to the ground, and I slid off her back to land on feet that had fallen asleep during our flight. "Gah, that stings," I said, stumbling and doing a little dance to get the blood flowing to my toes. "Sorry, Lugh, my manners are awful. Smokedancer, this is Lugh Lámfada, my, er—"

"I'm his elder sibling, 'though I'd ask ya' not ta' speak of it. Pleased ta' meet ya', dragoness."

Smokedancer stood tall before lowering her head halfway to the ground. The gesture carried a lot more respect than she'd shown Nuada, that much was certain. Apparently, she held Lugh in much higher regard than she did the other gods.

-Please tell him the pleasure is all mine.-

"Ah, she says likewise." I glanced around the court-yard, looking for a big, gray version of Clifford. "Did Failinis make it?"

The god pursed his lips and gave a small shake of his head. "Herne took 'im, likely fer' breedin', the bastard."

"Sorry I couldn't do more to protect him."

Lámfada's eyes narrowed. "Don't worry, I'll get 'im back, an' with interest."

"When the time comes, count me in. I've a bone to pick with the Hunter on that and other counts."

"I'll hold ya' to it, lad, but be advised—Herne is no pushover." Lugh inclined his head toward the dragon. "If ya' don't mind, I've some family business ta' discuss with the lad. There's clean water in the fountain o'er there, and I'll send out some livestock shortly."

Smokedancer swung her head to face me. *-I shall await you here, druid.-*

Hopefully, this won't take long.

-Do not worry yourself with my well-being. I am a

dragon, and dragons are patient. I shall be here when you are done.-

During that brief exchange, Lugh had already headed for a door in the fortress wall, so I hurried and fell in behind him. We entered into a long hallway that led off in both directions that ran all the way around the massive fortress, or so I assumed. The god entered an open door ahead, which led into a small, cozy room, filled with bookshelves, a table and chairs, a cot, and two armchairs that faced a fireplace.

"Have a seat, lad—ya' look dead on yer' feet." He gestured at one of the armchairs, before plopping down in the one opposite.

"This siege hasn't seemed to cause you any trouble," I said as I sat down.

"'Cept ta' keep me tied up here handlin' repairs, which is the whole purpose o' the exercise. I can't let 'em breach the walls—too much stuff here that can't fall inta' the other side's hands. S'what I get fer' bein' such a loner all these years. If I'd taken on some servants, or had Goibniu build me some golems—*ach*, if wishes were horses, beggars'd ride."

"That's funny, I heard that said differently."

"From your da, no doubt. Used to tell 'im he was sayin' it wrong, but the stubborn bastard ne'er listened."

I sat a little straighter in my chair. "You knew my dad?"

"Aye, he was a good man. Had the stones ta' go the

distance, he did, least until that blackhearted Fear Doirich got to him. Damned shame."

"I miss him," I said, a note of wistfulness creeping into my voice.

"Ye'll miss a lot o' things, afore this war yer' fightin' is done. Word o' advice," he said as he produced a crystal decanter from thin air, pouring the contents into two crystal glasses that had appeared on the table next to him. "Ya' need ta' learn ta' pace yerself, if yer' gonna be pursuin' this trickster business." The god leaned forward to hand me a glass, and I took it. "Real Irish whisky, not that piss they sell now. It'll warm ya' right up."

I took a sip and found it to be surprisingly good. Warmth spread through my body immediately, starting in my chest and moving out to my limbs. I held the glass up to my nose, sniffing the contents to see if I could detect any magic.

Yep, definitely enchanted.

I took another sip. "Damn, that sure hits the spot."

"Goibniu makes it. Says it's a healing draught, but all I've e'er seen him use it fer' is ta' kill a hangover an' remove lacquer."

"It's good. Heck, if I could bottle this back home—" I stopped myself before completing the sentence, as the mere mention of home made me long for a return. It wouldn't do to show weakness in front of Lugh, so I changed the subject. "You know about the trickster thing?"

"Ya' forget, I held the title amongst our pantheon fer' a time. Don't attend the meetins' anymore, as those feckers are as daft as a brush, an' twice as irritatin'."

"Click sort of badgered me into it," I said, staring into my glass. "Gwydion, I mean."

"He means well, but that one's trouble comin' and goin'." Lugh cocked his head and frowned. "Ya' know he means ta' turn ya' inta' a god, right?"

I scratched at my hairline and chuckled. "Yeah, I figured as much. I'm halfway there already, I guess, although most days it doesn't feel like it."

Lugh took a deep, contemplative breath, exhaling slowly as he slouched into his chair. "Ya' wouldn't be the first ta' walk the path ta' immortality, although it don't happen often wit' our kind. The Tuath Dé don't take too kindly ta' humans an' demigods that get all hopped up on their deeds, even though most of 'em started off the same."

"You're saying they weren't always gods."

"Not really, no. They stole their magic from our people—the Fomori—'an used it ta' make themselves powerful, like unto gods. O' course, I was born inta' it, as were you, even if not through both parents. S'why Máthair tried ta' protect ya' by hidin' it from ya'. Fat lot o' good that did."

"Well, I'm in it now. And I could use your help."

He smiled ruefully and gave a slight shake of his head. "Ya' should know, I'm onta' ya', lad. Yer' my brother, but not, as that'un died in the blast. Felt it when it happened, just as sure as I'm speakin' ta' you now."

I set my drink down on the armrest, giving my full attention to my half-brother. "That doesn't concern you? You're not going to rat me out?"

The look he gave me could have curdled milk. "Tattle on my own blood? What kinda' dicko do ya' think I am?"

"No offense, but you are a god in the Celtic pantheon. I don't have a very good track record with them."

Lugh leaned in with his right elbow on the armrest and his left fist knuckling his knee. "Look 'ere, lad, let's get one thing straight. We are *not* the Tuath Dé. We're Fomori, an' family. We do not stab each other in the back, we do not scheme against one another, and we certainly don't sell each other out ta' the other gods."

"Shit. Are you serious? I've been tiptoeing around the other you for years. Why didn't your counterpart tell me this before?"

"Who knows? Maybe because Ethlinn forbade him from doing so. The plan was always ta' hide ya' from the Tuath Dé as long as possible. Máthair knew that some o' them would want ta' kill ya' an' others'd want ta' use ya' as their pawn. Either way, ya'd be fecked."

I thought about how Niamh had used me to do her dirty work, and the many ways I'd been manipulated and harassed by the other gods. "Yeah, that's about the size of it."

"Gets old, don't it?"

"You got that right," I said, downing the whisky. "Which is pretty much why I'm here."

"Ya' need ma' help gettin' that Oak ta' do yer' biddin', am I right?"

"Sheesh, Lugh, it's like you're psychic or something."

"Watch it now," he said disapprovingly. "Jest cuz' we're related, don't mean ya' can get all cheeky with me." I waited, watching him expectantly. "O' course I'll do it. Can't fecking let the last druid oak die, can I? The Dagda would ne'er forgive me, fer' one. Have ya' planted more o' them yet, back in yer' own timeline?"

"Say what?"

Lugh scowled. "He didna' tell ya'? Yer' s'posed ta' take the Oak's seed 'an plant them all over the Earth—in secret, mind ya'—so's other druids'll have their own oaks and groves in years ta' come."

"Shit! No, he didn't tell me, probably because I pissed him off royal."

"Oh yeah?" Lugh said, raising an eyebrow. "How?"

"I, uh, helped Mom kill Aengus."

Lugh's eyes went wide as he began chuckling. "Ya' did whot now? Oh, fer' goodness sakes, that's funny. Not like the little shit didna' have it comin' to him."

"Maybe so, but the last thing I needed was another enemy in the pantheon."

"Pfah." The god waved the matter off as he settled back into his chair. "Give 'im a decade or so, he'll come around."

"I don't know, he was pretty pissed."

"Best way ta' clear muddy water is ta' let it settle. In the meantime, I'll show ya' some things 'bout that tree and druidry, so's ya' don't have ta' go beggin' after the hairy fella' once ya' get back there." He tossed his drink back, slamming the glass on the side table. "Let's start by callin' that great bloody houseplant home."

Lugh and I walked back to the courtyard, where Smokedancer was busily munching her way through a few dozen bleating, traumatized sheep. We left her to her meal and found an open area of the courtyard. Lugh indicated I should summon the Oak.

"Are you sure it's going to come when I call?"

Lugh shrugged. "'Course it'll come ta' ya'. It's a child, an' you're it's da. When ya' call, it'll answer."

"Yeah, but what if it doesn't want to listen to me?"

The Celtic god scowled at me as if I were the slowest student in the class. "Lemme ask ya' somethin'—when ya' were just a wee lad, did yer' parents ask ya' if ya' wanted ta' learn yer' letters an' figures? Or did they jest tell ya' ta' do it, an' ya' did?"

"Of course, they told me and I hopped my happy ass on the bus every day to school. But I was a human child —well, half-human, anyway. We're talking about a sentient, ultra-powerful magical oak tree. I mean, I've seen the Oak lay down the hurt on some serious players back home. If this thing doesn't want to mind, it'll do its own thing, and there's not much I can do about it."

Lugh glowered as he crossed his arms over his chest. "Jest do as I tell ya' ta' do, an' everythin'll be alright."

"Okay. Here goes nothing."

I closed my eyes and centered myself, slowing my breathing into the patterns that Finnegas had taught me before he passed away. Now that I was back to my old self, it took mere seconds to hit the sweet spot where I could tap into my power. Before I knew it, I was in tune with the land around me, aware of all the plants, insects, and animals in Lugh's courtyard. Smokedancer stood out like a beacon, and I even got a read on the beasts of burden and other animals that the rebels outside Lugh's fortress brought along with them.

Ignoring those distractions, I focused all my attention on connecting with the Druid Oak. Initially, the connection was tenuous at best, but it strengthened as I poured more of my will and intent into it. Soon that thin thread of magic and telepathy strengthened, growing into a thick umbilical cord of power connecting us together.

"Now that ya' have it," Lugh whispered in my ear, "pull it to ya'—an' don't take any lip off it as ya' do."

Figuring he knew what he was talking about, I metaphorically grabbed the mystical umbilical cord and pulled. Just as I expected, the Oak gave me some resistance, but then it came as I'd requested. When it portalled into the courtyard, I felt its magic as if it were my own. As I opened my eyes, the Oak shivered as if to express its displeasure at being summoned.

"Ignore it, lad. It's jest a child havin' a tantrum. Moreover, it doesn't know what's good fer' it. You're its da—and its mam fer' that matter—an' it's yer' responsibility ta' tell it what's good fer' it."

"You want me to scold it?"

"Nah, that'll jest make things more difficult. Coo at it a bit an' soothe it, then finalize the bond."

"Just like that? I whisper sweet nothings in the tree's ears, and simply claim it as my own?"

"Ye'll figure it out," Lugh said as he looked on with amusement. "You're a master druid, so this stuff ought ta' come naturally ta' ya'. Ya' jest have ta' be confident an' listen ta' yer' instincts."

Well, here goes nothing.

I wiped my palms on my jeans, then I extended my senses, telepathically communicating with the Oak to let it know I wasn't angry, and I meant no harm. This seemed to mollify it somewhat, but I still felt waves of anger and rebelliousness coming off of the tree from where it stood some twenty feet away. I continued to communicate with it telepathically, saying I'd not called it here to be punished, as it had done nothing wrong.

After all, the tree had seen its former master die. As Crowley had pointed out, that must've caused it no end of trauma and grief. The Oak had reacted the only way it knew how.

"Okay, I think I have the thing settled down. What should I do next?"

"Already told ya', lad," Lugh said with the slightest hint of impatience in his voice. "Jest reach out an' bond with it—I can't make it any clearer than that."

Right, just reach out and bond with it. Clear as mud.

Having no other option but to follow Lugh's instructions, I did just that—I attempted to connect with the Oak in the same way I did with my more mature oak back home. When I did so, the juvenile Oak responded with waves of resentment and fury. It was fighting me every step of the way.

Yet, as I continued to bond with the tree, I felt its resistance give way little by little. In many ways, it reminded me of how my dad used to get after me when I was young. I'd stomp my feet, cross my arms over my chest, and stick out my lower lip, refusing to cooperate. He'd give me that look—the look all dads gave their children when they were misbehaving—and then I'd shape up and behave.

Instantly, I recognized this as the same dynamic. The Oak was only a child, having been born just the year prior. Without the guidance of a parent to teach it right from wrong and guide it down the proper path, it was acting as any neglected child would. How foolish of me to think I could let it continue as it wished. I mean, honestly, what parent would abandon their child to its own designs?

As I continued the bonding process, all signs of the

resistance it had shown faded away, replaced by feelings of abashed resignation and repentance. Soon I found myself in full communion with it, and I quickly realized something else—when the Dagda rescued Jesse, he must've done something to facilitate my ability to bond with *this* Oak. All this time, all I'd needed to do was assert my authority and initiate the connection.

Astonished at this revelation—and feeling more than a bit hacked—I opened my eyes and stared daggers at Lugh. "You knew this all along, didn't you?"

Lugh's voice took on a weary tone as he replied. "The hairy old fecker knew ye'd come, jest as he knew he'd fall in battle. Paved the way fer' ya', he did, 'fore he passed."

The Dagda was many things, but he was no prophet. Meaning, an outside influence must have intervened, warning him of coming events.

"Don't tell me—Gwydion told him, right?"

"Aye, months ago. Popped in an' risked life an' limb ta' warn *Ollathair*. Lucky fer' him, the Bearded One didna' squash the squirrelly fecker flat on sight."

"You could've said something, you know."

The Celtic god of Being-Good-at-Everything smiled like the cat that ate the canary. "Ever since ya' were a stripling, ya've always been headstrong an' dead set on doin' things the hard way. O'er the years, Máthair an' I learned ta' jest sit back an' let ya' run yer' own race." Lugh inclined his head at the Oak across the yard. "Remind ya' of anyone?"

EPILOGUE

Once I'd expressed my gratitude to Lugh—without actually thanking him, of course—I transported myself and Smokedancer inside the alt-timeline Oak's Grove. Then I took us to the Void, with a brief pit stop to fetch Guts and his warriors along the way.

Why the Void? Because it was the safest place to go that I knew of, far from the influence of gods, fae, and vampires. The bottom line was that I needed time to think, and to rest. Due to the time differential inside the Grove, I could do plenty of that and still get back in time to rescue Crowley and kick Alarngar's ass.

Fucking vamps.

Regarding Smokedancer, she was happy as a clam inside the Grove, where she could roost and hatch her brood in peace. I wasn't fully read in on all the nuances of the lifecycle of dragons, but apparently, they carried their eggs long after they'd been fertilized, only laying them when they could nest in a safe place. I didn't need to know the details; all I knew was that protecting her felt right, and the Grove agreed.

As for the trolls, they were sort of tripped out over the whole teleporting thing. So, I took them back to their families, who had hidden in one of the larger cave systems in the Texas Hill Country. They swore they'd be there for me when I called on them, saying they owed me a life debt or some-such.

Honestly, my better nature said to just leave them in peace. But then my Fomorian nature reminded me that nice guys always finish last. The vamps weren't going to retreat into the shadows just because I asked them politely, that was for sure. Knowing I would soon ask the trolls to lay down their lives made me feel like a cold, hard motherfucker—but then again these were cold, hard times.

While I was resting, I visited Lugh a few times. He gave me lessons in advanced druidry that deepened my understanding of how we fit into the grand scheme. Part of the Dagda's plan was that we'd be caretakers of Earth, deepening our connection with the planet's energies until we could channel them at will. Through those lessons, I realized I had access to more power than I once thought—if I could learn to command it.

Interestingly, Lugh also claimed that we Fomori were naturally more in tune with Underhill than any of the Tuatha Dé Danann ever could be.

"Tis' *our* magic lad," he said. "Ne'er forget that."

I promised him I wouldn't.

The whole time I spent in the Grove, I kept reminding myself that the quicker I took care of business in the Hellpocalypse, the quicker I could get back to Fallyn and my friends. The knowledge that the vamps were probably still scheming back home haunted me constantly, increasing the sense of urgency I felt. Eventually I'd need to deal with those fuckers as well, and everything I learned here would inform the steps I took to prevent the Hellpocalypse from happening in my own timeline.

Then, maybe I could see about planting more druid oaks, in this timeline and my own. Which naturally meant I'd have to start training more druids to tend them as well. I couldn't very well let druidry die out with me—I was fairly certain that was *not* what Finnegas had in mind when he trained me.

No rest for the wicked. But one thing at a time.

Laying in the soft grass beside my new favorite swimming hole inside the Grove, basking in the false but very convincing sunlight, I considered all this and more. I'd nearly recovered completely from my ordeal with Boann, the curse had shown no signs of returning, and my grasp and command of druidry was stronger than ever. I was just about ready to return to the fight, but not yet.

Just one more day of peace, I thought as I drifted off to sleep.

The next thing I knew, someone was shaking me awake. "Wake up, lad! There's a dragon in yer' grove, an' some bastard's stolen yer' girl!"

"Huh? Click, what the hell are you doing here? Heck, how'd you find me?"

The youthful-looking immortal magician hopped from foot to foot with impatience, his face a mask of worry and distress. "There's no time, lad. Ya' must get back ta' your own timeline. Fallyn's life hangs in the balance."

Meanwhile, Smokedancer hovered in the background with a lungful of liquid lava queued up, ready to rain hell down on Click. I waved her off, sending her a telepathic "stand down" signal, and she flapped off to her nest. Slowly, I came to my full, awake state of mind, at which point Click's words registered fully.

"What do you mean, her life hangs in the balance? And why is it that every time you show up, things have gone to shit?"

Click looked over one shoulder and then the other before pointing a finger at his own chest. "Me?" he replied quizzically. "Are ya' takin' the piss? You're the walkin', talkin' wreckin' ball o' fate here. I'm just the benevolent mentor tryin' ta' make sure ya' don't blow up the universe afore ya' breathe yer' last."

"Fair enough," I said, scrunching my face into a crooked frown. "Now, tell me what happened to Fallyn."

Click gesticulated animatedly, causing the dark lock of hair that hung down his forehead to swing like a pendulum. "They snatched her, lad. Poof, gone. Where? I dunno. But we'll find her, that we will. I swear it."

"Who snatched her? And how? Fallyn's no slouch when it comes to taking care of herself, you know."

"Who d'ya think? Whoever set that water hag against ya' an' gave her the curse ta' cast, that's who. Very powerful, this person, an' sneaky enough ta' obscure themselves from my powers of augury."

"Okay, fine."

Click drew himself up as he looked at me askance. "Fine? Wha'd'ya mean, 'fine'?"

"I mean I'll time travel to the moment before she got taken and wreck whoever is messing with her, just as soon as I finish things up here."

The quasi-god palm-smacked me on the forehead as he leaned over me, eyes narrowed. "D'ya think I hadn't thought o' that already? Who taught time magic ta' who here, I wonder? Colin, this person stole her away usin' *chronjuration*—summoning a person or entity through space *an'* time. Not only is the spell untraceable, whoe'er took her is at the very least ma' equal in the high art of manipulatin' time!"

I hung my head, covering my face in my hands as I took several slow, calming breaths. "Well, shit—there goes my nap."

———

This ends Book 2 of The Trickster Cycle Trilogy. But never fear, Colin's adventures will continue in Book 3, Druid's Bane.

Visit my website at MDMassey.com and subscribe to my newsletter, so you can be among the first to know when the next episode drops!

Printed in Great Britain
by Amazon